Hacked to Death

Peter Budetti

This is a work of fiction. All incidents and dialogue, and all characters in the novel, are products of the author's imagination and are not to be construed as real. The novel is entirely fictional and is not intended to depict actual events or people. Any resemblance to persons living or deceased is entirely coincidental.

To

Melissa Marie
&
John Lorenzo

It's my great joy and
wonderful privilege
to have children that I
admire as well as love

Hacked to Death

Prologue

The fifteen thousand people packed elbow-to-elbow in the hot June sun were growing restless waiting for the guest of honor to arrive. They were drenched in sweat and weary after standing for endless hours, tired of hearing the Jefferson High School band pound out its repertoire of John Philip Sousa marches over and over, and had long since tuned out to the endless parade of minor local officials boasting about their pet projects. And on top of their growing impatience a palpable edginess began to spread through the crowd as people realized that, in addition to a heightened police presence, a small army of men and women in dark suits with curly black wires running from their ears were looking directly at each of them one-by-one, constantly scanning their faces with suspicious eyes.

At last the band broke into *Happy Days Are Here Again* and the throng sprang to life, raising a sea of banners and waving American flags. This was it, the moment they were waiting for. But their excitement was short-lived when they saw it was only Maryland Governor Francis X. Lenoir who emerged from the wings of the Paradise Valley Memorial Bandshell. He walked to the center of the stage in front of heavy curtains, waving and smiling as if the spectators were cheering for him. Lenoir extended his arms, encouraging the crowd to cheer louder and louder, then said, "OK, that's great, he can hear you. He knows you're fired up to see him. And I know you're not here to listen to me, so without further ado for a man who needs no introduction, Ladies and Gentlemen, Mayor Samuels, distinguished guests, and MY *FELLOW DEMOCRATS,* join me in welcoming *THE NEXT PRESIDENT OF THE UNITED STATES OF AMERICA, OUR OWN FAVORITE SON, A TRUE AMERICAN HERO, COLONEL ROBIN W. JENKINS!"*

As Governor Lenoir retreated off to the wings of the stage, the curtains opened to reveal a thick plexiglass cylinder twelve feet high with a curved front and a domed roof. Inside the containment capsule Robin Washington Jenkins grinned from ear to ear and waved briskly with his upraised right hand. Trim and athletic at forty-seven, with military-cut jet-black hair atop his six-foot-two frame, the legendary former football star and Marine skipped gracefully up the three steps of the podium to the lectern and its bank of microphones. Jenkins showed no signs of the severe injuries he had suffered in the firefight in Afghanistan when he had nearly died saving the lives of 17 fellow Marines, the act of valor for which he had been awarded the Medal of Honor. The crowd roared, hooting and cheering wildly and raising their cell phones aloft. Jenkins raised both hands and patted the air as if to silence the cheering, but inside he savored every moment—he was back home taking his victory lap. All the pundits and polls agreed: in just a few days he would be the Democratic nominee for president.

The broad smile grew even brighter as his perfect teeth glistened in the sunlight. Colonel Jenkins let the hometown crowd cheer and snap pictures for nearly five minutes. At last he said, "OK, OK, I love you all but that's enough. Enough!" Powerful amplifiers blasted his words so loud the excited throng calmed down enough for him to be heard.

"Well," he began, then paused, chuckling to himself as more than half the crowd turned their backs toward him like a military drill team executing an *about face*. The first time he had found himself suddenly speaking to the backs of thousands of heads he started to worry that something must have happened in the rear of the arena that distracted the audience's attention. Or that it was some sort of protest and people would start marching out. But now he knew it was a good sign: young and old alike were just turning around to snap selfies. He resumed speaking. "What do you think? *Are we going to win?*"

The crowd screamed its approval, chanting "Jenkins! Jenkins!" until he quieted them again.

"I can understand your excitement. I share it, you know I do. We've all had a deeply unsettling four years. All of us, the people of the United States who really care about this country, are desperate for relief. We've had enough of that guy—you know who I mean."

Jenkins would never say the name of the incumbent, President Hugo H. Dorzel. But he did not need to. A deafening chorus of booing erupted, which he let continue unabated for a full minute before continuing.

"That avaricious, foulmouthed, ill-tempered man cares only about himself, not about you and not about this wonderful country. He used his daddy's money to buy his way out of serving in the military. His deficits are bankrupting the nation just like he did his own businesses. He has undermined America's standing as the bastion of freedom and democracy in a troubled world. He has trampled on his duty to enforce the Constitution and laws of this country. He has destabilized one of the most brilliant creations of the Founding Fathers, the separation of power among three branches of government. Republicans in the Senate cower before him. His unscrupulous Supreme Court Justices rubber-stamp his disgraceful actions with unprincipled rulings. He has stoked the devilish flames of racism and given free reign to hatred and violence. He has no sense of decency whatsoever and no respect for women. He has trashed the moral authority of the presidency. He scoffs at the overwhelming evidence that global warming is consuming our planet and we may all be extinct before long. And all the while he has exploited the power of the presidency for his own financial gain and that of his billionaire cronies."

The crowd went wild with catcalls and booing. Colonel Robin W. Jenkins was their hero, their hope, the savior who would liberate them from the mindless tyrant who threatened to destroy the democracy they believed in. Once again he let them vent before speaking.

"I am ready to answer your call. They have drained the life from workers like you, stolen your money to fatten their bank accounts, choked off the opportunities for you to live decent lives and ensure that your children have hope for the future. We will restore the rule of law in an even and fair-handed way. We will hold him and his corrupt gang accountable for their crimes. We will right their grievous wrongs. You know," he said with a broad smile, "they call me 'Robin Hood' because we will make the disgracefully rich pay a fair share of taxes—well, *I love that nickname!* This country needs a Robin Hood instead of the robbers that have been stealing from the poor to make the rich richer."

More screams, wild cheering, prolonged chants of "Robin Hood! Robin Hood!"

"And that money will go to improve your lives and future— green energy, education, health care, mass transit, income supports. We will have an Attorney General who believes in enforcing our civil rights and antitrust laws. We'll stop cuddling up to the despots who would destroy us and we'll return to working with our friends and allies in international alliances."

He was well-prepared to take the reins. His team, a shadow cabinet he had cultivated for years, was primed to hit the ground running on January 20th as soon as he was sworn in. A moderately left-of-center cadre of dedicated and experienced men and women diverse in age, sex, and color. Americans who had grown up in all regions of the country. People who had known hardship and lived the American Dream. Patriots who had served their country. Optimists who clung to the faith that America would return to its historical path toward becoming the country the Declaration of Independence and Constitution promised. They were the best and brightest and most purely motivated. They believed in him and he believed in all of them.

The polls and focus groups confirmed that, yes, the populace was desperate to be rid of President Dorzel. There was just one hurdle for Jenkins to overcome once he locked up the nomination: selecting a running mate who would further strengthen his position. His supporters on the far left were exerting intense pressure on him to pick his closest rival, Annabaker Minion, as his running mate. But the polls and focus groups also showed that her presence on the ticket threatened to derail his candidacy. Too many moderates could not stomach her ultra-liberal views. She promised to nationalize the health care system, institute a massive wealth tax on billionaires, eliminate payroll and income taxes for the bottom one-fourth of wage earners, impose a 99% inheritance tax on big estates, break up mega-corporations, and—impossible for Jenkins to support—cut military spending by more than half.

Too radical, his gut and all the polls told him. Annabaker Minion was just too radical for America. He risked alienating key segments of his own base if he did not pick her, but he risked losing the election if he did. She was running a clear second behind him for the nomination and many of her followers were willing to support him in the general election, but only with her on the ticket. True, with her as his running mate, young voters might be energized. But a disastrous number of people would not vote at all, or they would support a third-party candidate and split the Democratic vote. Either way, Dorzel would remain in office for another four years. Jenkins could not take that risk. His inner circle was pressing him to dump

Annabaker Minion once and for all and pick one of the two middle-of-the-road candidates currently polling just behind her. But it would not be easy for him to keep Annabaker off the ticket.

He was running out of time to make a decision. What he did not know was that a far more serious and immediate threat was about to erupt. Some four rows into the crowd a tall, thin man with a dark beard typed a six-digit code into his cell phone and pressed the "send" button.

Nine Months Earlier

Chapter 1: New Career

Will Manningham lay in bed, staring at the digital clock on the nightstand. He watched it click off the minutes next to the little red "AM" dot from 1:37 until it read 2:00, then turned toward Sally and whispered, "Are you awake?"

"I am now," his wife mumbled, shaking her head and wiping the back of her hand across her eyes. "What is it?"

"I can't sleep."

"Duh!"

"Well, this is a big deal. I just don't know if I'm making the right decision. For me...for you...for us."

"Time to paint or get off the ladder, Sweetheart. We've been over this a thousand times. Either you take the job or you don't, but you need to get on with your life. *We* need to get on with *our* lives. It's just not like you to be so indecisive."

"I'm a numbers guy. I like to run the numbers until they point me in the right direction, but this time there are no numbers to run. I mean, I know all about the money, and how well off we'll be if things go well. And I calculated that the job has an eighty-five percent chance of working out. So that's all good. But what's driving me nuts is whether it will feel right. You know, will I feel like I've abandoned my promises to Mom and Dad and Barry?"

"You kept all those promises and then some, Sweetheart. You tracked down the Russian mob that murdered your mother and Barry. You busted up their ring that was killing people with phony drugs and medical devices. You've done your bit, you deserve to move on. But we've been through all of that over and over.

Nothing's changed. Either you stay with the government or take the job and get out."

"I guess that's part of it, too. I really loved figuring out who was stealing from Medicare and hurting so many people. And when I worked with Adrienne Penscal and the other Special Agents at the FBI, that was terrific—except for the part about you getting kidnapped and almost killed by the Russians, of course."

"Glad to hear you didn't enjoy that part."

"Sorry. My bad."

"Seemed to me that working in the federal government wasn't always fun for you, anyway. I remember you complaining all the time that you got less-than-enthusiastic support for your work."

"True, true enough. Every scam we uncovered that had cost the government millions and killed people was seen as an embarrassment to the program since they should have spotted the fraud in the first place. So we were pretty much a thorn in the Agency's side. But even if the follow-through wasn't great, at least we could run the computer analyses we wanted most of the time. Now it's all gone to hell since this lunatic Dorzel got elected. I don't know what I'm supposed to be doing anymore. The cast of characters he appointed, from the Secretary on down, doesn't want anything done, ever! All we hear from the Director when we find some kind of terrible scam is, *'That's not important, don't pursue it.'* Even Adrienne is frustrated over at the FBI. Dorzel's Attorney General is a total hack, he won't prosecute cases anymore unless they play well politically for the White House. They're actually screening the names of the crooks we spot against the lists of donors to both parties—and guess which ones we're authorized to go after! Then of course our hands are completely tied when it comes to looking at the Russian mob! Can you believe it? What a mess."

"I think you just answered your own question, Sweetie. If you can't do your job properly you should do another job."

"Yeah. You're right, as always. OK, enough is enough."

Will jumped out of bed and ran down the hallway into his office. A few minutes later he came back and bounced on the bed, waking Sally again only moments after she had drifted back off to sleep. "It's done!" he said, not bothering to whisper. "I am no longer an employee of the Centers for Medicare and Medicaid Services. I e-signed my resignation papers and sent them off to H.R. at CMS. And

I e-signed the contract and emailed it to Hank Cotter at *Cybersleuths, Inc.* That's it, your husband is now in the private sector."

Sally blinked twice and looked up at her tall, lanky husband. His flaming red hair flared straight out as though he had stuck his fingers into an electric outlet. "Congratulations, Sweetheart. Well done. Now come back to bed." Will slipped between the sheets and wrapped his arms around her. She patted down his hair, then walked her fingers playfully down his belly. "Hmmm…" she said, "seems like you might be in the mood to celebrate!"

"Well, we are both wide awake."

"Welcome to the private sector…*my* private sector, Mr. Manningham."

***

The next thing Will knew the digital clock read "8:07" and he heard water running in the shower. "Omigod," he said, jumping out of bed, "I can't be late on my first day!" He hurried back into his office and logged on to his computer. He was relieved to find a welcoming note from Hank Cotter:

> *Dear Will—*
>
> *Welcome to Cybersleuths, Inc. We're looking forward to a very productive working relationship. You can take it easy this morning— you have an appointment at H.R. at 9:30 to fill out a bunch of forms and the rest of the day you'll go through orientation. Come to my office at your lunch break and I'll introduce you to some folks and we can order in some sandwiches or something. We have some interesting matters we can share with you. Again, welcome. See you soon.*
>
> *Hank*

Another message was from the Human Resources department of CMS acknowledging receipt of his resignation forms and informing him that his access to the government's computer systems had been terminated and his files migrated into archives that he no longer had access to. It went on to say that his PIV card—the federal Personal Identity Verification I.D.—had been deactivated and he must return it, along with his keys, parking pass, and any work-related documents or other government materials in his possession within no more than five business days. The notice also reminded him that he remained under multiple ethical obligations and confidentiality restrictions, some of which would last for his lifetime, and warned him that he was subject to prosecution should he violate the relevant provisions of federal law. For further emphasis the last paragraph strongly recommended that he review those provisions and provided links to the statutes and regulations.

"OK, that's it, I guess I'm really finished at CMS," he said out loud. Sally had stepped out of the shower and heard his voice. She walked to the doorway of his office and said, "Are you talking to yourself again, Dear?" Will looked up and smiled at his wife. She looked beautiful, so fresh and alert and comfortable in the luxurious off-white bathrobe from *Restoration Hardware* that he had given her for Christmas several years earlier. Her short brown hair was wrapped in a matching towel.

"Talking to myself or my computer, not much difference. Hmmm…since you're still in your bathrobe, maybe we could continue our celebration…"

She walked over and kissed her husband on the cheek. "Good thing headquarters is in Denver or I'd be a couple of hours behind already. Anyway, I'm busy, no time for…*more celebrating*, sorry."

"Yeah, I should hustle down to my new office."

"What does your day look like?"

"Paperwork and training—orientation. But Hank mentioned some new matters they'll brief me on, so I might have some substantive work. We'll see. I sure hope I'm doing the right thing."

"It'll be fine. And if it isn't, CMS will take you back in a heartbeat—if they can keep the FBI from recruiting you, that is."

"Hope we don't have to find out."

Will dressed hurriedly, scarfed down half a cup of coffee, gave Sally a goodbye peck on the cheek and stepped out of the front door of their house. He walked down the path as far as the sidewalk, then instinctively stopped at the spot where his twin brother had been gunned down by Russian assassins who thought they were killing him. The horrific scene he had witnessed through the front window replayed itself in his head for the ten-thousandth time. The dark sedan, a flurry of gunfire, the bag of beer bottles flying through the air, Barry collapsing in a pool of blood. Will's body twisted inward at the memory, his eyes tearing up. Then he took a deep breath and turned around to look back at their house. A wave of nostalgia spread through him. How good it felt to be back in their own home, despite what had happened. He had once thought he never wanted to see this place again, especially not right here where Barry had been gunned down. But now it had the opposite effect on him—being here made him feel closer to his brother. And this was where he and Sally belonged. If they moved away that would be letting the gangsters win. Plus they had had enough of that FBI safe apartment with microphones and cameras everywhere, wiretaps on their phones, their internet continuously monitored. Will sighed with relief. Being back in their own home was reassuring at a moment like this, facing a serious transition in their lives with his new job. He took another deep breath, exhaled, then turned away. Time to begin the next phase of his life, with *Cybersleuths, Inc.*

***

Herman Piligree was very lucky to be alive. At least that's what his friends, his wife, and his doctor all said.

"Herman, if you weren't sitting right behind the Knicks' bench when you collapsed, you'd be dead," said his buddy Paul, who loaned Herman his extravagantly expensive season tickets. "I hope you realize I pretty much saved your life with those tickets."

"Herman, you turned so purple I really thought you were a goner," quipped his friend Pat, who had no filter for screening words that popped into his mind before saying them out loud. "Man, your body really jumped when they hit that defibrillator switch."

"Herman, Dear, I thank God for sparing you. I would be lost without you," said his wife, Alice, patting her chest with an open hand over her heart.

"Mr. Piligree, I have never seen anyone survive such an episode. At least, not for very long and not without serious brain damage," said Dr. Turnburg, who was not known for his bedside manner.

Herman took it all in stride. He knew he was lucky to be alive. More than lucky—now he was famous. He treasured the photo showing him being attended to while lying on the court at the Garden, the now-iconic picture on the front page of the New York Post under the headline, "KNICKS DIE, FAN SAVED." He was grateful to cardiologist Turnburg for keeping his heart going with that pacemaker. And he wouldn't need to borrow Paul's tickets any more—at tonight's game the Knicks would present him with a lifetime free pass.

New Yorkers wearing Knicks jerseys and caps packed the subway so full that Herman had to stand and hold onto a pole. A number of fans recognized him and offered him their seats but he smiled and said, "No thanks, my heart's fine now."

Just before the train arrived at Penn Station, Herman Piligree looked down and saw a tall, thin man with a dark beard take a cell phone out of his jacket pocket. The man typed something on the phone and pressed the "send" button.

Herman Piligree collapsed straight down, going from stiff to limp faster than a strand of spaghetti dropped into boiling water. The subway car erupted in chaos, people screaming, *"Oh my god, it's him,"* and *"It's that guy from the Knicks game."* Someone pulled the emergency handle, sending the crowd reeling as the train screeched to a sudden stop. A young athletic woman wearing a throwback Knicks jersey that read "19" below "Reed" elbowed her way to the fallen man, shouting, "Out of my way, I'm a doctor." She kneeled on the floor and administered CPR to the well-known basketball fan. But Herman Piligree's lifetime pass expired before it was ever used.

Chapter 2: Mother Russia

Alexandra Parushnikova was not happy being back in Russia. Sure, her mother's house in Novolugovoye was preferable to an American jail, that much she was grateful for. But she missed the high life she had enjoyed in the States as a well-paid detail rep for *Marquis-Herrant,* an international pharmaceutical and medical device company. Her fortunes had deteriorated quickly when the FBI discovered that *Marquis-Herrant* was a shell corporation, a front for the Russian mob reaping huge profits in a vast black market in counterfeit drugs and medical supplies. Fortunately for her and the other detail reps, the new Attorney General in the U.S. decided to go easy on the Russians. His loyal subordinates claimed that they did not have enough evidence to prosecute people at her level, that they could not prove that the detail reps knew that the devices and drugs they were pushing were dangerous, or even that they were counterfeit. And apparently it wasn't illegal in the U.S. for detail reps to use sex to encourage doctors to order medical supplies from a specific company. Money yes, sex, no, said the prosecutors. Legal commentators and the press scoffed at the prosecutors' arguments, but Alexandra Parushnikova got off scot-free. So she got out of the States safely and now was home with her mother.

It was very cold during her first winter back, much worse than she had remembered. From November through January the temperature stayed well below freezing for fifty-seven consecutive days, and snow fell every day. She had forgotten how depressing the constant darkness of Winter was with just three or four hours of sunlight every day, hazy light that barely broke through an overcast sky. And, maybe even worse than being cold and miserable all the time, she was horny. Her long blond hair and voluptuous body attracted lots of men but they were all flaming assholes. *Mudak,* she spat, every guy she met was a *pylayushchiy mudak*. And most of them were married. Not that she cared, but the way those guys ignored their wives and children just showed what assholes they were. Besides, she couldn't bring a man home with her mother in the house, so they all wanted to take her to slimy roadside motels where snaggle-toothed old hags rented rooms by the hour.

Making it impossible for her to have any privacy at home wasn't the only problem she was having with her mother. She had been generous with her mother when the *Marquis-Herrant* money was flowing in, but now the woman made it clear that she missed the frequent transfers of large sums of hard currency from her loving daughter in America far more than she had missed her loving daughter. Her mother had blown through her American dollars buying a new car and fancy clothes and throwing parties to impress her lady friends. She hounded her with a ceaseless litany of snide remarks: having her daughter come home in disgrace was an embarrassment she would never recover from; all the sacrifices she had made so her daughter could get those fancy degrees from Novosibirsk State University had been wasted; her snooty daughter sat around the house too proud to go out and get a real job and bring home even a few rubles. *Blah, Blah, Blah,* on and on.

Alexandra Parushnikova had had enough. Something had to change. But she figured her prospects of ever returning to America were as far below zero as the temperature outside the door of their home.

Then the call came. She recognized the voice: the woman known as Galina Khovanskaya who had recruited her for the job with *Marquis-Herrant.*

"Hello, Sasha," the woman said, using the Russian diminutive for Alexandra. "How are you getting along?"

"I'm cold and depressed like everyone else in this place. Why are you calling?"

"Would you be interested in something a bit more stimulating?"

"I'm listening."

"We should meet in person. Come to Berdsk. Do you know the café overlooking the River Berd?"

"Yes, sure. When?"

"Tomorrow at 10AM. I'll be in the coffee shop."

"Until then."

The next morning she cruised down the P-256 and across the bridge to Berdsk in the sporty Lada XRAY crossover SUV her mother had purchased with the money she had sent from the States. She was pleased that at least the woman had the taste to choose such a fine automobile. She arrived early, eager to find out what opportunity the recruiter had for her. She pulled into a carpark at the bottom of a small hill, exited the car, and climbed rapidly up the rise to the café. At the top she stopped to enjoy the sight of the crystal-clear waters of the River Berd breaking into whitecaps at its junction with the Ob. But she allowed herself only a brief pause. She was not there to sightsee, this was business. At least, she hoped it was business.

She was early, but the recruiter was even earlier.

As Sasha entered the café, a woman seated in a corner booth nodded at her without smiling, rose from the hardwood bench and stepped out of the booth to greet her. She was tall, about the same height as Sasha's five-foot-ten, but in her early fifties, some two decades older. She also had long blond hair, but unlike Sasha she was not a Russian beauty who turned men's eyes everywhere she went. Still, the woman had an attractive professional look, with slightly-tinted eyeglasses in a tortoise-shell frame perfectly suited to a face that was unforthcoming yet not stern. A half-empty cup of coffee sat on the table.

"Hello, Sasha," the woman said. "Good to see you again."

"Hello, Galina. It's good to see you as well." They hugged shoulders and kissed cheeks like old friends, but all the while Sasha was musing to herself, "*Galina, my ass. I wonder what her real name is?*"

"So, you had no difficulty finding this place?"

"Not at all. I have been here many times."

"And how is your mother? She must be pleased that you are home again."

"She is fine, thank you. Yes, she says she is happy to have her daughter with her. But I think she preferred having the money I used to send her."

The woman laughed. "Ah, yes. Daughters are fine, but some hard currency goes a long way here. Have you eaten? Would you like some breakfast?"

"I had only a cup of coffee before I left the house. Are you going to eat?"

"Yes. I was looking forward to some blinis with an omelet and kolbasa."

"I had grown fond of scrambled eggs and bacon in the U.S., but that sounds fine."

Galina signaled to the cook behind the counter. A handsome, clean-shaven, young man wearing a dark apron stepped out and approached their table. His long brown hair was drawn back into a pony tail. Sasha found her mind wandering to delights other than breakfast that he might bring her.

As soon as the man walked away Sasha said, "He's very good-looking. But we're not here to pick up men, are we?"

The corners of Galina's mouth turned up into a near-smile. "As you please, Sasha. But not until we talk. Talk turkey, as they say in the States, right?"

"A curious phrase. But yes, let's *'talk turkey.'*"

"We would like you to meet someone. Meet and get to know the person. Get to know him quite well, in fact."

"Who is *'we'* and who is this man?"

"At this moment all I can tell you about my employer is that I am no longer with the search firm that placed you with *Marquis-Herrant*. If our discussions progress satisfactorily you will learn more, but for now it is not possible for me to disclose who is offering you this opportunity, or who the man is."

"If I were interested, what would happen next?"

"First of all, you would be warm again—we have a beautiful training site in the South, in a lovely *gosdacha* on the Black Sea. Quite nice in the summer, and much more pleasant than this place even in the dead of winter. There you would receive your training. For reasons you will soon understand, all the sessions will be in English."

"And after the training?"

"You would come to Moscow. You would live in a beautiful apartment and attend many parties. And at one of those parties you will meet the gentleman we have in mind."

"Gentleman?"

"Some would not use that word," she laughed. "But a man, yes, definitely a man. A man who enjoys women. Especially women from our part of the world."

"What then?"

"You may be doing some traveling but I cannot say more at this moment. You will learn everything you need to know when the time comes."

"So if we are 'talking turkey' like the Americans, let's talk turkey. How much would I be paid?"

"You were satisfied with your compensation at *Marquis-Herrant?*"

"Quite so."

"Then you would be very happy, indeed. And so would your mother."

"And if I refuse this offer?"

"That is a choice for you to consider very carefully. I, personally, would not recommend such a decision."

"My mother might find a horse's head in her bed?"

She laughed. "We would do nothing to harm such a beautiful animal as a horse."

Alexandra Parushnikova laughed in return. "No, of course not. A rat or a dog, maybe. But I understand. And I have every reason to respect your advice in such a matter."

"Does that mean you accept?"

"When do I leave?"

Chapter 3: Hero and Heroine

As soon as the Chief of his Secret Service detail entered the hotel room Colonel Robin Jenkins knew something important was up. Captain Billy Jean Holliday pulled the door shut, turned the bolt and said, "Sir. We have a situation. We need for you to stay here until further notice. Please do not make any phone calls or use social media until we give the go-ahead." She walked over to the windows and pulled the curtains shut.

Jenkins remained calm. He was comfortable around the no-nonsense woman, a perfectly sculpted retired Marine. Once a Marine, always a Marine. Just like him, a Marine-for-life. Six-foot-two and as trim and athletic as when she rowed for Oxford against Cambridge during her Rhodes Scholar days, she had a commanding presence that inspired confidence that whatever was happening, she was in full control. With fellow Marine Billy Jean in charge Robin Jenkins knew he was safe.

"And what is the situation, Captain?"

"We're still awaiting details, Sir. But there has been an incident involving Ms. Annabaker Minion at her rally in Oshkosh."

Jenkins' mind was racing in several directions. Was Annabaker Minion dead? Of course he didn't hope that anything bad had happened to his opponent, but...well, that *would* solve his running-mate problem and he wouldn't get tagged with rejecting her. He immediately suppressed the rogue thought and said, "Do we know how she is?"

"First reports are positive, Sir. She has been sequestered and appears to be unharmed. We should have more information soon. For now, our main concern is to watch for any signs of a coordinated attack against you or any of the other candidates."

"How soon do you expect to know?"

"Any minute now, Sir."

"Can we turn on the TV?"

"Yes, just nothing that would allow a fix on your location."

Captain Billy Jean picked up the remote control and handed it to Jenkins. He turned on the television, but when the Fox News logo appeared at the bottom of the screen he snorted, *"Uff,"* and immediately began scrolling through the channels until the set was tuned to PNTW, the progressive news network. His usual preference was CNN or one of the three traditional networks or BBC, but if something involving Annabaker Minion had happened, PNTW would be all over it. She was the darling of that network, and it seemed that their aggressive young newscaster, Absalom Whitmore, devoted at least half of every show to coverage of Annabaker.

Jenkins had figured correctly: there was Absalom Whitmore sitting in front of a rear-projection screen that showed police restraining a packed crowd while a bulletin scrolled across the bottom announcing *"Breaking News: Annabaker Incident in Oshkosh, Wisconsin."* Then Absalom Whitmore held up one finger and said, "OK, we have some video." The image from the pool television cameras showed a thickset woman with a mass of densely packed black curls smiling and shaking hands as she worked the crowd. Annabaker Minion, as always, was venturing out of her security cocoon against the stern warnings of the Secret Service. She insisted that she was the "people's candidate" and needed to get close to the "real people." Besides, she was sure that the randomness of her spontaneous forays into crowds would protect her against planned attacks. Suddenly the video showed her bolting from the crowd and diving in front of the huge black Secret Service SUV that was trailing her. A jumble of mass confusion filled the screen, accompanied by piercing screams and screeching brakes. No sound of impact, and for several seconds, no sign of the candidate. Then Annabaker Minion was rolling on the street away from the SUV. The cameras zoomed in on her and showed her on the pavement with her arms wrapped around a small, lumpy bundle: Annabaker Minion was holding a small child in her arms and patting the child's cheek with her hand.

A woman ran up to Annabaker screaming, "Oh my god, oh my god. Mavis, Mavis darling, are you alright?" Annabaker handed the child to the woman, who was shrieking "I just looked away to see you, just for one second, just one second. Oh my god. Oh my god. Thank you, thank you!" Clenching the child in both arms she made an awkward effort to kiss Annabaker on her cheek. The candidate took both mother and child into her arms for an extended group hug, which triggered thunderous cheers and applause. Smiling from ear to ear, Annabaker returned to the crowd and shook hands and exchanged fist bumps for a few moments, then was led away by a phalanx of men and women in dark suits who escorted her into the very SUV that had nearly run over the child.

Robin Jenkins turned up the TV volume and heard Absalom Whitmore say, "OK, there you have it. False alarm. It's all good news. Annabaker Minion's campaign has just issued a statement saying that she was delighted that the child was not injured and that she simply did what anyone would have done under the circumstances. She saw the child dart into the street and just reacted. *What a woman!* She'll be continuing on with the rest of her schedule today, beginning in about three hours from now with a rally in Wauwatosa. Hold on—this just in from our advance team in Wauwatosa: traffic is building up rapidly with many more cars than had been anticipated. It looks like a lot of excited people are already teeming into town anxious to see Annabaker in person and congratulate her for saving that child's life.

"Now, it's very good news that the child is safe. We will have more details on who she is and just what happened very soon. And we'll see if we can line up an interview with Annabaker. But we must ask, *what went wrong?* How could the Secret Service let one of its SUVs nearly kill a child? What would have happened if Annabaker Minion had not rescued her?"

Jenkins turned to Captain Billy Jean and said, "Any more information on that situation, Captain?"

"Not yet, Sir. I will let you know as soon as I receive any details on the incident. But we have been given the all-clear as far as any threat to you, Colonel Jenkins."

"Well, I'm certainly glad that both the child and Ms. Minion are safe and sound. I intend to defeat her, but I want to do so fair and square."

Jenkins was operating on gracious-candidate autopilot, taking the highroad with the appropriate words, but the wild cheering on the streets of Oshkosh and Absalom Whitmore's report of people thronging to Wauwatosa reverberated in his head. The child's good fortune could turn out to be his misfortune. Annabaker Minion might emerge from the incident as a heroine in the eyes of an infatuated public. His Medal of Honor for risking his life to save 17 Marines in a distant land could be eclipsed by an image people could see in a video. The radical progressive era in Wisconsin was ancient history, but there were still enough diehard liberals in the state to swing elections—if they turned out to vote. This incident might draw them to the polls for Annabaker. He needed Wisconsin. If he lost to her in that state he would be hard-pressed to deny her a spot on the ticket. Or even worse—a wave of favorable free publicity might boost her into position to challenge his seemingly locked-up nomination.

Jenkins' political acumen soon proved accurate. It wasn't just PNTW that was hyping Annabaker Minion's heroism. The video was trending on social media and the airwaves were saturated with the images of her diving in front of a menacing SUV and rolling out on the other side with a little girl in her arms, followed by the mother screaming and the crowd chanting. Within hours the first two "instant polls" showed the race for the Democratic nomination in Wisconsin had gone from an almost-comfortable lead of 7 percentage points to a dead heat.

Colonel Robin W. Jenkins sensed disaster. Not just his candidacy but the Democratic Party itself would be sunk if Annabaker Minion were their candidate for president. The polls consistently showed that pitted against her, President Hugo H. Dorzel would be re-elected, possibly even garnering a majority of the popular vote, not just the votes in the Electoral College.

"Damn that little girl," Jenkins muttered, squeezing his right fist so tight his fingernails dug into his palm.

"Excuse me, Sir—did you say something?" Captain Billy Jean Holliday was troubled by the remark but showed no sign of reproach in her voice.

"Nothing, Captain. I'm just relieved that little girl is OK."

"As you say, Sir."

Chapter 4: Return to Zarya

Alexandra Parushnikova was delighted when she found out that her training would take place at Zarya Dacha, the historic dacha on the Black Sea where her grandfather had brought his "Little Sasha" as a surprise for her fourth birthday. The young child had been overwhelmed by the seemingly endless expanse of the brand-new mansion, sure that it had to be the biggest building on Earth. While her grandfather attended meetings with the Soviet leadership she wandered freely around the main house and guest houses. She swam in the enormous pool, watched movies in the private theater and played on the beach. But now her childhood fantasy of Zarya Dacha's massive size dissolved in the face of the reality around her. The grand palace of her memory seemed to have shrunk since her last visit as she saw the 4-story, 14-room resort for what it really was: an impressively lavish and magnificently positioned manor house overlooking the Black Sea, but on a relatively modest scale compared with the enormous buildings she had seen over the intervening thirty years. Even some of the grandiose mansions and showplace villas of pharmaceutical executives in the States dwarfed Zarya Dacha.

Still, the place was beautiful and quite comfortable. She was warm. And her mother was three thousand miles away. She would very much enjoy her training in the notorious mansion where Mikhail Gorbachev had been confined for three days under house arrest during the failed coup that led to the rise of Boris Yeltsin and ultimately the disbanding of the Soviet Union. Now with Russia's widely-condemned occupation of the Crimea, the peninsula—with Zarya Dacha and numerous other resorts—was under Russian control.

Ah, yes, her training. What was she there for? She still had only the vaguest idea of just what her new mission was to be. She had

had no further contact with Galina Khovanskaya after their initial meeting in Berdsk. Documents and tickets for her travel had arrived by courier. Her sizeable retainer and her mother's first stipend had been deposited directly into new accounts in the Novosibirsk branch of the Russian International Bank. On the appointed day her mother drove her in the Lada SUV for the 45 minutes trip to Novosibirsk Tolmachevo Airport, where she boarded the Aeroflot plane for the 7-hour flight to Simferopol Airport. She was pleased to be greeted on arrival by a stocky, reticent man in a dark business suit who proved to be highly efficient and evidently well-connected as he whisked her past the authorities with barely more than a nod of his head and drove her in silence for the short ride to Foros and Zarya Dacha. As she looked out the windows of the plush Mercedes sedan a vague familiarity of the scenery from her childhood visit wafted in and out of her mind.

At Zarya Dacha an attendant carried her luggage and led her up two flights to a small but elegant suite with a stunning view of the Black Sea. The room glowed bright red and gold, from the upholstered chairs to the thick curtains to the plush bedcovers on the ornately-carved and painted wood bed. An envelope with "Alexandra Arkadyevna Parushnikova" printed on the front sat on the mirrored dressing table. Inside, a single sheet of paper informed her that she had free access to the Dacha and grounds but should remain within the boundaries of the property and would receive her instructions the next day. When she started to dress for bed she had the sensation that she was being watched. She looked around the room and decided that the elaborate wall sconces and intricate stucco flowers on the ceiling no doubt concealed cameras and microphones. Although she had no qualms about exposing her voluptuous body under the right circumstances, she was suddenly filled with pique that some anonymous functionary was staring at her on a monitor, so she pulled her nightgown on over her clothes before removing her shirt, pants and undergarments. She felt as though she might be too keyed up or too exhausted to sleep, but when she climbed into the bed and curled up between the luxurious satin sheets she fell asleep as soon as she shut her eyes.

The following morning she awoke uncertain where she was. When her head cleared she remembered: Zarya Dacha, where she would undergo training for her new job. But then she remembered that she still had no idea what that job was. OK, all in good time—

for the moment what mattered most was that she was quite hungry. When she left the bedroom a dormant memory of the house seemed to emerge from some corner of her brain. The feeling guided her down an opulent cantilevered stairway directly to the elegant dining room where she had taken meals at a child-sized table in a windowed nook off to one side. She enjoyed the comfortable feeling of returning to eat in the familiar room, though this time she sat at a table for grownups. Very soon a second stocky, reticent man in a dark business suit who could have been a clone of the Mercedes driver came up to her, handed her another envelope labeled, "Alexandra Arkadyevna Parushnikova," then turned and walked away without saying a word. A nondescript young woman brought her a steaming pot of coffee and took her breakfast order. Sasha sipped coffee and stared at the envelope as though she could read the contents with x-ray vision, or take them in by osmosis. As if the cook had known what she would order, the young woman returned almost immediately from the kitchen with her eggs with kolbasa and blinis. When she finished eating, Sasha pushed the cup and plate off to one side and ripped open the flap of the envelope with her finger. A brief note told her to report to Room #9, just outside of the movie theater, in some three hours, at 11 o'clock.

That was it. No other details on her schedule or timetable. Still no explanation why she had been brought all this way. Maybe she was to learn the secrets of an international corporation that she would infiltrate. Or become privy to some dark scheme like pushing counterfeit drugs and medical devices for *Marquis-Herrant*. And what about the man she was supposed to get to know, the one that Galina had said might not be widely considered to be a gentleman?

OK, she thought, I'll find out more when they want to tell me more. She decided to spend the hours until her meeting exploring the grounds, then go for a long swim until time for the session. At least she was warm and comfortable, and a long way from her mother.

***

Harriet Handelmeyer's relationship with her family had been torn apart forever. When her kidneys failed and the doctors told her she would need a transplant she had hoped that she would not have to wait long since she had four siblings and they had always seemed to get along so well. But she was in for a shattering disappointment.

Her brother shook his head sullenly and said he was not in good enough health. Then, to her utter dismay, none of her three sisters were willing to donate a kidney. They said they were sorry, but they just couldn't face the surgery. Besides, who knew whether they might need both kidneys some day? So, estranged from her family, her best friend became a dialysis machine. A surgeon implanted a plastic tube between an artery and a vein in her arm to serve as an access port for her blood to flow through the device and be cleansed of the deadly toxins that her kidneys could no longer remove while she waited for some stranger to donate a kidney. Some stranger, a benevolent living person or a cadaver.

For the first few years Harriet Handelmeyer went into the dialysis center for her treatments. The regular trips were necessary if she wanted to live, but inconvenient and time-consuming. Three times a week she would take a bus downtown, then change buses to catch the one that took her to the strip mall that housed the dialysis center. Each treatment took some six or eight hours. She grew weary of spending nearly half her life just to be kept alive, so she was pleased when she was offered the opportunity to undergo dialysis at home. She wouldn't have to spend so much time traveling and the new machines meant shorter treatments with fewer aggravating side effects like nausea and headaches. She was not sure she would be comfortable handling things herself, but the dialysis company said they had trained many patients to carry out the treatments on their own. They would send a nurse to make regular home visits to check on her and service the equipment. And, they assured her that the machine would alert her, shut itself down, and notify the center automatically if it malfunctioned. She agreed to give it a try.

Everything went well for several months. She liked the cheerful, efficient nurse who came every Thursday and would sit and chat with her while she ran tests and made sure Harriet had enough supplies. Then one Wednesday a tall, thin man with a dark beard came to her door. He showed her an official-looking credential that identified him as a technician for the company that manufactured her dialysis machine and said that he was there to install a minor upgrade that needed to be done while she was undergoing treatment. Shortly after she hooked herself up to the machine he took a cell phone out of his jacket pocket, typed something on the phone, and pressed the "send" button.

The next day the nurse was bubbling over with the good news she was carrying when she arrived at Harriet's house: a kidney donor with a near-perfect match had been found. She couldn't wait to see the look on Harriet's face. She had brought some cheese Danish for them to celebrate together. She rang the doorbell repeatedly but Harriet did not answer. Finally she got concerned and dialed 9-1-1. Within minutes firefighters forced open the door and EMTs ran into the house. Harriet Handelmeyer was still hooked up to the dialysis machine but she would no longer have any use for a kidney.

Chapter 5: Cybersleuths, Inc.

Will Manningham climbed the five steps to the front entrance of the stately brownstone on Capitol Hill and pushed what appeared to be an ordinary doorbell button next to the oak double-doors. When he was immediately buzzed in he nodded with professional respect for the camouflaged sensor in the doorbell that had read his fingerprint. He walked through the doorway into what had long ago been the elaborate entry hall of an elegant row house but now was the central point of hallways that led in either direction to the four neighboring town houses. The old private homes had been connected and converted into the headquarters of his new employer, *Cybersleuths, Inc.*

Will followed a sign down a short flight of stairs to the Human Resources Department. A young man with a mass of dreadlocks looked up from behind a counter, rose, and extended his hand, saying, "Mr. Manningham. Welcome to *Cybersleuths*. Please follow me, we're all ready to get you through the process and into our system quickly."

Less than three hours later Will returned to the main level, then strode up the massive central staircase to the top floor and walked directly to the big office in the rear of the building. A brass nameplate on the outside wall read, "Henry J. Cotter, Senior Executive Vice President." The door was open so Will knocked lightly on the doorjamb. The man at the desk looked up, smiled and brushed a long lock of gleaming white hair off his forehead, then stood and walked over to his visitor. He was a couple of inches under six feet, but looked much shorter standing next to the six-foot-three Will. He extended a thick, beefy hand and said, "Hi, Will. Welcome to *Cybersleuths*. How's your morning been so far?"

"Thanks, Hank. I'm impressed—your H.R. is very efficient. All the forms were pre-populated with my particulars and all I had to do was glance at them and sign. And the training sessions on your systems were very informative." He pointed to the badge clipped to his coat pocket. "Got everything: badge, keys, health insurance, 401(k), W-4, you name it. That parking pass will be great in this neighborhood for the days I don't take the Metro. Uh…there was just that one part of the process…"

"I think I know what you're referring to."

"Yeah, it was a little unnerving giving a DNA sample for your cadaver identification files…"

Hank Cotter nodded, pursing his lips in agreement. "Everyone feels that way, of course. But, comes with the turf if you're going to be doing any field work."

"Understood," Will said softly as the image of his brother falling in a hail of gunfire flashed across his mind.

"In any case, glad things went well. Now about lunch—I hope you like Cobb Salad. It's either that or some vegan stuff." He pointed to a conference table nestled into a recess with a picture window that gave an impressive view of the U.S. Capitol and the National Mall. "Have a seat. The others are on their way."

"Thanks, a Cobb would be great. And, nice digs you have here, Hank."

"Yeah, we love it here. Construction took a long time with permits and all that historic preservation stuff, you know, but it turned out great. Much better than some high-rise on K Street. I'll take you to your own space when we're done. Only so many big offices in this building, but I think you'll like the one we have for you. Two big windows facing the Mall."

"As long as there's a ceiling and a door I'm sure it'll be fine. I can't concentrate in an open cubicle."

Just then three people walked into the office. Hank Cotter said, "Hi guys. Meet our new colleague, Will Manningham."

A tall, lanky, freckle-faced woman with bright red hair stepped forward and stuck out her hand. Will was instantly taken aback by her appearance—she looked so much like him she could have been a triplet separated from him and his twin brother at birth, or a sibling his parents had given up for adoption before the boys were born. He chuckled at the thought, not taking it seriously. Still, the resemblance was remarkable, and a bit unnerving. "Belinda," she said as Will took her hand, "Belinda Winnisome. We've heard a lot about you, Will. Good to meet you in person."

"Belinda's up to her gills on the project you'll be involved in. I think you'll like working with her. By the way, you have something in common—her PhD is from Princeton."

"Good to meet you, Belinda. Great school, Princeton. Math? Computer Science?"

"Pretty much both, actually. Electrical engineering, with a focus on computer science, and math."

OK, this is getting a bit creepy, thought Will. *She looks like a clone of me and Barry—and we went to the same college in the same program!* He suppressed the urge to inquire further about her background and family tree, just smiled and said, "Just like me! Wow, we really do have something in common. Let's chat about it someday."

"Sure, anytime."

Hank Cotter gestured toward the other two people, one man and one woman. He pointed at the woman and said, "This is Lauren Sveiks," and then to the man, "and Edward Hall. They will work with you and Belinda on our Russia desk."

"Pleased to meet you both," said Will. He towered over the diminutive woman who appeared to be under five feet tall. Will bent over to shake hands with her. She looked up at him with an ageless, cherubic face that left Will thinking she could have been anywhere from her mid-thirties to late fifties.

"My pleasure," she said, in a deep, throaty voice.

Will then turned to shake hands with the man, who said, "Ned, Ned Hall." Ned's voice was even deeper than Lauren's. Unlike the others, who were dressed casually, he wore a crisply starched white shirt, a brightly-patterned blue and yellow tie, and perfectly-creased dark suit pants. Young, Will thought, probably late twenties.

"OK, let's have a seat so we can talk and eat," said Hank Cotter. "Lauren, that's your vegan whatever. Cobb salads for everyone else. Will, you should know this is a real treat—we usually scarf down lunch at our desks, but today is special. And it's on the company."

"Yeah," said Belinda with a broad smile, "that never happens. Just like Christmas today."

For a moment Will thought he could hear Barry making the same remark. *Stop!* he told himself, *just stop that crap!*

The group ate in silence for a few minutes before Hank Cotter spoke again. "Will," he said, "everyone here has been very impressed with your work tracking down the Russian mob and uncovering how they've been stealing Medicare blind. Even more important than saving the government money—and I know this is how you feel—the consequences for patients have been terrible. Scores have died and even more have been seriously harmed from the mob's phony drugs and unnecessary treatments. Good work. But we didn't bring you here to focus on healthcare scams, not exactly."

"Now you tell me! But...healthcare's all I really know."

"Rest assured we had very good reasons for recruiting you. I'm sure you can understand why we couldn't tell you the details while you were still a Fed. You would have been under an obligation to report whatever we told you up through regular channels at CMS. But we have our own lines of communication with the government. This whole project is through a contract with Homeland Security."

"*Homeland Security!* OK, I get the picture. Well, I'm here, so let's get started."

"We'll start from scratch. I'll give you the big picture and Belinda can fill you in on the details and technical stuff afterward."

Will glanced at Belinda. She stared back at him but did not smile or nod or say anything. Will decided it would take a while to figure her out.

Cotter continued. "I thought of you, Will, because we're seeing something that does involve people's health in a bad way— they're dying suddenly, with no good explanation. Small clusters of people who just dropped dead. FDA and the Centers for Disease Control are stumped, so they reported their concerns to Homeland Security. They hired us, and we hired you. Clear enough?"

"Sure, but not much to go on. Do the deaths have anything in common?"

"Just one thing: the people who died had all been kept alive with medical technology."

"Like what?"

"Different things. Pacemakers, kidney dialysis machines, insulin pumps, implantable defibrillators. All fairly common technologies, generally reliable."

"You mean they failed out of the blue? Were they defective?"

"Not at all. Every piece of equipment in their bodies was retrieved at autopsy and tested extensively by the manufacturer. They were all in perfect working order. That's what got the manufacturers concerned and led to us getting involved. We repeated the testing in an independent lab and got the same results. Good as new, no defects."

"Any phony stuff? Counterfeit devices like the ones the Russians have been pushing through the black market?"

"No, totally legitimate. Everything checks out. The equipment came from different manufacturers. Each one traced the exact source and certified that it was their product before conducting the first tests. No contraband. No defects. No clue!"

"Why do you think the Russians are involved?"

"Truth is we're not sure. Homeland Security suspects that this involves the Russians but they haven't said why. And we have no real proof."

"Is there a money trail? Anything like that?"

"Again, we don't have a clue. We do not know if what we're seeing is about money at all. All we're certain of is that there are dead people who should still be alive."

"Interesting! Sounds like a challenge. What have you done so far?"

"Belinda can bring you up to date. Our approach should sound quite familiar to you."

"Sure, Hank," said Belinda, taking the cue. "So far we've been building links to data bases. We tied into files from the manufacturers on their products, including complaint records and reports to FDA. Health insurance billing records. National death registry. Lawsuits involving medical devices. Everything we can think of. We're looking for any signs of a pattern—you know, deaths in similar sites or linked to the same doctors or other providers or health care systems."

"Yup, just what I would have suggested. Sounds like a good start. Has anything turned up?"

"Nothing. No sign of any pattern. So far the deaths seem to be isolated events that are all totally unexplained and involve medical technologies. The only other thing they have in common is that they started in the last couple of months."

"Very interesting. So, why are you sure they aren't just random incidents after all?"

"We're not absolutely sure, just highly suspicious. FDA and the manufacturers have never seen an outbreak of sudden deaths from medical devices in absolutely perfect working order. Usually there's some flaw, some short circuit, some latent defect or damage. Or some medical complication like a surgeon who put in the wrong device or put it into the wrong patient. But here, we've discovered nothing like that."

Will ran his fingers through his long red hair. One fingernail began to pluck at a spot on his scalp as he thought about what he had heard. After a long minute he said, "I have an idea. What you've described sounds like a sniper taking random shots from different locations at different times with a few different weapons. Maybe we're dealing with target practice."

Chapter 6: On The Campaign Trail

Annabaker Minion loved campaigning for president now that she felt the tide turning in her direction. Ever since she was a little girl she had been driven by a sense of outrage that no one else seemed to feel. Everyone would just humor her as she ranted about how unfair the world was. About the sacrifice of lives and waste of resources to gratify the ravenous military-industrial complex. About the way her country had abandoned the noble sentiments in the Declaration of Independence that promised equality for all. About racism, misogyny, corporatocracy, xenophobia, religiosity, climate Armageddon. It seemed her list grew longer and more infuriating every day. Things were getting worse, much worse, and yet her message had only resonated with a handful of hard-core radicals. Chronic protesters who didn't bother to vote, except to shoot themselves in the foot by backing hopeless third-party candidates. And even those supporters were dwindling, dying off from old age. But now everything had changed. At long last the masses were finally listening to her, rallying to her causes, joining forces to combat the decline of civilization.

But why had her message finally captivated the public? She shrugged her shoulders and shook her head at the palpable irony. After a lifetime of being marginalized, a lone voice crying out in the wilderness to a small band of fiercely loyal followers, what was it that she had to thank for her sudden rise to prominence? A careless mother who didn't notice when her little girl bolted in front of a massive SUV, that's what! Annabaker happened to be in the right place at the right time while the TV cameras and cell phone videos were rolling. Now she was not just some radical wacko running for president, she was America's darling, their latest hero. A celebrity.

Sure, being a frequent guest on Absalom Whitmore's show had been great, but now it was hard to turn on the television without seeing Annabaker Minion. Morning talk shows, evening news shows, afternoon gab fests. And even more important, the videos had been streamed millions of times on social media and she had more followers than any of the other candidates—even more than that disgusting excuse for a president, Dorzel.

No matter. Who cared why things were swinging toward her? Don't people say that God works in mysterious ways? She was getting what she was due, it just wasn't coming the way she had expected. She deserved the attention, the praise, the spike in the polls. Not for saving the child. That was an instinctive reaction. Keeping a child from being crushed under her security detail's SUV was just random fate. Someone in the crowd might have jumped out and they would be the instant celebrity, not her. Screw how it happened, this was her rightful reward for a lifetime of devotion to all the right causes. That was why people were listening to her, couldn't get enough of her. She particularly relished a man-on-the-street interview when a guy in a C-suite suit said, "I always dismissed her as not being a serious candidate, but now I'm giving her a second look." That from some *man,* and a man in a suit at that!

Her popularity had surged, she was gaining on that militarist Jenkins. He could no longer ignore her. She was a player. Still, she had to acknowledge, there was one major problem looming in the polls: the numbers continued to show that in the general election Jenkins would unseat Dorzel but Dorzel would trounce her. One C-suite suit wasn't enough. Saving one child wasn't enough. Jenkins' military record resonated with middle-of-the-road America, the same folks who would never forgive her for going to North Vietnam with Jane Fonda or for arguing that the 9-11 atrocities did not justify the invasion of Iraq or the war in Afghanistan. She was riding high, but a hard core of swing voters could not stomach voting for her—they would stay home or shut their eyes, clench their teeth, and vote for Dorzel. If she won the Democratic nomination, Dorzel would be reelected.

So, if she couldn't crack through the view that she was a sure loser, what were her options? There were two, but she wasn't fond of either one: use her surging popularity to get on the ticket as Jenkins' running mate, or split off and run as a third-party candidate. Bolstering Jenkins' candidacy would be like running as a Republican as far as she was concerned. To her and her supporters he represented the failed Democratic policies that had helped Dorzel get elected: promise universal health care but settle for incremental measures and never take on the big-money interests; talk about helping the middle class while letting their tax rates go up and up; look the other way on antitrust enforcement while mega-corporations took over the world; give lip service to gun control while shying away from confronting the NRA where it counted. All the right words, none of the decisive actions that were needed. And on top of that, Jenkins wanted to increase the military's budget. How could she sign on to that agenda? The very idea of joining up with him stuck in her craw.

The other option, running as a third-party candidate, was far more attractive. She knew she could garner at least 15 percent of the vote, even more in some of the biggest blue states. The country needed a new party anyway, one that was true to progressive principles. No more limousine liberals or phony Socialists. It drove her crazy that Dorzel had gotten away with exploiting the populist fever that had fermented in this country for decades even though everything he did was making things worse for the very people who were conned into voting for him. The country was now living the paradox of *"What's the Matter with Kansas?"* on steroids. No matter, she'd bring the working-class around. They'd see that she would be true to the causes that would improve their lives. They'd rally around her.

Of course she knew the risk that she would pull a Ralph Nader and get blamed for the Democrats losing the election. Divide and don't conquer. But, maybe she didn't have to take that chance. Maybe even better—she could use the fear of a third-party movement assuring Dorzel's reelection to her advantage. If the polls continued to shift in her direction, the threat of her bolting from the ranks and forming a third party would give her enormous leverage to wrest the Democratic nomination away from Jenkins. And if that didn't work, what then? Would she really follow through on her threat and decimate the party?

She stared at herself in the mirror for a long minute. This was her time. She had to seize the moment. Which way to go? She took a long breath, exhaled, and told herself she didn't have to come to a decision, not just yet. Her immediate challenge was to continue to gain momentum and win the nomination. Plenty of time to choose between abandoning her principles and playing second banana to Jenkins or mounting a credible threat to split off and risk dragging the party under. She could wait. At some point the decision would make itself.

***

John Francis and Mary Anne Camieri were in seventh heaven—or, as John Francis, practicing his Italian lesions, would say, *settimo cielo*. They had just returned from a trip to his ancestral home town of Cammarata in Sicily and taken the bold step that they had been talking about for three years: they were moving to Italy. Cammarata was giving away houses for free, if the new residents agreed to renovate them. The house they selected was in a perfect spot on top of a hill, facing east with a stunning view of Mt. Etna from their balcony. They were on their way to their bank in Arlington, Virginia, to arrange for a transfer of the funds for the deposit that was required to assure Cammarata that they were buying the house in good faith and would actually restore it within three years. The bank asked them to come in to fill out some paperwork to convert the American funds, a little over $5,500, into Euros.

The couple knew that the renovation work would be demanding since the house had not been lived in for decades, had only one intact outside wall and part of the tile roof, and the ancient plumbing, and dangerously outdated electrical wiring needed to be rebuilt from scratch. But they were not deterred by the prospect of a prolonged construction project even though they had heard tales of woe from a few ex-pats frustrated with the Italian contractors and bureaucracy. They were thrilled with the prospect of leaving the U.S.—no matter how great the challenge of their Italian adventure, it would be better than continuing to live in a country with Hugo H. Dorzel as their president. America was no longer the land of promise that inspired John Francis's great-grandparents to emigrate from Cammarata during the agricultural blight in the late 1800s, or Mary Anne's parents to leave nearby Corleone a few years later. They even planned to change their names once they were settled, to Gianfranco and Anna Maria Camieri.

But the decline of the American dream was not the only reason John Francis and Mary Anne had decided it was important to enjoy their lives. Mary Anne had gotten a second lease on life after a near-death episode that occurred when she had gone into the hospital for a biopsy of a lump in her breast. The biopsy turned out negative, but during the procedure her heart started beating out of control. She would have died had the surgeon not reacted quickly to defibrillate her heart. Now her lifeline was a defibrillator implanted in her chest.

As the ecstatic couple emerged from the Arlington Metro and stopped at a crosswalk one block from their bank, a tall, thin man with a dark beard joined the small crowd waiting for the Don't Walk signal to change. He took a cell phone out of his jacket pocket, typed something on the phone, and pressed the "send" button. Mary Anne Camieri fell to the sidewalk, her body writhing in a grand mal seizure. EMTs arrived within six minutes but could not restart her heart. Gianfranco and Anna Maria Camieri would never live out their Sicilian dream.

Chapter 7: Back In School

Five-thousand miles from the headquarters of *Cybersleuths, Inc.,* in Washington, Alexandra Parushnikova was also beginning a new job. Just as Will Manningham had climbed a central staircase to Hank Cotter's office in the converted town house on Capitol Hill, she ascended a far more massive one in Zarya Dacha, then walked down a lavishly decorated hallway to Room #9. She turned the oversized carved brass doorknob and entered a space unlike any other she had seen in the elegant old Dacha: a small and sparsely furnished room that reminded her of the austere classrooms in her Soviet-era primary school. But this one was set up for a single student, a teacher, and a few observers. A simple blackboard behind an old wooden table in the front of the room. A chair for the instructor, three chairs against the walls, and a chair and desk for the student. For her.

She took a seat and glanced at the ancient wall clock that ticked softly as its pendulum swung back and forth: 10:55 in the morning, she was five minutes early. Just as the clock chimed eleven times the door opened and a man in a military uniform marched in bolt upright, followed by another man and two women. The man leading the parade looked like a Peter Sellers caricature of a Soviet general: bushy Stalin mustache, round Trotsky eyeglasses, and so many medals and ribbons she marveled at how he could stand ramrod straight with all that weight on his chest. She stood and turned to greet him, expecting him to bark commands in a loud, threatening voice. Instead, he smiled, extended his hand, and said, "Welcome to Zarya Dacha, Alexandra Arkadyevna Parushnikova. Ah, I should say, *'Welcome back'*—I know that your grandfather brought you here when you were a young girl. We trust your return has been comfortable so far?"

She reached out and shook the man's hand and said, "Very pleasant indeed, thank you..." She hesitated, realizing she had no idea what rank the array of stars and bars and leaves on his epaulets and lapels signified.

He smiled a knowing, friendly smile and said, "I am General Petyr Leonidovich Volodin. You may address me as General." He gestured to the others and said, "These are my colleagues, Gennady Yurievich Kedrov, Natalia Kostenka Anatolievna, and Valeria Klara Yakovna. Natalia Kostenka will be your instructor."

Alexandra shook hands and exchanged greetings with the three and said, "Please, call me Sasha if you will." She looked them over and immediately decided that she would have preferred Gennady Yurievich or Valeria Klara over Natalia Kostenka as her instructor. Gennady Yurievich was the oldest of the group, well into his sixties, but had the most relaxed demeanor. He was a stout man about her height, wore a wool tweed suit and white shirt with no tie, and had a well-trimmed white beard framing his peaceful, round Saint Nickolas face. He took her hand with his short, plump fingers and said, "Welcome, Sasha." Valeria Klara was much younger than either man, probably barely thirty years old. She had a trim, athletic body capped with blond hair drawn up into a tight bun. She wore a perfectly-tailored fashionable blue suit with a brilliant sapphire pendant on her lapel. "Greetings, Sasha," she said, nodding pleasantly as they shook hands. Then there was the instructor, Natalia Kostenka. Strikingly thin, she stood stiff and austere, cloaked in a dark striped suit with the top buttoned up to her neck. It was all Sasha could do to avoid staring down at the bony, fleshless hand that grasped hers with unexpected strength. The lips of her small, tight mouth barely parted as she said, "Natalia Kostenka." She seemed so other-worldly she might have been inhuman, an avatar.

"Well, then," said the General, "let us begin. Natalia Kostenka, if you please."

The skeleton of a woman stepped in front of the wooden table and said nothing until the General had taken a seat. Then, in a voice that somehow emerged with commanding authority through clenched teeth behind a narrow slit of lips, she said, "Be seated." She stared at Sasha like a raven contemplating its prey and, ignoring her student's request to be addressed as Sasha, said, in perfect and only slightly accented English, "Alexandra Arkadyevna, you are here on a mission of the utmost importance to the Russian Federation. And of

33

the utmost secrecy. Nothing you hear is ever to leave this room except as you are ordered. We expect you to honor these restrictions forever. I must emphasize this point: any breach of security would be a serious crime against the State. It would also be seen as a sign of disrespect, a failure to appreciate that we have been quite generous in the terms of your assignment. Your mother has also been well taken care of but she would not continue to be so comfortable should you violate any of these terms. Is that clear?"

Sasha understood fully what the woman was threatening: torture and death for her and extreme deprivation or worse for her mother. But she was not concerned about the consequences—who would she ever tell? And she was loyal to her homeland, of course she was. She did not hesitate to say as much: "Yes, quite clear. The arrangement is acceptable. I will do exactly as you say."

The woman lifted an attaché case onto the table and produced a short stack of papers that she handed to Sasha. "You will attest to your agreement by signing these documents. Pages 3, 13, and the final page require your full signature. You may initial the others."

"May I have a moment to look them over?"

Natalia Kostenka scowled at Sasha. Her lips parted a millimeter but before she could speak the General said, "Of course. Please take your time."

Sasha began thumbing through the pages but quickly realized she could not concentrate on the details in the many numbered paragraphs. There were numerous citations to chapters of law that listed sanctions for any violations. One clause in particular jumped off the page: "*subject to any and all penalties for crimes against the Russian Federation, without limitation.*" There was no doubt of exactly what that meant. Sasha had seen enough. No reason to continue reading—the die was cast, her life was in their hands. She picked up a pen, signed and initialed the sheets without looking further at the text, then handed the stack back to Natalia Kostenka. The woman returned the documents to her attaché case and said, "Very well, then. Let us begin."

Chapter 8: Searching for Patterns

"Target practice, hmm…" said Belinda. "Interesting thought, Will. Tell us more."

"Not really much of a thought, just something that popped into my head while you were describing the unexplained deaths. You said there seems to be no link among the people who died, at least not as far as you've identified so far. And the deaths involved very different medical devices. So what are the options? They could be entirely random events. In that case we might never discover a cause, and there might not really be just one. But what if they're not random, what if they have some purpose? That's what made me think of target practice with a weapon of some sort. The victims could be more or less random, but the common thread might be testing some new deadly weapon. In that case there would be a pattern we could discover if we figure out how and where to look. That's all I've got. As I said, not a fully developed thought, just a reaction."

As Belinda mulled over Will's words he was struck by the contemplative expression that came across her face, an eerily familiar look that reminded Will of the way Barry would react when he was considering something Will had said. Looking at Belinda, he could see his late brother staring off into space, pondering how to respond. This was too much. It was hard enough having a "phantom twin" forever lurking in his mind, like an amputee who still senses the missing limb. Belinda's resemblance to Barry unnerved Will so deeply that he did not hear her ask, "So, are you thinking this might be something like the sniper attacks around the D.C. area back in 2002?"

The sound of her voice snapped Will back into the moment. "Sorry, I got distracted. Did you say something about sniper attacks?"

"Remember the weeks when everyone was too scared to go fill up their car with gas or go to the grocery store or open their front curtains because people were getting shot out of nowhere? Are you saying these deaths might be like those?"

"Maybe…maybe so. As I recall, those shootings were not just target practice, but they did seem to be entirely indiscriminate at the time. Afterward, a variety of possible motives were suspected, right? Like terrorism or covering up one murder with a slew of others. In any case, what they had in common was that they were the work of the same killers, Malvo and Muhammad."

Belinda was silent for a moment, then said, "We do have one thread that runs through every one of the current deaths: the victims were all dependent on sophisticated medical devices. If someone figured out how to pull the plug on those devices, they could kill their targets by shutting them down or causing them to malfunction."

"Yup. Pacemaker stops sending impulses to the person's heart telling it to continue beating and the heart shuts off. Insulin pump stops pumping…"

"Or," interrupted Belinda, "pumps way too much insulin…"

"Exactly. Same result. Instantaneous death."

Lauren Sveiks spoke for the first time. "If I may," came the deep, throaty words, "I think you could be on to something. The medical devices were all different, yes, but they have one thing in common: wireless connectivity. Devices like that are all networked into a variety of systems. Hospitals, manufacturers, doctors, they all monitor implanted devices and record data from them remotely. Sometimes they transmit commands to the devices or update the firmware. The FDA has issued a number of alerts about medical devices being vulnerable to hacking. There have been numerous stories in the press about some serious incidents."

"Ah," said Will, "right! I remember when Dick Cheney was afraid that he might be assassinated by a hacker taking over his implanted defibrillator. He made his doctors disable the wireless function. Wasn't there even a TV show about something like that? You're saying Cheney wasn't just paranoid, it's a real threat?"

"Exactly. There was an episode of *Homeland*, but this is real life. The FDA has now recalled about half a million pacemakers that are vulnerable to cyber attack."

"Yes," said Ned Hall, "my contacts at Homeland Security say they have become so concerned about hacking into medical software that DHS is working with FDA to enhance the cybersecurity of devices."

"Very interesting," said Will. "But why would anyone hack into medical devices? Are we dealing with a Malvo or Muhammad who's gone high-tech? Or could the killers—if there are killers involved here—have a reason for murdering people?"

"Ransom," replied Ned. "A number of hospitals have been held hostage by cyber attacks on major systems. A widespread cyber attack on the National Health Service in the UK reduced hospitals to working with pen and paper for a while. In another incident some hospitals in this country were hit with ransomware that infected a device that injects dyes into patients to enhance MRI scans. There have been threats to block access to medical devices, steal personal health data, drain the power out of the batteries, or command the devices to malfunction in a number of ways."

"So, how easy is it to hack into someone's pacemaker or any other device? I mean, a couple of guys could go out and get guns and start killing people or kidnap someone for ransom, but can just anyone manage to hack into a pacemaker?"

"That depends on the device and, to some degree, how old it is. Different devices have different vulnerabilities. Some of the newer ones are pretty sophisticated. But you're right, it would take someone with a fair degree of technical savvy to pull it off."

"Have there been any incidents involving ransom that sound like what we might be seeing here?"

"Not really. If they're going after a particular person the hacker would need to locate the exact device they want to target. Most of the schemes I'm familiar with involve big systems, not individual people. For ransom to pay off you need to have a credible threat to someone with a lot at stake and a lot of money."

"So, did any of the people we're looking into receive any ransom demands? Or did the medical device manufacturers or healthcare systems get any threats?"

"Good question. We don't know yet about the deaths we're investigating, I'll check with Homeland Security to see if there have been other ransomware incidents."

"So this might not be target practice to prepare to kill a particular person so much as a way to terrorize device manufacturers and health systems," said Will. "Kill a few people to scare the bejeezus out of the big corporations so they'll comply with ransom demands when they know the threat is credible."

"Exactly," said Belinda, then went silent. Will saw the Barry look again, and shuddered slightly. After half a minute she said, "Sounds like we have two good theories, target practice and intimidation. If it's intimidation, then at some point someone has to take credit for the killings and issue a demand for payment. On the other hand, if it's target practice to prepare for going after a particular target there may never be anyone who comes out in the open, it'll be up to us to figure out what's going on and who's behind it. And who the ultimate target is."

"OK," said Will, recovering his composure. "Let's work from there and see what we can find that supports either theory. Belinda and Lauren, why don't you think about any data sources we can probe or other ways that we can find something that points one way or the other. Ned, you can run this by Homeland Security. And I'll see what I can find out from the FBI...I still have a good contact there."

Chapter 9: M.A.D.

Robin Jenkins was so angry he felt like spitting bullets. "Idiots!" he screamed into his empty dressing room. "*Fucking idiots!* I'm not the enemy, Dorzel is. Why can't they get that into their stupid heads? Our fucking debates are nothing but Mutual Assured Destruction, killing each other with friendly fucking fire. We're not even making the other side shoot at us. We're doing Dorzel's work for him, we're getting that asshole reelected. *Goddamn it all!*"

Jenkins was just about to kick over a small table along with the pitcher of water and half-empty glass sitting on top when he heard a knock on the door.

"Who is it?" he barked.

No answer. But after a moment the door opened and Annabaker Minion walked in.

"What the fuck do *you* want?"

"I just want to talk," she said, pulling the door closed behind her.

"You've done plenty of talking already tonight. I don't want to hear another word out of your mouth. You're a goddamn traitor, a mole for Dorzel."

"Calm down, Robin. I hate Dorzel as much as you do."

"Seemed like you were more interested in coming after me than dragging him down. What the fuck were you thinking, calling me a slave to the military-industrial complex? You know goddamn well I've gone against the extreme defense hawks many times, and it's cost me dearly. And what was that shit about me not wanting people to get health care? Have you read my fucking healthcare proposal? Jesus, Minion, what kind of bullshit was that?"

"I'm not sure those were my exact words, *Jenkins*. I was just drawing a distinction between your policies and mine. But I agree, I think things got out of control tonight, that's why I'm here."

"To apologize?"

Annabaker Minion smiled and shook her head. "Not at all. What's done is done, what's said is said. We need to figure out where to go from here."

"You know, all that crap you threw at me tonight will come back to haunt me in the general election. You gave Dorzel's crowd a million sound bites they'll aim at the undecided voters, the ones who'll figure a devil they know is better than a devil they don't know. And that same bullshit will scare away the progressives, they won't come out to vote. You might as well join the Dorzel campaign since you're shilling for that asshole."

"Are you going to keep ranting or are you willing to have a real conversation?"

Robin Jenkins felt his cheeks flushing, the arteries on both sides of his head pounding rapidly. He turned and looked away from her, only to see both their faces in the dressing-table mirror. "Goddammit," he mumbled, gritting his teeth. He turned back and said, "OK, what it is you want to talk about?"

"Can we sit down? And I'd like a glass of water, if you don't mind."

"Help yourself," he said, gesturing to the water pitcher and drinking glass that would have been lying in pieces on the floor if her knock had come a few seconds later than it had. He sat in the only chair in the room and pointed to the stool under the dressing table, saying, "And take a seat over there if you must."

Annabaker Minion poured herself a glass of water, downed it in one long gulp, then poured another and set the glass on the dressing table. She pulled out the stool and sat, then said, "I would like to put all of this to rest."

"Your dime, go ahead."

"You know that I've gotten a big boost in the polls and we're pretty much neck and neck now, right?"

"My people say you got a temporary bump from that kid thing in Oshkosh that'll disappear in another two weeks. I saw numbers today that say your little surge is already on the wane."

"Not what my people say—just the opposite, in fact. Be that as it may, what really counts are some other numbers. Have you seen the ratings from our debate yet?"

"No, why?"

"Instant reads show that we pulled in less than one-third as many viewers as the first debate. *One-third!* The numbers have been declining over the four debates. At this rate only our kids will be watching the fifth debate, and I'm not sure all of them will even turn on the television. I heard more people were watching re-runs of ancient episodes of *All In The Family* than our third debate."

"No shit! But I'm not surprised. Dorzel's voters always thought Archie Bunker had it right, they were too ignorant to understand he was a parody. Anyway, everyone's head is reeling from a constant diet of Dorzel insanity and we're just adding to the noise. The only ones who keep watching our debates are the ones who want to see us cut ourselves to pieces."

"I have a way out of this mess."

"Go ahead."

"You and I should team up and get the other seven to throw in the towel and support us. We make nice and turn our venom against Dorzel. Period."

"You want to be my running mate?"

"If it comes to that. Or you mine."

Jenkins thought his head would explode.

"What the fuck are you saying? You think you have a chance of getting the nomination? And you think that I would be your second banana if you somehow pulled it off? What have you been smoking?"

"I'm no more eager to be on the ticket with you than you are with me. But we're the only two with any chance of winning. And I've still got a shot at the nomination."

"You can't beat Dorzel. It would be suicide for the party to nominate you."

"So they tell me. But you can't win without me. Forget all the harsh rhetoric we tossed around tonight—you need the progressive faction and they won't vote for you if I'm not on the ticket. We need each other."

Robin Jenkins took a deep breath and tried to suppress his anger. The threat of being held hostage by Annabaker Minion made him furious but his battle-tested mind told him to get control, to think things through before making a decision. He went silent and sorted through what she was saying, what he knew, what his political instincts told him. OK, she wasn't entirely wrong. The radical left might torpedo him in the general election. Nothing was good enough for many of them, they had a long history of fucking things up by refusing to go along with reasonable compromises. If he picked a middle-of-the-road running mate a big chunk of the left might walk away, sit on some fucked-up sense of principle and turn their heads while Dorzel got another four years. Problem was, she wasn't entirely right, either. If he put her on the ticket she might turn off enough moderates to cost him the election. They'd sit on their thumbs rather than vote for her. Lose-lose either way. But he knew which way he needed to turn.

"Fuck this," he said. "I can't have you as my running mate. Out of the question. You're just way too far to the left for me to stomach. Anyway, I don't need you, I'll win without you. But I'll say this: if you stop attacking me now, then when I get the nomination we can talk about another role for you."

"Fuck that. I'm not about to be silenced for some vague promise. Besides, you haven't got the nomination, not yet."

"Well, god forbid you somehow get the nomination. The party would be doomed no matter who else was on the ticket, and it sure as hell won't be me. No deal."

"That's it, then."

"That's it. We're done here."

Chapter 10: Special Assignment

Natalia Kostenka hovered over Sasha, her raven eyes glaring from the dark, recessed sockets that haunted her bony face. When she spoke, the words punched through her slit of a mouth with blood-curdling menace. "You will look carefully at the screen, Alexandra Arkadyevna," she said, stepping to one side and clicking a button on a remote control that somehow had appeared in her right hand. An image flashed onto the screen, an image Sasha immediately recognized: Hugo H. Dorzel, the President of the United States of America.

Sasha stared at the screen, then turned and looked inquiringly at General Petyr Ilyin Leonidovich Volodin. He remained impassive, offering no sign that he would provide an explanation. She turned to Gennady Yurievich Kedrov and then to Valeria Klara Yakovna, both of whom also remained expressionless. The photo of Dorzel had come as no surprise to anyone but Sasha.

"This is your assignment, Alexandra Arkadyevna. You will meet this man and draw his attention to you. Doing this will not be difficult. We have every confidence that you are exactly the kind of woman that he is attracted to. That is why you have been offered this extraordinary opportunity to serve your country."

Her mind was in a jumble. What the hell had she gotten herself into? She was not shocked that the job might involve providing sexual favors—she had suspected as much when Galina Khovanskaya had recruited her again, and she had gone to bed with more than one doctor to push sales for *Marquis-Herrant.* But the President of the United States? Could they really want her to seduce the president? The very idea was so startling she struggled to take it in. She tried to focus on the man's image but a deep wave of revulsion filled her: he was a pig. Fat and slovenly, repulsive in every way. She could not imagine what act of sexual depravity he would want to do to her. Just being touched by that man would be disgusting, too loathsome to contemplate. The thought of him inside of her, of any part of him inside any part of her body, made her retch. Bile surged into her mouth. She forced herself to swallow the pungent liquid. She must calm down, gather her wits, figure out a way to get out of this nightmare.

But she knew there was no way out. The penalty for refusing to go along with whatever they demanded was clear: she would disappear. And she would not simply disappear. She would be punished for her crime, punished severely. Her mother would also pay a cruel price, maybe the ultimate one. She was entirely under their control.

"Do you have any questions, Alexandra Arkadyevna?" The words were cold, emotionless.

Sasha shook her head slowly. "None," she said softly, staring down at her feet. Then she looked up and said, "Yes, I do have one. Am I to be a spy?"

The three spectators chuckled. Sasha even thought she saw the slightest hint of an incipient smile on Natalia Kostenka's cadaverous lips. "No. A spy uncovers information that is meant to remain secret. We have many others who are taking care of that. You will be our liaison for information that both sides wish to share. Our intermediary, a go-between."

"But why, why should you need such a person? Surely you have some other way to speak with him if that is what you both desire."

"He does not trust his current channels of communication with us, nor do we. President Dorzel is convinced that his own security agency is disloyal and is working to bring him down. He is by nature quite paranoid, but in this case we have reasons to believe he is correct: several of the conversations in which he has shared state secrets with our president have been leaked. He entrusted a certain private attorney to carry messages between us, but that person proved to be quite erratic and thus unreliable as a confidential emissary. We cannot deal with him any longer."

"Is there no other way?"

Another brief burst of chuckles from the observers, but this time there was no trace of a smile on Natalia Kostenka's ghastly face.

"We experimented with a number of other methods and determined that we must have a courier we can trust. Having our own person embedded with him is the most reliable way to ensure that our communications remain private."

For a brief moment Sasha wondered whether the woman was being ironic by using "embedded," but quickly dismissed the idea. The woman was incapable of humor. And she went quiet and glowered at Sasha, making it clear she would provide no further explanation.

The General spoke up again.

"Natalia Kostenka perhaps feels it is not her place to go into details, but I can assure you that we have indeed explored many options. I will provide one example. You are familiar, are you not, with the American's passion for Twitter?"

"I have heard much about it, although I am not one who uses that form of social media."

"Then you know enough to understand what I am telling you. We developed a series of codes that we intended to use to exchange information hidden, as they say, in plain sight. The secrets were to be buried in his tidal wave of Tweets. But this proved impossible. When he tried to encode his messages to us they came out so garbled no one had any idea what he was trying to say. And he proved unable to decipher our encoded messages to him. That experiment was a complete failure, as were several others."

"Thank you, General," Natalia Kostenka said peremptorily, the self-important teacher reclaiming authority over her classroom. "And so we decided that the only way to be absolutely confident that our communications were secure would be to pass them through someone who could get close to him. We need to inject a third person between us, someone who can understand what he intends to communicate and carry messages back and forth without confusion or misinterpretation. Someone we can rely on without question." She paused for a moment. Sasha was astonished to see the woman's look grow even more grim and threatening than it had been. Then, like a venomous snake driving home its fangs, she spat, "You, Alexandra Arkadyevna. At least so long as you remain loyal to your Mother Russia."

"My loyalty is not to be questioned," Sasha said firmly, relieved that her voice did not betray the terror she felt.

"I must tell you that there are some who expressed doubts as to whether you were the most trustworthy person for this sensitive assignment. There are those in very high positions who would restore Mother Russia's dominion over the lands of the Union of Soviet Socialist Republics. They questioned your loyalty, and still do. After much discussion at the highest level those concerns about your loyalty did not prevail for the moment and we decided to entrust you with this most important task. But many eyes will be watching you quite carefully."

The General intervened again. "Perhaps that is enough for the first session. Alexandra Arkadyevna has much to ponder."

Once again the door opened just as the wall clock chimed. The stocky, reticent man who had brought her the envelope in the dining room entered, along with the woman from the kitchen. The woman pushed a cart with five place settings. The two servers removed the heavy sterling silver covers from the food and carried them out of the room.

"Good," said the General. "There is no need to rush the lessons. Alexandra Arkadyevna will be with us for some time. Now let us enjoy a pleasant lunch."

Sasha felt her stomach growling, but not with hunger.

Chapter 11: Special Agent

"Hi Will, welcome back. Have you finally decided that the F.B.I. is the place for you? We've kept your seat warm and upgraded your computer just waiting for this day."

Will grinned at the svelte, athletic woman who had been his colleague and had become a close friend. As always, Special Agent Adrienne Penscal's dark blue suit was sharply creased, her close-cropped brown hair perfectly combed, her eyes bright and penetrating. She occupied a special place in Will's heart, having protected him and Sally from the Russian mob after the botched assassination attempt that had killed his twin brother. And Will was forever indebted to her for risking her career by withholding important information from her boss so that he could carry out his unauthorized investigation that busted up the mob's operation. He was delighted to see her but he hesitated, unsure whether to hug her or extend his hand in greeting. She quickly resolved his dilemma, opening her arms and giving him a brief but enthusiastic hug. He stepped back, smiled, and said, "Not a chance, Adrienne. I'm all about making big bucks in the private sector now."

"Ha! You'll never convince me of that, but I do hope you're enjoying your new livelihood. So, what's up? You didn't say much on the phone."

"I thought this was something we should discuss in person. And, of course, I wanted an excuse to come back here and see you. Can we talk in confidence?"

"Sure, unless you say something that crosses the line into stuff I'd have to report."

"Actually, I'm hoping you already know about this and can provide more information than what we already have."

"Will, you're a private citizen now. I'll hear you out, but you know there's a limit to what I could share with you. Go ahead."

"Yes, I'm well aware of that, but my employer, *Cybersleuths, Inc.,* is working on this job for Homeland Security. The company has a special status of some sort that allows it to operate as if it's part of the government. We actually function pretty much as if we were government employees. I've been assured that DHS and FBI are cooperating fully on this."

"Hmmm…interesting. Tell me more."

"We're looking into a recent string of troubling deaths. Inexplicable sudden deaths of people whose lives were dependent on medical devices. Pacemakers, insulin pumps, implantable defibrillators, dialysis machines, all of which failed without explanation. At this point we're working on two theories. One, someone may, in effect, be taking target practice and testing some sort of new high-tech weapon. Two, the killings may constitute intimidation to support a demand for ransom. Sound familiar?"

"Maybe. What do you want from us?"

"We're interested in anything you guys know about the situation, but we're particularly wondering whether anyone has been threatened with a demand for payment related to deaths like this. We figured the hospitals or device manufacturers would report ransom demands to the FBI if that's what's going on, so here I am."

"I may have something for you, but I need to run this by our Division Chief, Garry Hollingshead."

Will remembered Garry Hollingshead well. The distinguished man, perfectly manicured with closely-trimmed silver hair and rimless eyeglasses, looked every bit the part of the senior FBI official that he was. Will was grateful for how supportive Hollingshead had been for him and Adrienne in the incident with the Russian mob—especially for not taking any reprisals against Adrienne for failing to inform him about Will's maverick investigation until after it was over.

"Say hello to Chief Hollingshead for me."

"Will do. Just stay here for a few minutes, I'll be right back."

Adrienne walked out and left Will alone in her office. He appreciated the gesture as a sign of how much she trusted him—FBI Special Agents do not leave just anybody unattended in their offices. After no more than five minutes she returned, sat at her desk and smiled. "OK, Will, we're good to go. Chief Hollingshead sends his regards and said yes, we are indeed cooperating fully with DHS on this matter. I am to regard you and *Cybersleuths, Inc.* as part of our team."

"Great! Feels good for us to be back on the same team. So, what have you got?"

"I don't know how many cases you're aware of, but we have identified a little over a half-dozen that we consider unusual. They stand out in a couple of ways. First of all, in the past when devices have failed and resulted in death we have always found the failures to be the result of a defect in the device. Sometimes the defects have been ones that the manufacturer already knew about but had not fixed, and sometimes they were ones that were only discovered when the device was examined and tested shortly after the incident. We tested the devices afterward and they were all in perfect working order. Totally pristine, no defects. That's very strange. Second, while fatal device failures do occur from time to time, they are relatively rare. Having so many within a short time frame is extraordinary. Statistically speaking, a cluster of deaths like this is too unlikely to be random." She smiled broadly and said, "I'm sure I don't have to explain the math to you, of all people."

Will nodded and smiled back. "Yup, I've run the numbers myself. As you say, a cluster like this is way beyond the limits of what would be expected. Any clues yet?"

"Short answer is no, we have no explanation for what is going on. In terms of your two theories, taking target practice to test some new weapon versus intimidation to support a demand for ransom, at this point I'd have to lean toward testing. To answer your question directly, there's no evidence of someone seeking ransom. No one has reported anything and we've conducted an exhaustive investigation of all the manufacturers, the health care systems and doctors who cared for the people who died, and the victims and their families. We've searched their homes and offices, interviewed everyone involved, traced their emails and texts, looked at everything on their computers, followed the money in their accounts. No hint of a ransom demand has turned up."

"OK, that's what I wanted to know, thanks."

"Another thing that points away from ransom is the seeming randomness of the events. If someone wanted to intimidate a manufacturer or even a group of patients we would expect them to focus on specific targets, the same device in multiple people or several devices from one company. But there's no pattern like that, none at all."

"That's pretty much the same conclusion I came to. So, target practice with some new weapon goes to the top of the list. But why? If they're not setting up a big payoff, why go to the trouble of killing people at random? What do your profilers think could be the motive?"

"Terrorism jumps to the top, of course. Unless someone takes credit early on, we often go for quite a while before we identify the group that's behind an attack. If the attacks get a lot of publicity we might get multiple claims of responsibility coming from groups that are aligned, or even from groups that would never do something together. So we're not saying anything to anyone about a possible connection among the deaths, not even to the families or the manufacturers or doctors. We are couching our investigations as routine, as normal regulatory oversight. In fact, our agents have not even identified themselves as coming from the FBI. People get nervous when a bunch of gumshoes show up on their doorstep so we've been operating under the cloak of the FDA to keep from raising suspicions. FDA wasn't exactly happy sharing jurisdiction with us, but they had no choice."

"Terrorism, huh? Makes sense. Not that terrorism makes sense, but the terrorists could be holding back until they're ready for some mass attack, some sort of cyber 9-11. Then they'd reveal who they are."

"That's one possibility, yes."

"Any other thoughts?"

"Not anything that's well-formulated yet, just mulling over a variant on what we've said so far. Some terrorists, of course, have a definite purpose in mind, however misguided their goals are. But other terrorists are really anarchists. They do things to disrupt society without any clear motive. They conduct massive disinformation campaigns to set people on edge, provoke them to turn against each other, all without any discernable purpose other than creating disarray. Government can't govern properly when society is in turmoil. I think you know what the result can be."

"Strong-arm takeover to restore law and order?"

"Exactly."

"We're heading in that direction already in this country, Adrienne. Dorzel would like nothing better than to unleash storm troopers to keep him in office rather than submit himself to the will of the people in an election."

"You're a private citizen, Will, you can say whatever you think. But that's not for me to comment on. I need to do my job and stick to the script, as you well know."

"Understood, enough said. No more politics. So where do we go from here?"

"Maybe *Cybersleuths, Inc.* could help us be sure we're not missing any deaths. There really is no reliable system for tracking the cause of death back to a medical device. So far we've had to depend on doctors and hospitals reporting their suspicions back to the FDA like they're supposed to, but that's pretty much hit-or-miss. We'd appreciate it if you could come up with a better way to get the full picture."

"Sounds like my kind of project. I've already got two very good analysts searching for data sets that might be useful."

"I can help you there, at least in part. We have access to detailed information on every medical device that's been implanted in anyone in this country. We'll be happy to share that with you."

"Excellent, that'll be a great place for us to start. We'll brainstorm about how to tie that in with other data bases and structure our analyses."

"And we'll let you know when the next person dies."

Chapter 12: Taking the Lead

"Colonel Jenkins, Mr. Ackroyd is here to see you."

"OK, Captain Billy Jean, please show him in."

"Right away, Sir. I will wait outside the door."

"You're welcome to stay, Captain Billy Jean."

"Thank you, Sir, but I'll be close by if you need anything."

Captain Billy Jean Holliday had sat in on only one meeting between Jenkins and his campaign manager, Andy Ackroyd, and had decided that was one meeting too many. It wasn't just Ackroyd's profuse vulgarity—she was a Marine, there were no words in the English vernacular she hadn't heard millions of times. And it wasn't just that he and Jenkins were discussing politics—she was exposed to political chatter all day long, that was fine as long as she didn't participate. But she drew the line at hearing about the dirty tricks Ackroyd was always trying to get Jenkins to approve. Better she just didn't know about some things.

She opened the door to the makeshift office in Jenkins' hotel suite, ushered Ackroyd in, and shut the door as she stepped out of the room.

Ackroyd swore like a drunken sailor but otherwise he was not at all like the bulky, cigar-chomping, whiskey-swilling Edward G. Robinson stereotype of a political hack. Slender, almost frail, Ackroyd didn't smoke or drink, and he wore heavy black-frame eyeglasses with lenses as thick as the bottom of Coca-Cola bottles. He walked over to Jenkins and stood, waiting for the candidate to speak.

"OK, Andy, what's up? Why were you so anxious to see me?"

Ackroyd took the questions as permission to sit in one of the upholstered armchairs. "It's good news, Colonel. Pretty fucking good news: we're surging in the polls. You're up twelve points and rising against that wacko Minion for the nomination, and doing even better in the head-to-head against Dorzel. The numbers are all good everywhere we need them, all the right states, the right precincts, everywhere. It's a fucking lock. We can start calling you 'Mr. President' soon."

"No such thing, you know that, Andy. But still, that is good news. What happened?"

"You want to start with asshole Minion or asshole Dorzel?"

"Minion. Last I knew she was gaining on me."

"Yeah, well, she took a tumble."

"How come?"

"Well, you know that thinktank report saying that her socialist schemes would hurt the working class more than the billionaires?"

"That report? That's old news. And who pays attention to thinktanks anymore anyway?"

"We put out a lot of…of, uh, what you might call publicity in all the right places. You know, some hard-hitting ads on TV and in newspapers and a lot of…uh, social media. And we worked on the big unions and got them to pull their support."

"What else? That doesn't sound like enough to give us a big swing in the numbers."

"Veterans. A big chunk of the undecided vets have turned to you. About fucking time they came around, you're a war hero and she's a fucking peacenik. They're responding to the information we're putting out about how she would destroy the military."

"Is there more?"

"Do you really want to know?"

"Oh, Christ, are you saying we spread some kind of shit around about her?"

"No, Colonel. Not shit, not really. Just the truth…more or less. But maybe I should spare you the details?"

"You're right, I don't want to know. At least not until you get wind that something we did or said is coming back to bite me on the ass. But for god's sake, be careful. You know I want to play by the rules."

"Sure, sure, I hear you. What I will say is that our social media people are getting better and better at this. All kinds of new information for them to digest, high-tech analytics."

"What about the bump against Dorzel?"

"More like a steady rise than a sudden bump. Main point is that we're way beyond the margin of error now. Your lead over Dorzel is stabilizing, locking in comfortably. Minion's losses plus a continuing flow of the undecideds to you are swelling your margin. You're pretty much home free. Democratic nomination, then the fucking presidency."

"Dorzel must be going nuts. I'm sure he was hoping that Annabaker would push me out of the running and he'd have an easy time against her."

"Yeah, that's exactly what he was counting on. The latest numbers still show that Minion wouldn't have a chance against him, not the way the electoral college works. She'd pull in a lot of votes in California, New York, a few other places, but she's got too many negatives in too many places between the coasts. Easy pickings for Dorzel. You bet he's going nuts—you should take a look at his Tweets. Now that he's pretty far behind you and Minion is out of the picture, he's saying the polls are all fake news."

"I can't read his stuff, makes me want to puke. What's he saying about me?"

"Even for that fucking Dorzel he's sunk to a new low. He's re-tweeting those phony rumors about your military service, those bullshit claims that you weren't the one who saved all those Marines. All that crap has been totally discredited, over and over. The shit is absolutely false, but Dorzel keeps repeating it."

"How could anybody believe that crap? You know that I never wanted to take credit for anything with my squad, but, goddammit, all 17 of the survivors wrote testimonials about me on their own. They were the ones who pushed for me to get the Medal of Honor, I never asked them to do anything like that."

"Yeah, that asshole is spreading the fucking lie his usual way, tweeting that *'some people are saying'* that you were actually responsible for the deaths of the Marines who got killed, and that one of them was the real hero. He claims that several of your buddies spoke to reporters anonymously about this and now you're trying to silence them, keep them from telling the truth."

"Swiftboating all over again."

"You got that right. Tear somebody down by telling lies about their strongest points. Go for the things that people admire about them to tarnish their image, split their supporters. Ever since that strategy worked against John Kerry in 2004 it's just gotten worse and worse. Now we've got a president who passes along all kinds of shit, the bigger the lie the better. But it seems to be backfiring this time—your lead is just growing no matter what kind of crap he puts out."

"Sounds like he's getting more desperate as the polls move our way. I wonder what he'll do next to try to get rid of me."

"It'll be bad, whatever it is. And we know the Russians will be helping him. But don't worry, we'll be ready for anything."

"I sure as hell hope so."

Chapter 13: Porn Films

When lunch ended and the servers had wheeled away the carts with the trays and dishes, Natalia Kostenka resumed her post at the front of the classroom. The woman had barely nibbled at her food and looked as though she had not eaten in months. And yet when she spoke it was with that curiously forceful monotone. "Now, Alexandra Arkadyevna, you will watch some more pictures."

The lights dimmed in the classroom and to Sasha's horror a stark naked image of Dorzel appeared on the screen. He was standing in front of a naked woman who reclined on a luxurious overstuffed couch. But the image was no still photo. Natalia Kostenka pressed the "play" arrow on the remote control and Dorzel sprang to life— and sprang to cover the woman with his body. The scene continued for about ten minutes, then a similar one appeared in a different setting, with a different woman. More videos followed, a gallery of sexual acts some of which Sasha had never heard of and could not have imagined.

Sasha had been with men who wanted her to watch pornography but seeing other people having sex had been of no interest to her. Until now. She was disgusted by the Dorzel videos but also found that she was intrigued by them—or, at least, intrigued by how dramatically they chronicled Dorzel's physical decline over the years. The date and time stamps on the films showed that surveillance of Dorzel's sexual activity had been underway for decades. The recordings began with a much younger Dorzel, probably in his forties. Over time, the movies and videos displayed the deterioration of his body like time-lapse photos: pendulous rolls of fat spread across his belly and buttocks, his hair thinned and receded, his skin dimmed to a fleshy sallow color then brightened to an unnatural orange.

After one hour Sasha had seen enough depravity. And she had grown weary of listening to Natalia Kostenka's deadpan commentary on each scene.

"Stop, please, no more," Sasha said.

The instructor replied with no emotion, "Quiet. You must watch. And learn."

Anger surged through Sasha. Once again she felt bile squirting up into the back of her throat. Only her absolute determination not to lose control in front of the instructor and onlookers allowed her to continue watching.

Once Sasha had gotten past her irritation at being forced to watch Dorzel amuse himself at the expense of countless women, she realized that the visuals had been recorded in many different settings, as well as over a long period of time. Most were in the kind of fancy bedrooms one would expect in luxury hotels, while others appeared to be in offices or corporate board rooms. The formal, austere look of a few gave Sasha the distinct impression that those encounters had taken place in government buildings. Some three hours after it began, the marathon porn show finally came to an end.

Sasha sighed with relief. Regaining her composure enough to speak, she said, "These videos are most extraordinary. How did they come into your...our...possession?"

The General answered. "President Dorzel is very fond of two things: women and luxury, especially when the women and luxury are provided at no cost to him. It has proved to be remarkably simple to arrange assignations for him in various hotels and other settings all over the world. As you can see, our highly competent technicians have been quite successful at making these recordings for many years, long before he decided to run for president."

"Does he know that you have them?"

"Ah, yes, for sure. He is well aware that we possess these videos. We first demonstrated their existence to him some time ago when we sought his cooperation on a business matter, a transaction that was vital to our tourist industry. He is quite vain, especially about his *manhood*. As you are familiar with such matters you will no doubt have observed for yourself that the films are not, shall we say, flattering to that part of his anatomy. He is so anxious that such images never be seen that he acceded to our requests. Since then they have proved quite useful, first in other business matters and now in his presidency."

"And will you be filming me when I am with him?"

"Perhaps."

"Perhaps? You will not tell me?"

"There may be situations in which it would be advisable for you to know that you are being filmed, and others when it would not be advisable. You have a job to do and we expect you to do it well no matter the circumstances. Whether you are being observed should be of no concern to you."

Sasha thought for a moment, then said, "What you say may indeed be true. The man is disgusting. He is so repulsive that I could not possibly take pleasure in having…relations with him. But you are quite correct. I have a job to do, and when I am required to be with him I will at all times be doing no more than carrying out my responsibility. Going through the motions, as we say. So yes, it should make no difference to me whether you are watching or not."

"Satisfactory."

"What is the information I will be carrying?"

"Mr. Dorzel has been quite useful to us as President of the United States and we strongly desire that he remain in that position for at least the next four years."

"Why do you say 'at least' four years? Is not the American presidency limited to two terms of office?

"Do not be misled into believing that the American Constitution is immune from being changed. Or circumvented, for that matter. Our own president faced a similar limitation but, as you know, he showed that it was not insurmountable, and he has remained in office. A strong leader has many different ways to bring about such changes. But that is a matter for another day, another time. We are committed to taking all measures necessary to assure this man Dorzel's reelection. For that reason we have an urgent need to communicate clearly about information that will assist that effort."

"Such as? I know very little of American politics."

"Your mission requires no special skills other than the ones we know you possess. Our expert analysts are continuously making assessments of the need to undertake actions that will guarantee his reelection. Their reports help guide our strategy, in particular our use of social media and the information that we provide to the press. We are devoting great resources to our propaganda operations. But we must have immediate access to him so that we can be sure we are working in concert with the actions his campaign is also undertaking.

It is imperative that we are of a single mind on the most sensitive matters. We must know if he feels that he is in danger of losing the election and if so whether we should initiate certain additional actions."

"Actions such as?"

"We have devoted many resources to keeping him in office, but they may not be sufficient. If he is in danger of losing we will take additional measures to intervene. Our propaganda methods have been extremely successful, but we have certain other tools at our disposal. They are new and powerful tools, but we wish to use them only if it becomes necessary. That is all I will say for now."

"And what will I be bringing to him…other than what will be required to gain his attention?"

"You will be given the details as the moment requires. No matter what you are discussing with him we must be absolutely clear with respect to what we are telling him and what he is telling us. This is of utmost importance with this man, and has proved extremely difficult to carry out. You must communicate with him in a way that we are confident he understands what you are saying to him. And equally, that we understand what he has in mind and wishes to tell us. You will also remind him that we will be watching carefully to assure that he remains steadfast on our arrangement."

"You are telling me that I am to hold the President of the United States accountable?"

"You will remind him that he has been, and remains, accountable to the Russian Federation. Our hold over him has been quite strong but he is impulsive to an extreme and may take actions that prove to be against his own interests. He may become overconfident knowing that his supporters will follow him anywhere like ducklings and tolerate his behavior no matter how crude or ignorant. But you will remind him of the danger he faces if we turn against him."

"I do not understand how it is possible for us to have such power over this man. The whole world knows that he has been with many women, why would he betray his own country and obey us just to keep some videos from being seen?"

"At the start what drove him to cooperate with us was his vanity, which has always been the most important thing to him. As I said, he was so terrified of having the images of his manhood displayed everywhere that he went along with our initial request. It

59

was some consolation that the bargain was financially profitable not only for us but also for him. But the actions that he took to make the deal successful were corrupt practices under American law for which he could have been prosecuted. Then we came back for more, and more still. We drew him in deeper and deeper. By the time he decided he wanted to be president we had not only the films, we also had substantial documentation that he had committed many crimes over the years. He needed to continue our arrangement to keep from being sent to jail. You will recall that the opposition party was in power when he began campaigning for president. If we had released our files he would have been arrested in very short order. As president, now he controls the prosecutors. They will not turn against him so long as he is in office."

"This is all extremely difficult to comprehend."

"We understand. And yet, you must adjust to the situation quickly."

"When am I to begin my work?"

"Soon, quite soon."

Chapter 14: Sleuths and Aggregators

Belinda Winnisome motioned for Will to join her in front of a bank of monitors. "Check this out," she said, pointing to one of the screens. "I'll start with a general overview of the Big Data we collect. Some sources will be familiar to you, pretty mundane now but we still use them. Then I'll demonstrate how we get and use some of our more recent additions that may be quite new to you. I'd be surprised if you were able to do anything like our latest work when you were inside the government—at least not inside Health and Human Services. NSA, Homeland Security, they're a different story, but not HHS. Too many privacy restrictions."

She began scrolling through the types of databases Will had spent many hours searching: birth and death records, criminal files, newspaper and other media archives, on and on through the trove of data files and information sources that had been central to his work. When she added in highly confidential financial transactions she said, "I believe you may have had access to records like these when you were at the FBI, right?"

"Yup, all of that looks familiar. All too familiar."

"Even the FBI, however, is generally limited to using such files only when they are related to a specific target of interest."

"True, but we had pretty wide latitude when we got search warrants from the FISA court."

"Of course. FISA warrants are very useful in some cases. But here we have no such restrictions. Homeland Security gives us *carte blanche* access. We get pretty much everything whether it's on the open internet or buried in the Dark Web. We started by developing search engines that scan through much bigger Big Data than you've ever had access to. For example, we can see far more detailed records of financial transactions than even the FBI can get."

"Very impressive. You said that's how you started—tell me more about what came next."

"Having access to so much data through Homeland Security was great, but we had to put in a lot of effort to package it to make it useful for specific purposes. So we moved beyond doing all our own searches. There are lots of data aggregators out there—commercial tracking services that collect massive amounts of information on just about everything that happens in our lives and sell it on the open market. IP addresses, location data, business and personal communications by email, text or any of the other emerging social media formats. Truly countless numbers of blogs and web pages. Every time someone clicks on a link—that's now called 'clickstream data.' And we have access to all of it, whatever they have. They are willing to sell everything."

"Isn't that expensive?"

Belinda laughed, a chuckle that gave Will a shiver down his spine—for all the world that chuckle could have been Barry smirking at his twin's naiveté. Will shook off the shiver and stifled the disturbing thought to force himself to focus on what she was saying.

"It would be prohibitively expensive…if we had to pay for it. But we have access through Homeland Security, and they get everything. I have no idea what they pay for and what they, uh, just get somehow. Of course, as you know, amassing all the data in the world doesn't make us smart or useful. Our real value comes from what we are able to do with all this information."

"Can you show me an example of what they collect and how you use it?"

"Of course. How about I use you as the guinea pig, OK?"

"Me? Not sure I want to see, but sure, go ahead."

Belinda opened a new screen that appeared disarmingly simple, much like one of the early search engines such as AltaVista or Lycos before Google engulfed the cyber universe like a giant electronic amoeba. She typed in "Willford Manningham" and hit *Enter.* Within a few seconds a list of people appeared. There were a number with names such as "William Manning" but only one "Willford Manningham." She clicked on Will's name and then selected *Profile* from the drop-down options. The screen blinked once, then offered her another set of options. She selected *Personal Characteristics.* The response amazed Will: the computer instantly generated a dossier on him that was no mere list of his activities or the simple facts of his life, it was a detailed portrayal of his very being. Screen after screen displayed his preferences down to microscopic detail: one that caught his attention was a line that revealed that he liked spicy food. Not just his penchant for fiery food or even that he laced almost everything with hot sauce, but the astounding fact that he used only *Louisiana Hot Sauce* and shook the bottle some four times at each meal.

"So now they know you like spicy food, what brand of hot sauce you like, and how good a customer you are. They can do lots of things with that information. Get you to buy more, or nudge you to switch to a different brand. Or bombard you with ads for restaurants that sell spicy food."

"OK, I get the picture. What else?"

"You'll love this." She returned to the Willford Manningham profile options and clicked on *Employment History* and then *Past 24 Months*. The computer announced that Will had worked for the Centers for Medicare and Medicaid Services in HHS until recently; had interviewed for a position with *Cybersleuths, Inc.*; and left CMS to work with that private company.

"So did that program hack into CMS and also into your own personnel files?"

She shook her head. "Not at all. It was not necessary to do any hacking. All we had to do was analyze the massive amounts of data on Willford Manningham that we have access to. In this case, our computer used geomapping data that tells us where you have been, and for how long. Data from your smartphone's GPS, from multiple systems in your car, your smartwatch, the taxi company, where you used your Metro card, where you logged into Wi-Fi, the cell phone towers you connected to, how long you spent at each location. When you consistently showed a regular pattern of long days at CMS locations our algorithms concluded that you worked there. Then as you started making phone calls to us and coming here for a couple of hours over a period of weeks our analytics on your phone usage deduced that you were interviewing here for a job. Now it knows that you're here all day just like you used to be at CMS, but you don't go to their offices anymore. Bingo: you changed jobs and work here."

"How about the hot sauce thing? I mean, for goodness sake, I didn't even realize I usually shake the bottle four times at each meal."

"That's a really simple deduction based on the quantity of hot sauce you purchase using a credit card and the average number of meals. Would you like to see a list of your favorite foods in every restaurant or fast food outlet?"

"No thanks, I've seen plenty already."

Will had developed many profiles of people he was tracking, but this was a series of quantum leaps beyond anything he had ever created. He knew that sophisticated profiling like this was possible but he had no first-hand experience working with databases with so much specific information. The thought of anyone knowing everything about him sent a chill down his neck: this was all about him, Will Manningham, a private person, a solid citizen, not some Russian mobster or corrupt government official. A line from *Killing Me Softly* started playing in his head—the computer was *singing his life with its words.*

"So this is why we don't really refer to Big Data anymore, we mainly talk about artificial intelligence, AI. We have access to so many inputs other than data files the only thing that matters is what we can do with them. Remember how you learned in Statistics 101 that discovering that two things are associated with each other does not mean that one causes the other?"

"Of course—teams wearing green uniforms might win more often than teams with white ones, but the color of their uniforms doesn't cause one team to win and the other to lose. And winning or losing doesn't cause the color of their uniforms."

"Exactly. But it turns out that if we pair that factoid with untold billions of other pieces of information that might seem to have no conceivable relationship to winning or losing and we analyze them all simultaneously we can predict with great accuracy which team will win. No need to worry about whether A causes B if we know that B will happen nearly 100% of the time when A, and C and D and a mindboggling number of other items are present."

"OK," he said, "got it." He shook his head to clear his mind. He had to adjust to the new reality, put it to work, not worry about the intrusion into his own life. After a quiet moment his brain went to work. "That gives me an idea. Let's run your analytics on all of the people who died when their medical devices failed. Maybe we can find a common thread."

"Brilliant idea, but I'm afraid you're going to be disappointed—that's exactly what we've already done. We drew a complete blank. Nothing at all came up. None of them were in the same place at the same time in the past year. No lines of communication among them, on-line or by phone. Not even any significant common purchases. No links among the manufacturers of the medical devices involved or the doctors. So far they seem to be an entirely random assortment of people with no connection whatsoever."

"Ouch. Back to square one. More like square zero. Let me think a bit."

Will was silent for a full minute, then his eyes opened wide and the freckles on the fair skin of his face disappeared in a red flush of excitement. "Here's a thought: they do have the most important thing in common, the way they died. If the deaths were caused by the same person they would have needed details on both the victims and their devices. So you found no lines of communication or other connections among the victims or through their individual healthcare providers or device manufacturers—but what about with a third party? What about seeing if there is someone they all have in common who obtained information about them or their devices from the manufacturers or the doctors?"

"Now that's another brilliant idea and this time it's one that we hadn't thought of! It shouldn't be too complicated to construct a way to answer that question. We need to see whether someone has been in touch with all of them. Or, more likely, has been hacking into the information systems of their doctors or the manufacturers of their medical devices. And probably into their personal files, their emails, texts, calendars, whatever."

"Yes, we need to construct a neural network. You know, like a detailed map of the brain and the complex web of neurons that connects it with different parts of the body. That way we will identify any links between the people who died and some common point. It'll give us a picture of whether there's a common hub that sent out feelers to sources of information on the different victims."

"That sounds like something in Lauren's bailiwick," said Belinda. "I'll talk to her about it, she's our expert on neural networks. That's the way to identify any connection among the deaths that we've missed. Brilliant, Will!"

"Thanks, but I have one more thought: if we find such a common hub maybe we will identify other targets we don't know about yet."

The look that came over Belinda's face was eerily reminiscent of Barry mulling over something provocative that Will had just said. He was distracted again. Would he ever get over seeing his brother in his new co-worker?

"Yes," he heard her say as he returned to the present. "Targets that have been already been attacked but we don't know about. Victims that aren't on our list. But...I hate to say this...we might also identify some people who are still alive and haven't been attacked yet, but are in their sights for a future attack."

"*Oh shit*, what a terrible thought! But of course you're right. Let's just hope we find them in time."

Chapter 15: Leaving Zarya

The moment that Sasha dreaded came much sooner than she had expected. She had just taken a seat in the dining room and was enjoying her first cup of strong coffee when Natalia Kostenka glided up behind her as quietly as a shadow. Sasha had no idea anyone was looking over her shoulder until she heard the commanding voice say, "Alexandra Arkadyevna, you will leave Zarya Dacha in one hour."

Startled by both the unexpected voice emerging from nowhere and the even more unexpected command, Sasha gagged on a sip of coffee and barely managed to avoid spitting it back into her cup. She covered her mouth with a thick, soft napkin and coughed twice, then turned to look at the instructor, who did not move from behind her.

"Where am I to go, Natalia Kostenka?"

"Milan. The airplane to Milan leaves in three hours."

Another surprise: Milan, not Moscow. "Milan? Why am I to go to Milan?"

"You will find out soon enough. You will be accompanied by Valeria Klara. She will provide all the necessary information. Return to your room as soon as you have eaten and collect your things."

"Collect my things? Will I be returning here?"

"That is not the plan."

"Why am I to leave Zarya Dacha after just three weeks?"

"Enough questions. That is all for now. Do as you are told. Valeria Klara will meet you at the main door in fifty-eight minutes."

The wisp of a woman turned and exited the dining room just as the waiter approached the table and set a covered plate and a small basket of sweet vatruska breakfast rolls in front of Sasha. "Take it away," she said, dismissing him with a wave of her hand.

"I am instructed to tell you that you may not be eating again for some hours." He lifted the cover from the plate and retreated into the kitchen.

Sasha stared at the eggs, kolbasa, and blinis. She had no appetite, but understood that she should take the waiter's admonition seriously. The trip to Milan would occupy most of the day and she did not want to be starving for so long. She ate several mouthfuls of eggs and blini, then took a bite out of one of the vatruska rolls, savoring the sweet cheese filling despite her agitation. Then she patted her face with the plush napkin and headed back to her room to pack.

Milan! Well, there were worse places than Milan, and she had always dreamed of traveling to Italy. And she thought she would enjoy being with Valeria Klara, and especially enjoy being far away from that Natalia Kostenka. Questions filled her head as she hurried up the stairs to her room. Why would she have to leave Zarya Dacha so soon and on such short notice? Why was Valeria Klara to accompany her? And Milan—why Milan? She gasped at a sudden thought: would Dorzel be meeting her there? She could not get the images of that disgusting man and those women out of her head. Was that what awaited her in Milan?

Sasha looked around her room and wondered whether she would ever see it again. As she hurriedly folded her clothes and packed them carefully into her suitcase she glanced up at the elaborate wall decorations with their hidden cameras and microphones. She sighed and gave in to the inevitable: her life was no longer her own, she would never again have any sense of privacy. Everything she did would be watched, and recorded. Everything.

Valeria Klara Yakovna was waiting when Sasha arrived at the main entrance. Once again Sasha was impressed by the woman's fashionable outfit: red pants, a light green blouse, and a white jacket with a brilliant ruby pendant on the lapel. She greeted Sasha with a broad smile and said enthusiastically, "Ah, Sasha, so we are off to have a bit of fun, yes?"

"Hello to you, Valeria Klara. But I do not know the purpose of this trip, only that we will go to Milan."

"*Si, Milano!* Do you like my outfit, the Italian *Tricolore?*"

Valeria Klara's lighthearted mood relaxed Sasha a bit. She laughed, "*Si, bella!* But I still do not understand what we are doing."

"I will tell you all that I know, but I do not know everything. Here is the driver to take us to the airport. Let us get on our way and I will talk to you in the car."

When the two women had settled into the back seat of the Mercedes, Sasha looked at Valeria Klara more closely than she had before. She was youthful and attractive, and not only well-dressed but also exceptionally well-groomed. Her makeup highlighted deep blue eyes that Sasha had never noticed before. Her hair was no longer drawn back into a bun but hung free to her shoulders in a sculpted array of blond curls. When she spoke she exuded an enthusiasm that she had never shown in the presence of the stern Natalia Kostenka.

"Now, Sasha, you must take it easy—this little trip of ours is entirely for fun: we are going shopping for your wardrobe. First in Milan, then perhaps to Rome, and Paris. If we still do not find what we like, we will also go to Stockholm or Barcelona."

"We are going shopping for clothes? In those cities?"

"Yes, the fashion capitals of Europe. Of the world. You must be appropriately dressed to carry out your mission."

"Those cities are so very expensive. We could spend a fortune on clothes if we go to the houses of the famous designers. How are we to pay for such clothes?"

Valeria Klara laughed, displaying a set of perfectly aligned white teeth more brilliant than any Sasha had ever seen. "Ah," she said, "that was a matter of some discussion. Natalia Kostenka argued that you and I should only look at what the designers presented at their showings and make notes and drawings. Then our seamstresses in Moscow would create similar articles at a fraction of the cost. But the General dismissed that idea. He said that you would be greatly embarrassed and your mission could be jeopardized if you were to be discovered wearing cheap knock-offs. So we are authorized to spend freely."

"Why would anyone notice what I was wearing?" Sasha asked the question, but she knew the answer.

"You are to be noticed by a particular person, a person who attracts a great deal of attention. That is the heart of your mission, as you are well aware. And the women he is seen with also attract much attention. So the General is correct—if the press found out that you were wearing an outfit copied from one of the famous designers it could become a scandal that would undermine your mission."

"And all of this is to be paid for by the Russian State?"

"Of course. Natalia Kostenka will be watching the bills with her devilish eyes, but the fashion houses will know only that you are a woman with an unlimited line of credit. They will no doubt assume that you are supported by some billionaire. One of our new Russian billionaires who supports many women in style."

"And after we make all these extravagant purchases will I ride off leading a herd of elephants laden with treasures? What is to happen in Milan?"

Again the perfect teeth and laughter. "Ah, you make a little joke. That is good! No, you will not be carrying the clothes with you. You will select the outfits that you wish to have, the fashion houses will take the necessary measurements, and we will put them on hold until we have finished our shopping tour. At that time we will have some of the clothes tailored and delivered to you and will cancel the others. Unless," she added with a mischievous grin, "you wish to buy them all just to spite Natalia Kostenka."

"And what is it that you do not know?"

"Ah, yes. I do not yet know where you will be going at the end of our trip. That will be decided in a few days. It is possible that you will be going to Moscow. To be seen in your new clothes."

To be seen in the clothes in public, thought Sasha, and later to be seen in private with no clothes at all.

Chapter 16: Legacies

Annabaker Minion got a roar of approval from the crowd when she shouted her trademark slogan: *"No More War!"* The throng took up the chant: *"No More War! No More War! No More War!"* She felt like she was back in 1969, the March on Washington to end the Vietnam War, the first time she felt the power of mass protest. These were her people, they loved her and she loved them. She was their shining star, the one who was *taking it to The Man* for them. Dorzel was evil, Annabaker Minion would stop his treachery. She would bring an end to the nightmare, undo the horrific damage he had done to the country. Annabaker Minion could do no wrong, they'd do anything for her.

Except vote for Robin Jenkins. That was the one thing her admirers would not do. If they no longer had her to lead them toward something they believed in, if they had to choose between Dorzel and Jenkins, their enthusiasm for her would be swept away in a tidal wave of despondency. They'd walk away, drop out, leave the two warmongers to battle it out. Compromise was collaboration, out of the question, better to have a devil who wore his wickedness proudly than a false prophet who would change nothing.

Somewhere deep down inside of her, Annabaker knew how wrong that was. She knew because of her sister, and because of their father. Her sister, Charlene, the dedicated public servant. Charlene, who worked tirelessly for all the same causes Annabaker believed in, but in a very different way. Charlene, whose hero was Frances Perkins, the first woman cabinet member, the Secretary of Labor under President Franklin D. Roosevelt who oversaw the implementation of Social Security. Charlene, the patient, hopeful one who believed in working inside government to make things better. She had spent years in the bowels of the Social Security

Administration and later as a staff member for Democratic committees in Congress. Charlene, who had helped bring about very real incremental improvements in Medicaid and Medicare and was sure that eventually the United States would fill in all the gaps and everyone would have health insurance.

Charlene was the heir to their father's legacy. He had enlisted in the Army to fight against the Nazis and survived D-Day on the beaches of Normandy. Then he returned to finish college and go on to law school. He spent his career as a professor of Constitutional Law, a tall, distinguished gentleman professor in three-pieced suits who inspired generations of students with his lectures on Civil Rights. He wrote countless law articles, and later op-ed pieces, on the critical importance of the balance of power among the three branches of government to keep any one faction from seizing total control. Yes, Charlene was their father's daughter.

Annabaker knew that as much as their father had loved her, if were still alive he would be a resolute supporter of Colonel Robin Jenkins and not his own daughter. Jenkins was a decent person just as her father had been, a family man, faithful to his wife and a good father to his children. Jenkins was a Marine who understood the human side of war, not a crazed, irrational wild man like Dorzel who had no idea what war was about and had no business commanding the awesome might of the American military. And even as she attacked Jenkins during their debates she knew full well that he really did want people to get healthcare, to make a decent living, to have a future for their kids. Like Annabaker, he decried the way Dorzel was bankrupting the country to further enrich his insatiably money-hungry cabal and risking nuclear war to feed his ego. And like their father, Jenkins still had an old-fashioned belief in the American Dream. Ideals like equality under the law. Life, liberty and the pursuit of happiness still meant something to him.

Annabaker had not ignored the lessons she had learned from her father and her sister. She was no political ingénue. Dorzel had to be stopped, but she knew full well that things would not improve on their own the day after the election even if she were to be elected president. It would require a great deal of serious work by devoted people like her sister and father to right the wrongs Dorzel had wrought. That meant that well-meaning people would have to work together. To cooperate. To agree on goals and compromise on means. To put an end to the license Dorzel had given to hate groups to unleash their blind intolerance.

But Annabaker was their mother's daughter, the heir to her mother's legacy. Their parents had met in law school, and while their father was fighting his way up the academic ladders, their mother had taken on the cause of every underdog in society. She had joined the Freedom Summer Project in 1964, leaving the girls at home with their father while she went off to give legal advice to college students registering voters in Mississippi and working for civil rights in Alabama. She marched on Selma with Martin Luther King. She fought Nazis and fascists and racists and landlords as a brilliant, fiery, take-no-prisoners counsel for the American Civil Liberties Union. She led countless fights for women's rights, against glass ceilings in the corporate world and for freedom of choice in the private world.

Yes, Annabaker Minion was their mother's daughter. She loved and respected her sister and her father, but she was not about to abandon her people any more than her mother would have. Those people counted on her, she kept them going. And here they were—thousands and thousands of them chanting her slogan, urging her on. This was her calling, she needed to keep the fires burning. If Jenkins wouldn't meet her halfway—fuck that, more than halfway—then she'd have to keep fighting him. She would never sell out. Never.

Chapter 17: Brainstorming

"OK, guys, the FBI has given us access to some additional data that I've done some runs with and..."

Will stopped suddenly and blushed, embarrassed that he may have committed a sexist *faux pas* by addressing Belinda Winnisome and Lauren Sveiks as 'guys'. "Uh, sorry, uh...uh, ladies...you know...I didn't...uh...I mean..."

Both women laughed at his clumsy apologies.

"A lot better than 'gals'" Lauren said. "That's what those asshole professors in grad school used to call the women."

"No offense taken," added Belinda with a chuckle. "You're good."

"OK then. Thanks. Now, as I was about to say, you both know that there's no single system to track all individual deaths back to specific medical devices. Record-keeping is strictly *ad hoc*, one at a time. The death registries are quite complete, that's not the problem. But there is no comprehensive data base designed to link the death registries with implanted medical devices. The files that the doctors and manufacturers keep on their own patients and devices are decentralized and maintained in unique proprietary data systems that cannot talk to each other. In fact, they're designed that way specifically to protect privacy. Doctors and hospitals are supposed to file reports with FDA and the manufacturers when they suspect a death was caused by a device, but reporting is voluntary and incomplete—nobody wants to think they caused a death, let alone bring that to anyone's attention."

"So," said Lauren, "how can we make any headway then?"

"The FBI gave me access to a complete set of information on patients and devices. Every patient that's ever had a medical device implanted."

"How'd they do that if the files are all decentralized and the doctors and hospitals don't always report when they should?"

"They gave me access to many separate sources. Medical records, files from the manufacturers, billing information from health insurance companies. A zillion different data points. I pulled it all together into a usable file."

"Cool," said Lauren. "I was thinking we'd have to hack into a lot of medical records and corporate computers to identify everyone who's had a device implanted."

"Yeah," said Will. "Much better to be doing the work at the request of the FBI than having the FBI come after us for some massive data hack. Anyway, they asked us to see if we can connect the dots in a more systematic way, and that's what I've been working on. Belinda brought me up to speed on how the data aggregators are tying together incredibly detailed data from an almost infinite number of sources for commercial purposes. I'm hoping that we can use all of that to come up with a creative way to tie it all together."

"What exactly are we looking for?" asked Lauren.

"Three things," said Will. "First, are we missing any deaths that were associated with medical devices? Second, and this is something Belinda and I have been talking about, can we use all the massive data from the aggregators to identify any connections among the deaths? And third, can we spot potential targets who are still alive? This has some obvious urgency if we are to keep them alive."

"I've been thinking about this since we talked," said Belinda. "Let's walk through those three questions stepwise. As far as the first one, I think the solution may not be all that difficult since the FBI has given us access to all the data on everyone who received the various medical devices. We already have access to the death registries, so all we have to do is scan through the death records for any matches."

"Yes," said Will, "I did that part already. It was pretty much straightforward. I tied the data from the FBI on who got a medical device with the death registries and generated a comprehensive master list of all the people who died after having a device implanted. I was thinking I would eliminate all the ones who clearly died from other causes, you know, like traffic accidents."

"Not so quick," said Lauren, interrupting Will. "If someone was at the wheel when their pacemaker shut down…"

"Ah, good point. OK, let's work off of the master list I compiled, everyone who had had a device implanted by the time they died. Now we needed to identify any connections among the deaths"

"I told Lauren about that like we discussed," said Belinda.

"Great. So, Lauren, I'll describe what I'm proposing to do, then you can let me know what you think."

"Sure," said Lauren. "Go ahead, Will."

"I figured it would be feasible to find some common node somewhere. But the common node may be one or two or even more steps removed. Picture a neural network that has neurons coming out from the brain and branching off in many different directions. But all the branches stem from the control center in the brain."

"Sure," said Lauren. "I've built many neural networks like that looking for terrorists with a central command but a lot of independent cells."

"Exactly. Although in this case, the cells aren't aware they're part of the network. They're targets, not active players."

"Ah, important distinction."

"So, the common node may be one or two steps removed. For example, let's say there's a control center behind the whole scheme. We'll call that Point A, the brains behind it all, the common node that everything else connects to. So strands from Point A would connect with Points B, C, D, E, and so on. Point B in turn would connect with hundreds or thousands of people with one type of medical device, say, pacemakers, and collect information on each one of them and their devices. Point C would connect with, let's say, people with insulin pumps and collect the same information. And so on for Points D and E and so forth for other medical devices. The map is not just one huge branching network, it's a bunch of them, each with a separate threat back to point A. Points B, C, D, and E do not connect directly with each other, only with point A. Does that make sense?"

"I think so," said Lauren. Belinda nodded her agreement.

"So," Will continued, "let's say the mastermind behind this whole thing is sitting at Point A running some master computer somewhere. Once it has all the information it needs on people grouped around Point B it generates detailed directions on how to tell a pacemaker to stop pacing someone's heart. It does the same thing for Point C to learn how to command an insulin pump to overdose someone with insulin. And Point D for a defibrillator to shock someone repeatedly. But the master computer that houses Point A is running the show."

"Exactly," said Lauren.

Belinda asked, "What if the master computer disguises itself depending on the messages it's sending and receiving? You know, it looks like a PC in Vermont for one signal and a MacBook in New Zealand for another."

"Good question," said Lauren. "I was just about to ask the same thing. That raises the bar on our challenge, for sure. But we've got lots of experience tracking messages back through a jumble of proxy servers. We can use all kinds of proxy information to point toward a common source. That is, whoever's operating the computer at Point A might route the signals all over hell and back so they don't appear to be coming from the same place, but we can still use characteristics of the signals and patterns of usage to be reasonably sure they're all from the same source."

"Good," said Will. "That's what we'll do if the signals suggest that the servers are being camouflaged. Now, what about the third question, the most urgent and troublesome one: can we spot potential targets who are still alive? Any thoughts?"

"That's by far the biggest problem," said Lauren. "Thanks to your contacts at the FBI we now have access to information on everyone with an implanted device, but there are millions of them. We need some clue to help us sort through all the possible targets and predict who might be at risk. For example, if we find some common characteristics among the ones who died, that could guide our search."

"Or," said Will, "we discover who's sitting at Point A. Some evil Wizard of Oz controlling everything. Once we know who's in charge we might be able to predict who the next target might be. Until then we're stuck just sitting back waiting and watching for the next person to die."

"Not a good option," said Belinda.

"No," said Will, "not good at all."

Chapter 18: Shopping Spree

By the time the two women arrived at the Milan Malpensa
Airport Sasha was glad she had at least nibbled at her breakfast—she
had eaten nearly nothing since leaving Zarya Dacha more than twelve
hours earlier. Her expectations for service on the Aeroflot flight from
Simferopol to Moscow had been low, and they were duly met. But
she thought the airline might at least serve a decent meal on the
connecting flight to Milan. Instead, she was reminded that when
Aeroflot said economy, it meant economy.

Now she was hoping their hotel would have a restaurant with
good Italian food. But who knew how long it would be before they
would be sitting down to eat? She groaned at the thought that they
would have to suffer for hours in an endless line to make it through
Italian customs, an ordeal she was not looking forward to enduring
on an empty stomach. To her great surprise, the fully automated
passport control system made their entry into Italy remarkably
efficient. Soon they were passing through the main hall of the airport
skirting past the throng of men of all colors and ethnicities
aggressively hawking ride services into the city. Sasha dismissed them
with a wave of her hand and said to Valeria, "Let's go to the official
taxi line."

Her companion smiled and said, "That, my dear Sasha, will
not be necessary." Valeria pointed to a trim young woman wearing a
stylish white suit and red beret who held up an iPad displaying their
names in a giant black font.

"Buongiorno, ladies," she said. "I am Livia. Welcome to
Milano."

"Hello, Livia. I am Valeria Klara, and this is Alexandra
Arkadyevna."

"Good to meet you, Livia. Please, call me Sasha."

"I am delighted to meet you both," she said in slightly-accented English as they shook hands all around. "Please, follow me. My colleague Paolo will collect your bags."

Sasha turned to look at Valeria, who smiled at her with a knowing grin and said in Russian, "What else did you expect for a billionaire's mistress and her attendant?"

Sasha replied with a smirk, "So why didn't we fly first class then?"

"No one on the plane knew who we were. Or," she chuckled, "who you are *going* to be. Not yet. In the future it will be all first class or private jets, you will see."

They both laughed and followed Livia through the dense crowd to the carpark and up to a stretch limo whose engine was idling. Sasha's weary eyes opened wide when she recognized the enormous car waiting for them. "Holy god in heaven," she said in Russian, "that limousine is a Lamborghini Aventador! I have seen photographs of movie stars riding in such cars in the magazines I used to read in the States, but I never imagined I would ride in one."

"Nothing but the best," laughed Valeria, also in Russian. "We have an image to create." Then in English to Livia, "Thank you so much. We should be quite comfortable."

The fastidiously attired Paolo opened an oversized side door of the limousine and offered his arm to each of the three women in turn, but they all politely declined his assistance as they climbed into the passenger compartment. Sasha and Valeria sat in plush leather side couches facing each other, while Livia took a freestanding seat in the middle of the floor that was mounted like a captain's chair so she could swivel back and forth between the two Russians.

"Please, make yourselves at home," said Livia. "There is champagne and, of course, caviar on the ice. If you are quite hungry, there are some tramezzini, delicious small Italian finger sandwiches. The chef awaits you at the hotel and will prepare any of his specialties that you request. But if you would prefer to go to the spa first and perhaps have a massage or sauna to recover from your long trip, just let me know and I will make the arrangement."

Sasha shook her head in amazement. Valeria saw the surprise on her face and admonished her in Russian, "You must get used to such luxury. You must appear to be a woman who is accustomed to lavish treatment, not some starstruck peasant from a remote village."

Sasha flashed back to her mother's house in Novolugovoye. They were not peasants but they had scraped by from day to day, enduring long lines for scarce food supplies. To them, going into nearby Novosibirsk had felt like a trip to the big city. Her only taste of glamour had been her magical visit to Zarya Dacha with her grandfather. Back then they had no idea that limousines like this one existed—when her mother was at last able to buy the Lada SUV it seemed the height of luxury. But Sasha had indeed come a long way from that life and knew she would have no trouble adapting to this new one. No trouble adapting to whatever was expected of her.

By the time she had guzzled her third glass of champagne on an empty stomach she felt the alcohol going directly to her jet-lagged brain and decided it was time to have something to eat. She pulled a tray of tramezzini out of the refrigerator compartment, selected one each of tuna, porchetta, and shredded beef, and devoured them rapidly. Between bites of the little sandwiches she took tiny spoonfuls of caviar, washing them down with sips of sparkling mineral water. Afterward, she was not aware that she had dozed off until she heard Livia calling to her and Valeria as the limousine slowed to a stop. Sasha looked out the window and blinked twice to take it all in: they had pulled up in front of the world-famous Armani Hotel Milano. This time she was glad to accept Paolo's help leaving the limo, steadying herself on his arm before trying to walk. She was, she hoped, no more than fashionably drunk as would be expected for someone in her position riding in a Lamborghini Aventador.

After freshening up a bit in their ultra-modern suites Sasha and Valeria soon were gazing at the panoramic view of Milan from the modernistic top-floor restaurant. They giggled like giddy schoolgirls on a field trip as they savored a cornucopia of Italian specialties from the antipasti buffet and drank two bottles of an exquisite Barolo vino. At last they collapsed in their beds and did not awake until after the sun was high in the sky over the Duomo.

After a late breakfast they set out on their shopping extravaganza. They did not have to walk far, since the hotel was in the heart of the Via Montenapoleone fashion district. Valeria had arranged personal viewings at a long list of famous shops, starting with Armani and on to Prada, Versace, and more than half the list of renowned designers. She was in her element. Every style she requested was perfect for Sasha, every outfit exactly what suited their mission. Valeria had exquisite taste for elegant clothes that oozed sex appeal. After viewing countless evening gowns with impressive displays of décolletage, Sasha was surprised when a model walked out in a dress with a high Roman collar that seemed inexplicably reserved—until the model turned around and Sasha gasped at seeing a very different kind of cleavage. The nearly backless dress was cut so low it revealed several centimeters of the slit between the woman's buttocks.

Valeria laughed at Sasha's reaction. In Russian she said, "I am told that this gown is reminiscent of a dress that Guy Laroche designed for a movie many years ago, long before you or I were allowed to see such films. Do you think you might like such a gown?"

"I think I would be reaching around scratching nervously all night," Sasha replied. "Let us not purchase that one."

Their shopping soon fell into a routine that continued every day. They visited one shop in the morning between ten and one-thirty, then one or two shops after the extended midday meal, generally from three-thirty or four until eight or so. The first few days they viewed evening gowns and sporty outfits. Then one day was devoted entirely to lingerie. Thongs barely more than g-strings, so weightless Sasha could shut her eyes and not feel their weight in her hands. Teddies that left nothing to the imagination. Another full day was spent looking for outer garments: fur coats and faux fur coats, brightly colored raingear, coats for decoration and coats for foul weather. Two more days were taken up shopping for shoes. Valeria impressed Sasha with her ability to remember what they had selected and pick shoes that were perfect complements to the outfits. By nine or ten in the evening each day they were worn out, but never too tired to head to one of the many Michelin-star restaurants in Milan for a spectacular dinner before returning to their Armani suites at one or two in the morning.

Over dinner one evening at the end of the long week Valeria looked up from her food and said, "So, Sasha, have you seen enough?"

"I cannot describe how I feel. The clothes are beautiful and this has been great fun, but I am exhausted. Can we pause for a while, please?"

"Of course. So I take it you are satisfied with Milan. Do you wish also to visit the galleries of Rome, Paris, Stockholm or Barcelona? Or anywhere else?"

"I would prefer to stop with Milan. Do you think I have enough to begin my mission?"

"For now, yes. Quite sufficient. As things progress, we may need to do more shopping depending on…the demands on your presence. We shall see what is needed when the time comes."

"So, what do we do now?"

"We remain in Milan to complete the fittings. Then we will go to Moscow to await word about when you will be called upon to display your elegant new wardrobe."

"And when will that be?"

"The time is not set, but I am told it is in the works. The word could come at any moment."

"Then I need some more champagne."

Chapter 19: POTUS

"Hi, Will. Do you have time to drop by headquarters? There are a couple of things I'd like to go over with you. And...I'd like your advice on something."

"Of course, Adrienne. What's up?"

"I'd prefer to discuss this in person. OK?"

"Sure. It's a nice day, I'll walk over—I could use the exercise. See you in about half an hour."

"Perfect, thanks. I'll clear you to come in the back way."

"I'm on my way."

Will wondered what on earth Special Agent Adrienne Penscal could possibly want his advice on. As close colleagues they had often asked each other for work-related suggestions. And he considered her a friend. But this sounded...well, it sounded *personal*. He shook his head and smiled, blushing with embarrassment at the memory of the last time he had tried to guess where she was going with something personal and had quite wrongly inferred that she was coming on to him. What could it be this time? A career move? Maybe she was interested in leaving the FBI and coming to the private sector? Internal FBI politics? Whatever it was, he would be glad to share his thoughts. Time enough to think once he knew what she had in mind.

He headed out of the conjoined brownstones housing *Cybersleuths, Inc.* and immediately felt glad he had decided to walk the not-quite two miles to FBI headquarters. He took a refreshing breath of crisp Autumn air and smiled at the leaves on the trees that glowed like gold in the bright sunshine. He headed west on C Street NE, then angled up northwest on Massachusetts Avenue, around Columbus Circle past the regal Union Station, and on to E Street NE, which became E Street NW when he crossed North Capitol Street. From there it was a straight shot to the back entrance of the J.

Edgar Hoover Building just over 9th Street NW. He walked up to the guard house and waited at the turnstile until he was signaled to advance to the security booth. The guard studied his driver's license, typed a few keystrokes into his computer, then looked up at Will with what was on the verge of becoming an hospitable smile. "Very good, Sir, you're cleared."

Will entered the building through heavy steel-and-glass double doors that had to be at least eight inches thick, dropped his cell phone and the other contents of his pockets into a small plastic bin and set it on the conveyor belt, and walked through the metal detector. He collected his belongings, all but the cell phone for which he was given a claim check. The guard inside the screening area handed him a badge with an oversized "V" to alert everyone that he was a visitor. He hung the badge around his neck on its chain and could not help reminiscing about the weeks and months he had carried full-fledged FBI credentials, however temporary his assignment there had been.

This time Adrienne greeted him with only a firm, friendly handshake—apparently, hugs from FBI Special Agents were only for reunions, not routine visits.

"Hi Will. Thanks for coming over."

"I never say no to the FBI."

"You always say no when we ask you to come work for us," she said with a grin.

"Fair enough," he said, smiling back. "What's up?"

"A couple of things. First, business. How's the investigation going? Were the files we gave you useful?"

Will was momentarily distracted—what did she mean by '*first*' business? What would be 'second?' Then he answered, "Actually we're making some headway. Those files should be very helpful, thanks again."

"Tell me more."

Will spent the next half-hour describing the work he was doing with Belinda Winnisome and Lauren Sveiks. He started with the three questions they were pursuing: deaths they had missed; tying together massive data to identify hidden connections; and, looking for potential targets who were still alive.

When he reached the third question Adrienne said, "Yes, that has been troubling us greatly. Just like any case involving a serial killer, we always want to prevent the next murder from happening.

Unfortunately, that's the hardest part. All too often we're stymied until the killer slips up, and by then another murder has taken place. Any hopes there?"

"We don't know yet. Our predictive analytics can't predict anything until we have good data to feed into them and some clue to help focus the search. Hopefully that will come if we make progress on the first two questions. So far, though, nothing."

She thought for a long moment, then said, "You know, law enforcement is all about evidence, not feelings or intuition or theories. Nothing other than cold, hard facts. But somehow this particular situation bothers me. I have nothing solid to go on, and yet I can't help feeling that we're building up toward something big, some real game changer. And we aren't going to be prepared for it when it happens."

Will nodded. "Yes, I have the same feeling. Like 9-11. After the fact we saw all the dots that we should have connected ahead of time, but didn't. We had more than enough information to have had a good shot at preventing those atrocities, but we didn't pull it all together until it was too late. That's what's driving us to do everything we can to answer that third question right now: who's next? One person, or a cyber attack on a massive scale?"

"Those two aren't mutually exclusive. One key death could trigger widespread killing in retribution."

"You mean like the assassination that set off World War I?"

"Exactly. That's why we've diverted a very large part of our resources to monitoring as many terrorist groups as possible. Electronic traffic and leads from our assets in all the hot spots are at an all-time high. But nothing concrete. Keep me posted if you come up with anything. We're counting on you guys."

"We're not all guys," Will quipped, smiling sheepishly as he recalled his little *faux pas*.

"Ha! You don't have to tell me that, my friend. And, speaking as a friend, as I mentioned, I would like your advice on something."

Get ready, here it comes. "Sure, but as I always say, free advice is worth what you pay for it. Shoot."

"Remember that first time you were here in my office and you were admiring the photographs I have on the wall?"

"Sure, very impressive." Pointing at a large framed picture positioned prominently among her photos and other mementos he said, "Especially that one of you and the Director with that great inscription."

"Well," she said, hold up her hand with a narrow gap between her index finger and thumb, "remember how I told you that I had come *this close* to having a picture taken with POTUS and then he got pulled away just before it was my turn?"

"Of course. What a bummer that must have been!"

"You can say that again. I let myself get all excited that I was almost there, and then what a letdown, a dull thud. Anyway, remember also how I said recently that you could say or do whatever you wanted to as a private citizen but I had to keep my nose out of politics?"

"Sure."

"Well, that's it, that's what I want your advice on. The Director has been invited to a formal reception at the White House and he has extended an offer for Chief Hollingshead to accompany him with a handful of agents. We will definitely get a photo opportunity."

"I thought Dorzel was at odds with the FBI."

"At first, yes, he sure was. But he's got his own man in there now as Director. And you know the president, consistency is not his defining characteristic, especially when shifting positions serves him."

"So what do you want from me?"

"I've always wanted a picture with the President of the United States...but I don't want to get anywhere near this particular president. And I don't want a photo of him on my wall for the rest of my life. But it won't play well upstairs if I say no to the Chief and the Director. And who knows if I'll ever get another chance with a different president. Any thoughts on what I should do?"

"Wow, that's a tough one. When you say it won't play well upstairs, just what do you mean?"

"The Director could take it as a slight to the president and maybe as an inappropriately political statement. I could get tagged like football players kneeling during the National Anthem. I'm not so worried for myself, although it could be a black mark as far as future promotions. But the Director might take it out on Chief Hollingshead and I wouldn't want that to happen."

"Hmm...complicated. Truth is, it *would* be a political statement, right?"

"Partly, yes. But Dorzel is just not someone I want to be around. You know his reputation with women. What if he tried something or made some crude remark? Even the thought of shaking hands with him makes me queasy. I might not be able to control my reaction."

Will laughed. The idea of Adrienne Penscal losing control over anything was so foreign as to be humorous. "Fortunately, they'll make you check your weapon at the front door."

"Come on, this is serious. Give me some ideas. Some words of wisdom."

"I'm a numbers guy, not Dear Abby, but sure, here's my reaction: this feels like something personal because you can't stand Dorzel and you've always coveted a picture with POTUS. But the reality is that you're being asked to do this in the line of duty, and you never shirk your duty. That's just not like you. I know it's not an order, just an invitation, but there's a high expectation that you will accept. And you'd definitely make waves by declining. So grin and bear it is my advice. You can decide later whether to hang the picture on the wall, or not."

"Grin and bear it is what Dorzel always says to women," groused Adrienne under her breath. Will was astonished to hear her say something like that. She had always been the consummate professional no matter how distasteful her assignment, but the thought of shaking hands with Dorzel seemed to have undone her.

"It's a handshake and a photo, Adrienne, you're not being asked to…you know, to do anything more."

"You're right, Will. I don't want to let Chief Hollingshead down and I don't have to hang the picture on the wall if I don't want to. OK, thanks for the free advice. It was worth the price," she added with a smile.

Will was pleased to see that she had gotten over her pique.

"No extra charge."

Chapter 20: Moscow Calling

Natalia Kostenka had told Sasha and Valeria in no uncertain terms that as soon as their buying spree was finished they were to stop their massive infusion of rubles into the Italian economy and leave Milan immediately for Moscow. But after they had been in Milan for nearly a fortnight they were having such a good time they decided to figure out a way to stay a few extra days. Valeria hit upon the idea: they would have plenty of free time to enjoy themselves if they told Natalia they needed to stay in town for fittings on the articles they had already selected and didn't schedule any more visits for time-consuming viewings of the collections at additional salons.

The delaying action worked almost to perfection. They decided to start by doing the things at the top of their Milan lists: Sasha wished to see Leonardo's painting of The Last Supper, and Valeria was determined to attend an opera at the Teatro alla Scala. Both sites required tickets that were often scooped up weeks or even months ahead of time, but that posed no problem for the ever-enterprising Valeria, who handed the hotel concierge €100 and told him that he should get the tickets and not worry about the cost, just add the charges to their hotel bill. He promptly arranged for a guide who spoke fluent Russian as well as English. Very early in the morning of the following day the man met them at the ancient Dominican convent of Santa Maria delle Grazie for what, to Sasha's delight and amazement, turned out to be a near-private showing of The Last Supper. That afternoon the guide took them on a tour of La Scala before handing them fourth-row tickets to a performance of Verdi's La Traviata. They were in heaven.

Then the fun came to a sudden end. The instant Sasha saw the look on Valeria's face at breakfast the next morning she knew something had happened. In Russian, her companion said, "We must leave at once. He is coming to Moscow next week."

Sasha felt as though she had been kicked in her belly. She put her hand over her mouth and ran for the ladies' room. After fruitless attempts to purge her empty stomach she splashed cold water on her face until she no longer felt woozy, then returned to the restaurant and stared blankly at Valeria. Her companion took Sasha's hands in hers and said reassuringly, "The first moment will be the worst. You must remember that this is your job, you are on a mission. Then you will find a way to put up with whatever must happen."

Sasha nodded, but could say nothing.

Valeria nodded back, a look of understanding on her face. Then a glint appeared in her eyes as she said, "At least you will travel to Moscow in style. I booked two seats in business class." The glint in her eyes was soon joined by a mischievous grin. "Natalia Kostenka will poop in her drawers when she sees the bill. Those tickets cost over €1,000 each. That is some five or six times the price of coach, which that joyless woman would have had us buy. I would have purchased first class but this is the best Aeroflot offers on this route. After all, your new image is priceless, you cannot be seen traveling with peasants who carry live chickens in their bags." She laughed, thoroughly enjoying her triumph over the ghostly Natalia Kostenka. Sasha smiled back at Valeria and snorted a muffled laugh, suppressing her apprehension over what was soon to happen.

The three-and-a-half hour flight from Milan to Moscow seemed longer to Sasha than the day-long journey to Milan from Zarya Dacha. The flight was smooth except for a half-hour of turbulence as they rose over the Alps, but Sasha was sick to her stomach for most of the trip for other reasons. Several times Valeria encouraged her to take advantage of the excellent food and drinks that Aeroflot provided to business class customers, but she could not even look at food and had no interest in any more champagne or wine. They had left Milan in brilliant sunshine just before three in the afternoon, but flying east it was after eight-thirty and the sky in Moscow was a dull grey-black wall of gloom when they landed. The darkness surrounding them mirrored Sasha's grim mood. What had she gotten herself into? How could she bear to have intimate relations with that pig? For no particular reason she thought of her mother and grew angry. The woman was enjoying herself at the price of selling her daughter off to be a whore, happy that she had given birth to a very high-priced whore who kept her mother in style. She bit her lip to gain control. This was not her mother's doing, this was her own. Her mother might be enjoying the fruits of Sasha's degradation but she had made all her own choices. There was no one to blame but herself.

When they landed at Sheremetyevo, Moscow's A.S. Pushkin international airport, they were indeed given VIP treatment. The vast throng of passengers in coach were held back on the plane until the business class section was empty. They were ushered into a comfortable reception area where courteous, efficient officials whisked them through passport control and customs. The driver who awaited them was yet another clone of the stocky, reticent men in dark business suits from Zarya Dacha. He led them to a large black Mercedes sedan, at which point Valeria muttered, "Not like the limo in Milan, but not bad."

Sasha was quiet for most of the drive. As the Mercedes got closer to the City Center she looked out at the mix of buildings they were passing. She saw rows of ultra-modern low-rise apartment buildings and glossy skyscrapers pock-marked with older residences that had seen better days. They came to a stop near the Moscow River in front of a five-story modern building with an unusual eye-catching design: the façade of each floor displayed huge bay windows alternating with long, curved balconies that gave the rectangular structure the appearance of rounded corners. "We are here," announced the driver, the first words he had spoken on the trip.

The two women rode the whisper-quiet lift up to the top floor and entered one of the apartments. Sasha stood still and shook her head in disbelief at the stunning view. Through floor-to-ceiling bay windows that opened onto a long balcony they saw the brightly-lit Kremlin, framed by the Moscow River and the lights of the city. The apartment had an open floor plan so that the living and dining areas and the kitchen all offered the panoramic view. They walked down a short, curved hallway and entered the master bedroom, an oversized space with the same spectacular view. The Scandinavian-style bed was enormous, fully in proportion to the big room. Its California King mattress was tastefully framed by the light maple slats of the eight-foot high headboard and low footboard. The master bath was done in shiny white tile that seemed to reflect the polished chrome plumbing fixtures and white ceramic of the Japanese toilet, French bidet, Italian Jacuzzi bathtub, and walk-in shower with water jets on three sides. The rest of the apartment included a study, a sitting room featuring a massive television screen, a second bedroom, a powder room, and a number of walk-in closets.

"Ah," Sasha said to Valeria when they finished looking around, "this is quite nice. Am I to live here?"

Valeria said, "Yes, this is your apartment."

"And is that second bedroom for you?"

"I, alas, will be with you only temporarily, to see that you settle in properly for your assignment. Then I will be sent elsewhere."

"Where will you go?"

"I do not know. Perhaps nearby for a period, perhaps back to Zarya Dacha, perhaps somewhere else."

Sasha realized that she had come to like Valeria very much. Valeria seemed more a friend than a government watchdog. She would miss her when she was gone. Their weeks in Milan had been a lighthearted holiday, two young women off on their own, enjoying the high life with a nearly unlimited expense account. But now the harsh truth came home—Valeria was, indeed, a government watchdog, and soon other watchdogs would replace her. And Sasha would be left on her own. On her own in a beautiful apartment that, despite the sleek design with no scrollwork on the walls and ceiling to conceal cameras and microphones, was no doubt wired to record her every move.

"So," said Sasha, sighing at the thought of the men sitting at their monitors observing her and Valeria, "what happens now?"

"There is to be a reception three days from now that the man will attend. You will be introduced to him. We expect that you will attract his attention and he will wish to…as we say, see more of you."

"I will be ready."

Chapter 21: Targets

Assassination! Will couldn't get the word out of his head ever since it came up in his conversation with Adrienne. What if the deaths so far were practice runs for an assassination, like The Jackal shooting at a watermelon to adjust the sight on his rifle so Charles De Gaulle's head would be sure to explode with a single shot? The whole Dick Cheney paranoia about being hacked to death coming true? But who, who could the target be? And only one target, or many? How could he figure out whether that was the story? He had to find a way.

As he often did when puzzling through a new problem, Will stared at his monitor to think, never conscious that the fingernail on his right index finger was searching through his long red hair seeking out the small crusty plaque on his scalp. The wandering fingernail would pick gently at the scaly growth until Will found inspiration and needed all ten fingers to enter a torrent of keystrokes into the computer, countless commands to build the algorithms, then more entries to correct errors and make changes and additions, a growing cascade back and forth as ideas were transformed from brainwaves to computer language.

Like most of his best ideas this new one was simple: scan the FBI files of everyone who had an implanted medical device against lists of public figures who might be potential assassination targets. Start with the president, Cabinet members, leadership of the House and Senate, and Supreme Court Justices, then add others as they came to mind. Will wrote a short program commanding the computer to pull up the FBI data and run it against lists of public officials readily available from the Library of Congress.

Within two hours of his fingernail's first scratch at the plaque on his scalp, he had results. Too many results. President Hugo H.

Dorzel was on the list—one pacemaker, implanted some nine years earlier. So was the vice-president, four of the nine Supreme Court Justices, and about one-third of both the Cabinet and the Congressional leadership. It seemed that nearly everyone in a seat of power was being kept alive by a medical device somewhere in their bodies. He reflected on the advanced age of so many public figures and realized he should have anticipated that a high percentage would have implanted devices. For a moment he felt overwhelmed, discouraged. Then he noticed that about half of the devices were not ones that would be vulnerable to murder by hacking: artificial hip and knee joints. But the rest of the devices were ones to be concerned about, including two implantable defibrillators like the one that kept Dick Cheney alive but caused him so much angst. He was surprised to see that three people on the list had deep brain stimulators in place, one for epilepsy, the other two for Parkinson's disease. What came as no surprise was that the most common devices were insulin pumps and cardiac pacemakers.

OK, he had the list—what did it tell him? Were these really possible targets for assassination, or just miracles of modern medicine? What to do next? He needed help. Will texted Hank Cotter to see if he was free for a chat with him and his small group. Hank replied immediately that he'd be available any time in the next two hours. Will sent messages to Belinda, Lauren and Ned asking them to join him in Hank's office. Fifteen minutes later they were all gathered around the conference table with the spectacular Capitol view.

"Thanks, everyone," began Will. "I had a conversation recently with my friend, Special Agent Adrienne Penscal at the FBI, to update her on our progress. We talked about how we're using the data files she had provided to us on every individual with an implanted medical device." Will decided not to mention Adrienne's perplexity over whether she should attend the reception with President Dorzel. "She raised a specific concern about something growing out of our 'target practice' scenario: whether the deaths so far might be building up to a major incident, perhaps the assassination of a public figure."

"Just like in *Day of the Jackal*," said Belinda. "Loved that movie, what a classic thriller."

Will laughed and said, "That's exactly what came to my mind! I've probably seen it ten times." The laugh sounded genuine but it was Will's way of covering up the cringe that he felt at her remark—

he had indeed watched the old movie many times, but always with Barry. Once again struggling to put Belinda's resemblance to his dead twin out of his mind he sucked in a breath, paused, then continued. "Anyway, I thought about what to do to test Adrienne's idea. So I cross-checked public figures against the FBI files and identified several dozen possible targets. At that point I was stumped. So I wanted to see if any of you could come up with a good way to proceed."

"What have you found so far?" asked Hank.

"The implanted devices include a lot of artificial joints, which we don't really need to be concerned about. That leaves a bunch of defibrillators, pacemakers and insulin pumps. And there are three people with a device we hadn't focused on: deep brain stimulators."

"Interesting," observed Ned. "Those gadgets control electrical currents in the brain much like pacemakers do in the heart. I suppose in the age cohort of our nation's leadership it's to be expected that a few of the old geezers would have Parkinson's disease. That's what the stimulators are for, right?"

"Two of them, yes, but one is for epilepsy. That person is the youngest in the group, just over forty years old."

"Now that's really interesting," said Lauren Sveiks. "Could be very damaging to a political career for someone to have seizures in public. Shouldn't be that way, but that's the unfortunate truth in our society."

The group nodded in agreement.

"So," Will said, "any reactions? Ideas? Suggestions?"

"Have you said anything to your FBI contact?" asked Hank Cotter.

"Not yet. I'd like to have something concrete to tell her."

"My quick reaction," said Hank, "is that Dorzel is the most likely target. POTUS is the one official who has the big-time protection that makes him almost invulnerable. The others usually have a handful of federal agents assigned to protect them, but nothing like Dorzel has with the Secret Service. So unless you're dealing with the president's level of security why go to so much trouble to prepare for killing a public figure when you could shoot them with a rifle or toss a hand grenade into their entourage?"

"That makes a lot of sense," said Will. "If we're really dealing with an assassination attempt."

Belinda looked doubtful. "Who would want to kill Dorzel and also have the technical capacity to carry out something like this?"

"Lots of people hate the man," said Ned.

Will answered, "Yes, that's for sure, but if this is all to line up an assassination we're talking about an extremely sophisticated arrangement. Advanced technology, detailed planning, all done in total secrecy. You've got a good point about Dorzel but who could pull this off?"

"Top of my list would be the Russians," said Hank Cotter.

Belinda shook her head. "I agree that the Russians have the capacity," she said, "but they love the guy. Why would they want to knock him off? He's the best friend they've ever had."

The group went silent. Five of the best brains anywhere searching for a response.

"Let's think this through," said Will. "Maybe Dorzel is no longer their best friend. He's irascible, unpredictable, maybe he's done something to turn them against him."

"Or," added Belinda, "they've gotten everything they wanted out of him. But why get rid of him when they don't know who might come next?"

"You know," said Will, "that reminds me of a comment Adrienne Penscal made when we first talked about possible scenarios. She pointed out that terrorists often do things to disrupt society just to create turmoil and undermine people's confidence in government. Instability and anarchy serve their purpose."

"That's certainly what we've seen from the Russians with their disinformation campaigns," said Hank Cotter. "They sow mistrust to send Western democracies into disarray. Set people against each other, strengthen their hand by weakening the other side. Dragging us down is its own goal. Putting someone like Dorzel in office is a valuable bonus. It's a lot easier to screw with another country's stability than to actually do the hard work of rebuilding their own disastrous economy."

"Let alone eliminating official corruption," added Lauren Sveiks.

"OK, said Will, "do we all agree that the Russians are likely candidates for the evil mastermind, if that's what's going on here?"

"I'm still not so sure," said Belinda. "I mean, I buy them as being able to pull this off, but I'd still like a better explanation than chaos for chaos' sake. I think there has to be a target, but Dorzel doesn't seem like someone who would be in their crosshairs. So we shouldn't stop with Dorzel. Yes, it's so hard to get at the president that it might take a scheme this complex to assassinate him, but there could be other people who are extremely well protected and whose death would serve their purposes a lot better than losing their buddy Dorzel. We also shouldn't ignore the possibility that someone else entirely could be behind this, not just the Russians."

"Like who?"

"Our own government, for starters," said Ned.

"Wow, talk about mistrust of government!"

"Don't write it off too easily. We all know what our own intelligence agency is capable of."

"True enough," said Hank Cotter. "We can't rule anything out yet, but let's not start by questioning our own government."

"You know," said Belinda, "what Ned just said reminds me of a rather unsettling experiment I read about a few days ago. A group of very well informed people were subjected to repeated disinformation messaging over a period of a few months. The topics were things they knew a lot about. At the start, they realized that what they were hearing was not true, but it was presented so skillfully that they began to have some doubts about their own information. All the subjects found the experience very disquieting."

"Ouch," said Will. "The big lie theory. Keep repeating a big lie over and over and pretty soon people will start to believe it." He paused, shaking his head. Then he said, "Other thoughts?"

Silence again. Brain cells grinding away so frenetically to connect the right synapses their labors were almost audible.

Hank Cotter spoke up after a long minute.

"OK, we have one somewhat plausible but flawed scenario so far: the Russians are out to get Dorzel. Strongest support for that is that they are the ones who are capable of pulling off a high-tech assassination. But there are lots of holes in that story, especially how it would benefit them. Anyway, let's start there. Will, I'd like you to pay another visit to your friendly Special Agent. See if she can come up with any reason to believe that Dorzel and the Russians might be on the outs. Maybe he's done something we don't know about that would turn them against him and make them want to get rid of him. Depending on what she says maybe we'll know whether to push this one further. And in the meantime, all of us need to continue to think of other scenarios. Who else besides the Russians? Besides Dorzel? Don't rule anything out until you know enough to rule it out."

"Got it," said Will. "I'm always happy to chat with Adrienne. Let's see if she can help us decide whether we're barking up the wrong tree." Recalling how she had confided in him about her quandary over the Dorzel reception, he added, "If she knows something, I think she might just share it with me."

Chapter 22: Beauty and the Beast

Valeria Klara knew exactly which evening dress Sasha should wear to her first meeting with Hugo H. Dorzel: the skin-tight floor-length gown in a clingy, sparkling red silk blend. A tantalizing slit below the waist on one side revealed nearly the entire length of her long left leg. The bodice consisted of two slender straps that criss-crossed over her chest, each covering only a narrow sliver of her buoyant bare breasts. Like most of the clothes from Milan, Valeria had selected this one, insisting over Sasha's objection that it would be perfect to attract Dorzel's attention. Looking at herself now in the mirror Sasha grudgingly conceded the point—any man who could look away from her in that dress could not be drawn to her by any outfit. Her long blond hair billowed up through a diamond-and-platinum tiara, then down to her shoulders in perfectly curled twists. The matching choker would draw the attention of other elegantly-clad ladies to her slender neck, but the men would never notice it as their eyes made a rapid descent from her face to her décolletage.

"I was quite right to trust your judgment, Valeria Klara, this dress is exquisite. You have impeccable taste."

"That is, I trust, one of my humble talents. Yes, the gown is well suited for a formal state reception—elegant, and tastefully provocative. If this man is a real man he will be unable to resist you."

"And will you be my companion for the evening?"

Valeria laughed. "No, my dear Sasha, you will be attended by an officer from the General's staff, Major Maxim Grigorovich Dragomirov. He is handsome and an excellent dancer."

"But will the president think that I am taken when he sees me with such a man?"

She laughed again. "Not at all. Even if he did, we do not believe that would concern him in the least. Perhaps it would excite him to steal you away from a handsome officer of the General's staff. And should anyone inquire, you will say that the Major is your cousin, and make it subtly clear that he is not your love interest."

"Do you expect that he will...that I must be with that man the same night?"

"Yes, unless he is called away for some matter of state. But even then he might well ignore even the most critical matters until he is finished with you. We have never known him to pay more attention to official business than to a woman. In any case, the arrangements have been made for you, as you say, to be with him that very evening."

Sasha fully understood what Valeria Klara meant: recording equipment was at the ready in some bedroom, with a gang of observers awaiting the images of her and the President of the United States to appear on their monitors. But she no longer felt her stomach churn at the thought of being intimate with the man she knew all too well from those disgusting videos. She had come to terms with her fate. This was her job, and she would do it well. After all, this was not to be a one-night stand. This was only the beginning. She was to entice Dorzel into lusting after her so dearly that he would insert her into his inner circle. She must become the eyes and ears and mouthpiece of the Russian State in the White House. That was her real job; everything else was just the means to fulfill that responsibility. And to assure that her mother would remain safe and sound back home in Novolugovoye.

When Sasha opened the door to her apartment to greet Major Maxim Grigorovich Dragomirov she was instantly taken aback by his striking appearance. Valeria Klara had said he was handsome, but she had not done the gentleman justice. At least six-foot-two, with a square-jawed face right off a patriotic war poster, he was magnificent. He wore the dark evening dress uniform of the Russian Army. Gold braid encircled the insignia of the General's staff pinned on the right side of his chest, ribbons and medals covered nearly half of the left. He greeted her with a mock salute, smiled a entrancing smile, and said in a radio announcer's deep yet soft voice, "Ah, my dear cousin, the most lovely Alexandra Arkadyevna Parushnikova. Major Maxim Grigorovich Dragomirov at your service. I am delighted to be your escort this evening,."

"And I am most grateful to you for accompanying me, my dear cousin."

"Let us be on our way, then. We are in for a full evening."

"Perhaps," she said, with no hint of the irony she felt. "Perhaps quite full, indeed."

He helped her into her long wrap coat. The soft cashmere felt good against her skin and the fur collar fit perfectly over the diamond choker.

"May I, cousin?" he said, offering her his arm.

"Of course, cousin."

They descended in the lift without speaking. As they approached the glass front doors of the apartment building Sasha saw that this time they would be riding in a real limousine, a dark black stretch Mercedes limo. Not a Lamborghini Aventador, she thought, but a car that would announce her as a person of high status.

When they pulled up in front of the vast Kremlin compound a uniformed guard saluted, opened the limousine door, and helped Sasha exit gracefully. Male and female uniformed guards snapped to attention and saluted all the way through the maze of buildings until they reached the Grand Kremlin Palace and entered the most majestic room in the complex, the Georgievsky Hall. Two more uniforms peeled off from a line of guards and greeted them with salutes, then opened the ornate doors and escorted them in.

Sasha looked around in disbelief at the grandeur and size of the great room. Remembering Valeria's caution not to come across like a peasant gone spellbound in the big city, she struggled to keep her eyes from opening wide and exposing her intense feeling of being far out of her element in this place. Dedicated to honor the Russian Army, the Hall of Saint George was enormous beyond anything she had imagined. It was some 200 feet long and nearly 70 feet wide, but what accentuated the monumental size of the space was a vaulted ceiling some 60 feet high from which hung a series of colossal gold leaf-coated chandeliers. Columns with statues depicting victorious warriors formed the endcaps of an endless series of large, angular vaulted recesses like the apses in a cathedral. Panels in the ceiling were lavishly decorated in stucco and gold, and the walls held plaques commemorating the exploits of thousands of national heroes. Luxuriously upholstered benches lined the sides. An ensemble of some two dozen musicians in one corner played patriotic and traditional folk tunes in the background. Long bars with a glittering array of bottles and glasses filled the other three corners of the cavernous room. Uniformed waiters and waitresses were everywhere, some carrying silver trays with glasses of champagne and vodka, others with delectable appetizers.

They had arrived a little after nine but the evening was still early. Dignitaries, many in military uniforms and some whom she recognized as important leaders of the Party, continued to flow through the big doors. Two legendary cosmonauts, one man and one woman whose faces she had seen in newspapers and on television since she was a little girl, stood at the center of a circle of fawning guests vying to get close enough to touch the pair. As yet there was no sign of Dorzel, or of their own president.

About ten o'clock the ensemble switched from Russian standards to dance music. Valeria had understated Major Maxim Grigorovich Dragomirov's talents by simply describing him as a good dancer. Sasha acquitted herself well on a dance floor, having gone through the ballet training that had been obligatory for all young girls even in the poorest state schools so that the State could identify dance prodigies for the Bolshoi very early on. But the Major was truly gifted, so smooth in his movements and light on his feet that trying to keep up with him she felt like she was plodding through snow drifts wearing heavy boots. He remained gracious throughout, complimenting her after every dance.

Midway through a waltz everything changed. The crowd hushed and the dancing came to a sudden stop when the ensemble abruptly interrupted Shostakovich's Waltz No. 2 and broke into the ruffles and flourishes that signaled the arrival of the most important guests. Every head turned toward the grandest of the side alcoves where the presidential guard stood at attention. The doors in the center opened and the crowd broke into a deafening cheer as the two presidents emerged, laughing heartily and shaking hands with the guests as the ensemble played the Russian Anthem followed by Hail to the Chief.

Even at a distance of some fifty feet Sasha was struck that Dorzel was much fatter than she had anticipated. She had seen him naked many times on the videos and knew he had gotten more and more obese over the years, but now she saw that he bulged out of his tuxedo. His jacket hung wide open, his belly flopped over the curled-up cummerbund that could not contain his waistline, the bottom stud of his dress shirt had popped out of its button hole.

Her next impression was that Dorzel was shorter than she had expected. The videos had shown him largely in horizontal or various awkward positions, and even when he stood next to a woman Sasha had had no way to judge his height. All she knew were the official statements that he was six-foot-three. But standing next to the Russian president, who projected a immense he-man image but was well known to be five-foot-seven, Dorzel clearly did not tower over his counterpart by anything like eight inches. Ah, she thought, picturing him in the videos, he is lacking in height as well as in other parts.

Within a few minutes the crowd formed into a reception line to await their turn with the two presidents. They sorted themselves into position in order of their military rank, status in the party, fame, or wealth. The group in front stepped back to let the Cosmonauts and three compact, muscular young men take the places of honor at the head of the line. Sasha glanced inquiringly at Major Grigory, who whispered that the three were the stars of the Russian national ice hockey team. She nodded but said nothing, returning his words with raised eyebrows and a slight palms-up shrug that spoke for her: would they make it through the long line or was their effort doomed before it got started?

The Major winked back at his ersatz cousin. He gestured with a raised index finger for her to wait a minute, then skirted the line and headed directly toward the area surrounding the two presidents. He walked up to one of the stone-faced guards and mouthed a few words. With no change of his rigid expression the guard nodded slightly, indicating with his eyes a position in the line less than twenty guests from the front. The Major nodded back and returned to Sasha. "Come with me," he said with a smile. She put one gloved hand on his elbow and they walked with complete poise along the line to the spot where the guard now awaited them. The guard saluted again, then held up one hand to open a place ahead of the next group in line, two older men accompanied by two much younger women. The men stood still immediately at the guard's signal, one of them shushing his companion with a stern look when she started to protest the loss of their spot in the queue.

When their turn came Sasha quivered at the sight of Dorzel close up. His small round eyes bulged from ovals of white skin that cut across his eerily orange face, marking a pale stripe like the outline of a skier's goggles. As quickly as the little eyes opened they rolled around in their recessed sockets and shot down past her face and the diamond choker to her cleavage. His stare lingered for an eternity, burning at her breasts like laser beams until at last he turned his face to say something to the interpreter. The interpreter uttered a few words directly into the ears of the Russian president, who responded with a lascivious grin and a slight, but distinct, nod of approval.

That first sordid night would later evoke memories for Sasha that were sometimes merely disquieting, but more often unnerving. The rare moments when her mind was being merciful she would recall only a blurry, chaotic jumble of disagreeable sex, followed by a great sense of relief when she found herself alone in the bed the next morning. But most of the time her memories were horrific. Long after she had endured many nights with the man, that first encounter would replay in nightmare images of mounds of flesh dripping with torrents of sweat, everything steeped in a strange off-orange color. She would see herself trying to escape in slow motion, thrashing around in air that had thickened into a viscous soup. Sensations would flow through her in short bursts: a cold shudder when he first touched her with his short, stubby fingers; desolation at being led away from the Major like a condemned prisoner; searing pain in her scalp as Dorzel ripped out clumps of hair when he clumsily yanked the straps of her dress over her head and snagged them on the tiara; more wrenching pain when he reached up under her dress and grabbed brutally at both sides of her crotch; feeling suffocated as she gasped for breath and prayed silently for relief while he smothered her under his flabby body.

That first night would never go away, but it was only the beginning.

Chapter 23: Personal Life

"Hi Adrienne, it's me again."

"Hi Will. What's up?"

"There's something else I'd like to run by you. Can I come over to FBI headquarters this afternoon?"

"Sure, any time after 2. And I'm glad you called—I also have something I've been meaning to speak with you about."

"A follow-up on the topic of our last conversation?"

"More or less."

"Keeping me in suspense, huh? No problem, see you between 2 and 3."

"That works. See you then."

A few minutes after 2, Will stepped outside and looked up to a dark, threatening sky. He decided to risk walking over to the J. Edgar Hoover Building but one block from Union Station he felt the first drops of rain—big, heavy drops that thudded on his head like acorns. He considered hopping on a Metro train, but realized he'd have to walk several blocks at the other end and had neglected to bring either a raincoat or an umbrella. So he jumped into a cab at Union Station, bracing himself for bitter complaints from the driver about how long he had waited at the train station for a good fare only to get stuck with a short ride. The irate taxi driver did not disappoint, cursing at Will in at least two languages until, to his scornful delight, his passenger stepped out of his cab into a monumental downpour at the Hoover Building. Will jogged to the guard station, then stood waiting at the turnstile long enough to get thoroughly drenched. Once he passed through screening he headed for the nearest men's room to dry off. No paper towels in the eco-friendly bathroom, however, only high-powered hand dryers that blew hot air straight down. He pulled off his jacket and shirt and held them under the blasting air to dry out as best as possible. He thought he'd better not remove his pants in an FBI bathroom, so he went through mounds of toilet paper to wipe his shoes and pants legs, then looked in the mirror and used his long fingers to rearrange his hair and not look quite so disheveled.

Not a good start, he thought. But his situation improved rapidly when he arrived at Adrienne's office. She greeted him with a mix of amusement and concern, saying with a perceptible smirk, "I thought you would be smart enough to come in out of the rain, cybersleuth. Stand right there just a minute." She handed him two large bath towels from a cabinet in her built-in wall unit. "Semper paratus," she said.

"Quite fitting," he replied, recognizing the motto of the Coast Guard, "and some people might very well need water rescues out there today. Thanks much."

"No problem. I am always prepared with towels for when I use the fitness center downstairs."

He wiped his face, hair and clothes vigorously. When he started to sit down she handed him another towel and said, "Here, sit on this."

"Thanks," he said, draping the towel across the back and seat of the chair. "OK, who goes first?"

"You called me, so you start."

"Fine. I'll cut right to the chase: do you have any reason to suspect that Dorzel and the Russians are not getting along anymore?"

"Why do you ask?"

"We're working our way through the various scenarios. As we considered the possibility that the deaths are target practice in preparation for an assassination, two questions came to mind. First, who has the technical resources to carry out such killings, and to do so on American soil? The Russians immediately jumped to the top of the list. Second, what target would require such a complex way of murdering someone? Dorzel jumped to the top of that list. He's the only one with the extremely high level of security that might warrant an entirely new method of assassination. Other public officials are much more vulnerable. They have security details and take precautions, but their protection is nothing like what shields POTUS. Same is true for celebrities and even for billionaires. So putting those two factors together, one working hypothesis is that the Russians are preparing to knock off Dorzel. But that raises the very big question of why they would want to kill him, since he's become their BFF. Our special relationships with the UK and Europe have fallen by the wayside under Dorzel but our official deference to Russia has grown exponentially. That's why we'd like to know if the FBI is aware of something that might have turned them against each other, to the point that the Russians would want to murder him. Do you have anything that can help us rule this scenario either in or out?"

"The short answer is no, we have nothing that would help rule that scenario in. The longer answer is that, if anything, we have indications of an even stronger alliance between Dorzel and the Russians that would cut entirely the other way. As far as we can tell they would have no interest whatsoever in getting rid of him."

"Wow, I didn't think they could get any closer. Can you tell me what those indications are?"

"I'll tell you what we have, but it isn't all that much. When I say 'indications' I mean just that—indirect signals, nothing solid."

"Like?"

"I'm sure you know that we've had a pretty good fix on the traffic between the White House and the Kremlin for many years. Once Dorzel took office we saw a big surge in the flow back and forth. That's continuing to rise, but now our assets inside the Kremlin also report that they're seeing a lot of activity that suggests a new initiative focused on this country."

"What kind of activity?"

"The Russians have assembled teams of analysts to interpret a substantial amount of incoming material. Teams that report to the highest levels of their leadership."

"So do you know where the new stuff is coming from? Or what it's about?"

"No, not yet. But the bottom line is just what I said—the connections have not diminished. However the Russians are managing to get the new information, they're getting a lot. And its flowing through channels we don't have our fingers on yet."

Will leaned back against the towel. His index finger ran through his still-damp hair to its favorite spot on his scalp while he thought about what Adrienne had just told him. After a minute or two he said, "OK, I get the point. Whatever is going on, it clearly doesn't support the hypothesis that the Russians are preparing to kill Dorzel. So that leaves us wondering who else they could be after.

And whether it really is the Russians who are behind whatever is going on, or somebody else."

"On that second point, I can't tell you to rule the Russians out. They may not have a motive to assassinate Dorzel, or we may not know what their motive is, but they clearly would have the technical capacity to pull it off. And assets here in this country who could carry it out."

"Any other groups who could do it?"

"Maybe the North Koreans or Chinese. But we haven't detected any intel that points in their direction."

"Terrorists?"

"Too sophisticated for any of the international ones that we know about. Setting up the infrastructure for a scheme this complicated requires a lot of planning and communication. We're monitoring the terrorist organizations that could conceivably pull something like this off, but we haven't seen anything that indicates any of them are involved. They're mostly decentralized in small cells, not a structure that would support a complex scheme like this."

"So no leads on the international front. How about closer to home?"

"It's always possible that there's a domestic group that has been below our radar, techno-savvy mad geniuses who hate Dorzel or whatever, but none that we can identify so far."

"OK, so we don't rule out the Russians but we should start thinking about other possibilities. How about the second point? Any suggestions on who else they might be after if it's not Dorzel?"

"We've got nothing more than you do. We agree that the level of sophistication and complexity of the hacking attacks— assuming that's what they are—would be what's needed to get to the president, and that no other targets would be so difficult to assassinate. We're still thinking about other possible targets but we have no one in mind as yet."

"Anything else going on with the Russians?"

"There is one thing, a big uptick in their waves of propaganda as we head toward our elections. Bots that push phony rumors on social media every day. Two, three, four different versions of every conspiracy theory out there about the Democrats. Incredibly realistic doctored photographs."

"Ah, thanks, got it. Enough on that front for now, OK? Keep me in the loop if you come up with anything."

"Of course."

"Now, your turn—what was it you wanted to talk to me about? Something about that POTUS reception?"

To Will's surprise a look of reserve, almost shyness, came across Adrienne's face. She lowered her head and hesitated.

"What is it, Adrienne? You can say anything to me, you know that. Just blurt it out."

"Thanks," she said, looking up directly into his eyes. "OK, here it is: I've decided to attend the reception with POTUS."

"Good. So why the reluctance to tell me?"

She smiled, blinked her eyes twice—a gesture that came across to Will more like she was clearing a speck of sand off a contact lens than being flirtatious—and said, "I'd like you to go with me."

Two thoughts raced through Will's mind and collided with each other. One was a flashback to that disconcerting moment long ago when he had mistakenly thought Adrienne was hitting on him. No, he told himself, don't go there, whatever she's thinking, that's not it. The other was an image of Sally—what would his wife say about such an invitation?

"Uh...uh..." he stammered, utterly at a loss for words.

Adrienne's smile turned to laughter. "I'm not asking you out on a date, Will." Then she got serious. "It turns out that this is a more formal event than we had expected. And the invitation is for us to bring a plus-one. Everyone else has a spouse, but I don't have anyone...well, not anyone I can bring."

Will got the clue immediately. For as long as he had known Adrienne Penscal she had never said a word about her personal life. Never a mention of a boyfriend, a husband, or an ex. Lots of pictures of people on the wall but they were all of colleagues, dignitaries, family. Now he knew, and he understood. A reception with President Hugo H. Dorzel, the Director of the FBI, Chief Hollingshead, and some of her colleagues would not be an appropriate coming-out party.

"That would be great, Adrienne. I'd be happy to go with you. I'll have to run it by Sally but I don't expect any problems on her part. For any other president she might be jealous that I'm going to a big event at the White House with another woman, but she'd be even more ambivalent about going to this particular one than you are. And she has a lot of respect for you—you did save her life, after all. So I'm delighted to be your companion. Thanks for thinking of me."

"I'm the one who should do the thanking. So, thanks for accepting. As I said, it's black tie. Do you have a tux?"

"Fortunately, yes. I was going to rent one when Sally and I got married, but they said I could buy it for not much more than the rent because they were phasing out that style. So I might look a bit outdated, but it should do."

"I'm sure it'll be fine. Of course I don't have anything to wear, I'll have to go shopping. Something fairly fancy but still professional. That'll be a challenge, I'm not much of a clothes shopper."

Adrienne's comment brought a question to Will's mind. He said, "Why black tie for a reception with the FBI? Aren't work-related events usually business attire?"

"President Dorzel apparently likes to get dressed up. And this is not just an event for the FBI, there will be lots of other guests."

"And you're sure you'll get your POTUS photo?"

"Sure as I can be. Dorzel wants publicity showing that he gets along with the FBI now. But who knows?"

"I hope it works out for you, all things considered."

"Exactly. All things considered."

They shared a knowing smile. No words were necessary.

Chapter 24: The Next President

Captain Billy Jean Holliday announced the arrival of Andy Ackroyd in the monotone she reserved for her least-favorite visitor: "Mr. Ackroyd is here to see you, Colonel Jenkins."

"OK, show him in. You are welcome to stay, you know."

As usual, signaling her resolve to avoid hearing Ackroyd's latest dirty trick scheme, she said, "Yes, Sir. Thank you, Sir. I will be just outside the door."

Even before the door was fully closed Ackroyd jumped into his rapid-fire spiel. "More good news, Boss. New York Times just endorsed you. Strong stuff in both directions, up for you, down for Dorzel. You're the one to save the nation from that horse's ass."

"They called him a horse's ass? The Times."

Ackroyd spat out a laugh. "Not in so many words, nah. But lots of shit about how he has proved to be even more unfit to be president than anyone's worst fears. *'historically unprecedented incompetence; divisive rhetoric encouraging race and class warfare; international laughing-stock…'* Want to hear more?"

"Not about him. What about me?"

"Really good shit. They say you should definitely be the next president. Let me read one…whoops, sorry, it starts off with more on Dorzel: *'Hugo H. Dorzel is not making this nation great, just the opposite. He is undermining the greatness that has taken two-and-a-half centuries to create and nurture. Colonel Robin W. Jenkins represents an opportunity for this nation to once again live up to the values that make it great.'* How's that?"

"All good, sure, but what does a newspaper endorsement get you these days? People spend all their time on-line, not reading newspapers."

Ackroyd showed a toothy smile. "You got that right, Boss. Perfect segue, you're really gonna love what I've got now." He pushed his heavy black-frame eyeglasses up on his nose as he said, "Something even better than a newspaper endorsement: new data. Not just polls, brand new stuff. This shit cost us a fortune to buy into, but this is where the action is these days for campaigns. People don't have land lines, they screen their calls on their cell phones, they walk away from pollsters outside their grocery stores, they delete surveys in their emails without opening them. But like you said, they go on-line constantly. That's exactly where the new shit comes from, companies who grab everyone's data and pull it all together. They see more of our shit than a proctologist."

"What do you mean? What data are they collecting?"

"Everything. They know what Google searches we're making, where our GPS has been, what kind of tuna fish we're buying and whether we mix it with mayo or mustard."

"What the hell good is that for us?"

"Profiles, Boss. Deep, deep profiles about every one of us. It's a big business now, collecting and analyzing search patterns and building profiles. These guys are billionaires overnight. They pull in everything about us and then figure out what it all means. It all started out predicting what products we'd buy and how to market other stuff to shift us from one brand to another. Pretty soon the guys we're working with hit upon the fact that a political campaign is just like any other marketing campaign. You, Colonel Robin Washington Jenkins, you're the goddamn product. They figure out who'd vote for you and why, and how to market you."

"How? How can they know what a voter is going to do?"

"It's all about tying things together, shit we never think about. Stuff we don't have any idea means anything, but it does. For example, let's say you're interested in the race for president between Dorzel and Jenkins. So you do a search on 'Jenkins vs. Dorzel.' You don't know it but you've just told the political world that you are likely to vote for Jenkins."

"How? Just by doing a search?"

"Yeah, a search in which you put Jenkins in first. Seriously. If you put Dorzel in first, chances are you'd vote for him. That little bit of info combined with all the other shit they have on you and millions of other people tells them how you're going to vote. The difference might be whether you wear black shoelaces or brown ones—if you put enough details together you get patterns nobody knew existed."

"Shoelaces? Give me a break! OK, I could maybe understand the thing about putting in my name or his first in a search, at least that has something to do with voting. But what the hell could the color of shoelaces tell us about how someone's going to vote?"

"Like I said, it's not the shoelaces, it's tons and tons of little pieces of information all tied together. It's a new world, Boss. Artificial intelligence."

"Sounds like a bunch of bull to me. What makes you think it really works?"

"You know me, Boss, I was really skeptical when these guys came to us to sell their system. But they convinced us real quick. Believe me, it works. They showed how their shit predicted the outcome of the last election—they predicted that Dorzel was going to win, and exactly where and how he would take the election. They were the only ones, no one took them seriously because all the polls predicted just the opposite. That was the first time they had access to enough data or whatever, and now they've got even more. They're making polling obsolete. Forget margins of error of five or ten percent, they're making predictions down to a tenth of a percent. It's fucking unbelievable. Now we're using their shit to adjust our messaging strategies. And it's paying off big time."

"What do you mean? How's it paying off?"

"The numbers show that you've got an absolute lock on the election. We already had a pretty good idea that you were in the lead, but with this powerful shit there's no doubt about it. You know how the pollsters have always tried to explain away why their predictions went wrong? Why they didn't know Truman would beat Dewey? Or that fucking Dorzel would win? Their favorite excuse has been that people say one thing then do another when time comes to actually mark their ballots. Or they make up their minds at the last minute, or they come up with some other reason. Well, we don't have that problem anymore. With this shit we know what they're really going to do when push comes to shove. And you're going to win. You're going to get the nomination and massacre Dorzel."

"Don't count the votes until the polls close on the general election, Andy. I'm not president yet."

"Yeah, yeah. You're right." He paused.

The hesitation was so out of character for Andy Ackroyd that Jenkins raised an eyebrow and asked, "Too good to be true, huh? I was waiting for another shoe to drop. What more do you have?"

"OK...well...there is one more thing, Boss. Dorzel's people are crazy but they're not stupid. They have access to the same kind of shit we do, and they know they can't beat you. They totally know it. So they're getting more and more desperate, pulling out all the stops."

"Like what? If you're so sure what people are going to do, how can they change that?"

"For one, they can keep people from voting at all. All the fancy numbers tell us is what somebody's going to do when they get into the voting booth, but they can't do anything if they never get there. The numbers tell the Dorzel people who's going to vote for you if they get a chance to vote. So those scumbuckets now know exactly which polling stations to close, whose voter registrations to revoke, that kind of thing."

"Those bastards. Such fucking hypocrites, talking about American values then making it impossible for citizens to vote. What can we do about that?"

"We've got our fingers on the same spots, filing all kinds of lawsuits, beefing up voter registration efforts. Doing everything we can. But...there's more."

"What the hell else?"

"Their biggest card would be to keep you from getting the nomination."

"How could they do that? Didn't you just tell me I'm even stronger there than in the general election?"

"Yeah, sure I did. Right now you're a shoe-in for the nomination. If I were working for Annabaker I'd be drafting her concession speech already. By the time the first-ballot is over you'll be nominated by acclamation. But...well, Boss, I hate to think this way, but the Dorzel people are crazy enough to try anything to stop you. Anything at all."

"What are you saying, Andy?"

"I don't think you're going to like this, Boss, but we can't take any chances. They might come after you. We need a whole new level of security."

"More security, are you kidding? I can hardly take a piss without three people watching me. Everywhere I go I'm in an armored car, we never take the same route twice, we set up tents that are a block long for the car to drive through whenever we pull up at a hotel or somewhere. What the hell more can we do?"

"Like I said, you're not going to like this. You can't do any campaign events out in the public any more. The Dorzel crowd have guns that could hit you from miles away. They're even crazy enough to enlist suicide bombers. We have to take some really drastic measures."

"I'm not going to stop campaigning in person, Andy. That's out of the question. I survived combat in a war, I'm not afraid of a bunch of crazy jerks. Enough is enough already."

"Listen to me, Colonel. Enough is *not* enough, not anymore. They will go to any lengths to stay in power. You've got to make it through the election so we can sweep into office with a huge majority and take both the House and Senate. If something were to happen to you and Annabaker got the nomination instead, Dorzel would get reelected for sure. Her radical positions make her completely unelectable. And we'd never get the Senate. You are in combat again, and you need to be prepared for real warfare. Just a different kind of war. There's an enemy out there, and they could be coming after you, believe me."

Jenkins shook his head but said nothing. Then, "What do you have in mind?"

"Again, you're not going to like this. If you're not willing to stop having public rallies we need to do something much more drastic. Listen to me, Boss. We want you to pretty much live in a bubble, a bulletproof bubble. Everywhere you go, you'll be protected."

"Fuck off. That's not going to happen."

"This is not just me talking, Colonel. The Secret Service is very concerned. If the Dorzel folks sent a bunch of storm troopers to one of your rallies lots of people could get killed. Not just you, families in the crowd wanting to see you."

"They're already setting up metal detectors at the rallies, no one can get a gun in."

"We're not talking about cowboys with six-guns on their hips, Boss. We're worried about a gang of crazies with assault weapons shooting their way past the security stations. The only thing that will stop them is if they absolutely cannot get to you."

"OK, stop. That's all for now. I hear you, but I need to think it over. We don't have any public rallies until the end of next week. I'll let you know."

"Tomorrow at the latest, Colonel. Otherwise we won't have time to get things in place and we'll have to cancel the rally."

"Tomorrow, then. I'll sleep on it But don't even think about cancelling until I get back to you."

"Yessir, Boss. I told you you weren't going to like this."

"You got that right. I don't like it, not one bit."

Chapter 25: Proshchay

The morning after her ordeal at the Kremlin with Dorzel, Sasha was sitting in a hot tub still nursing her sore bottom when she heard a knock on the door to her apartment. She left the tub, wrapped herself in a soft white robe and went to find out who could be visiting, hoping against hope it was not Dorzel. She glanced through the peephole and sighed with relief at the sight of Valeria Klara. Good, she thought, maybe they would spend the day together, two girls doing something normal, help her unwind from her night in hell. But when she opened the door and saw the downtrodden look on her friend's face she knew that this was not to be a friendly social visit.

"Valeria Klara, I am so happy to see you—but something is troubling you. Come in and tell me what it is, please."

Valeria stepped forward, wrapped her arms around Sasha, and kissed her on both cheeks. "We must say farewell, Sasha."

"Farewell? Are you going away?"

"Not I, my dear. It is you who will be leaving Moscow."

Sasha stumbled back a couple of steps, then steadied herself against the door jamb. "So soon? And where? Where am I to go?"

"May I come in and perhaps have a cup of coffee?"

"A thousand pardons. Of course, of course. Come, sit down and I will make you a cappuccino. It is still morning so we will not violate the Italian rule we learned in Milan that cappuccinos may only be served before noon."

"No matter the time of day, a cappuccino would be wonderful."

Sasha led the way across the big room into the kitchen area and pushed a button on the side of the expensive multi-purpose coffee maker Valeria had insisted they purchase. Within seconds the

116

machine was spouting puffs of steam and filling two large cups with coffee extract and foamy cream. They took their cups into the seating area and Sasha said, "Now, my friend, tell me what is to happen with my life, if you please."

"Your seduction of the President of the United States proved to be quite a success. He begged our president to send you to him. So that you could '*continue to get acquainted*,' I believe is the way it was told to me. But my friend in the president's office said that Mr. Dorzel spoke about you with words she would not let cross her lips, and that the men laughed in a most objectionable way about your first night together."

"I cannot take any credit for a seduction. The door to the bedroom had barely slammed shut before the man began ripping at my dress. He was so clumsy and in such a hurry he could not manage to untie the knot that held the straps of that beautiful gown together. He pulled so hard to get them over my head that they caught on my tiara and ripped out clumps of hair. My scalp still hurts so much I may not shampoo for many days."

"You will need to shampoo your hair—and wash yourself all over—very soon. I am to tell you to prepare to leave by the end of this month. Seventeen days, and you will be gone."

"You have not said where it is that I am to go."

"You will go where he is going: to America, to Washington."

"To live? Or just to visit?"

"You should expect to stay for some time."

"But you will not be joining me there?"

"That is correct. You are, as they say, on your own now, my dear Sasha."

"And where is it that I am to live?"

"Ah, you will have a very nice apartment of your own. I am sure you have heard of the place: it is called Watergate."

"*Jesus, Mary, and Joseph!*"

Both women laughed at Sasha's outburst, a laugh that broke through the tension.

"The building is not new but I am told that the apartments have been brought up to date and are quite comfortable. You will have a balcony that opens up on a river just as you do here. But that river is called the Potomac, not the Moskva."

"Am I to I sit in my apartment all day and wait for him to call?"

"Not at all. You are to be issued a visa and a special work permit, and you will have a respectable job. The U.S. State Department has been most accommodating in opening up business opportunities for Russian companies so it was easy to arrange all your credentials. You will be employed in your old profession as a representative of a pharmaceutical company and you will call on doctors all over Washington. The company is based here in Moscow. Here it is called Farmatsevticheskaya Volga but in America it is known as Pharma Volga."

"And will I be expected to…to use the same methods to entice the doctors into purchasing from that company that I used before?"

Valeria grinned. "No, you are to reserve such favors for the president. You will have, shall we say, a workload in the company that will not be too demanding."

"I see. If you are not with me, how will I receive instructions and pass along information?"

"You have been assigned to the Security Service. Someone in the Service will establish connection with you shortly after you arrive."

"That is it? I am to be sent on my own to await instructions?"

"Not at all. You are to undergo intensive training over the next seventeen days, beginning this very afternoon. The training will be conducted right here in Moscow at the headquarters of the company."

"But then we still have seventeen days together before I leave!"

The gloom returned to Valeria Klara's face. "No, my dear, I am not to see you again. I already know so much about your assignment that I am never to be in touch with you again. I only hope I do not know too much."

Sasha shuddered. "No! You are not in danger, are you?"

"I do not know. I do not believe so, but I will be watched very closely. It would be most unwise for me to have any contact whatsoever with you."

Sasha slumped back on her chair. Deep down she was not surprised by what she was hearing, but the reality of her new life was sinking in. The party was over. She was at work now.

"I understand. I am saddened that we must part, but I understand." Then a frightening thought came to her: "And my mother? Will she be safe? May I communicate with her?"

"Yes, but you must follow a protocol that you will soon learn. No other contact would be acceptable."

"I will truly be alone, then."

"Not *all* the time," Valeria Klara said with a sympathetic but ominous look.

Sasha nodded. "No, not all the time. But his is not companionship I look forward to."

They sat in silence, each taking a final sip of cappuccino. Sasha set her cup down and said, "And now? Where am I to go this afternoon?"

Valeria Klara reached into a folder she was carrying and pulled out an envelope. She handed it to Sasha and said, "You will report to Farmatsevticheskaya Volga by two o'clock this afternoon. Here are the directions."

Sasha tore the envelope open. A plain card had the address of the company—to her surprise it was in the Central City, not Yermakova Roshcha or another of the industrial areas.

"Do you know why I am to go to the center of Moscow? Why would a pharmaceutical company be located there?"

"No, I do not know. Perhaps that is where the company's executives are, not where the manufacturing takes place. In any case, you will know soon."

Valeria Klara stopped talking. She rose from her chair and said, "And now I must leave. This is goodbye, Alexandra Arkadyevna Parushnikova, my dear Sasha. We have had fun, have we not?"

"We have indeed. I will miss you, Valeria Klara Yakovna. I wish you well."

"Let us hope that Natalia Kostenka will not be conducting your new training," said Valeria Klara. Both women laughed, hugged one last time, and parted. Sasha watched her walk down the hall and whispered, "proshchay moy drug," farewell my friend, as Valeria stepped onto the elevator. She felt an unexpectedly sharp pang of remorse. Whether it was because she was losing her only ally or because she was entering a new life she did not know. She sighed and shut the door to her apartment.

Chapter 26: Targets

Will scratched at his head, trying to reconcile the fact that Dorzel was the most likely target of a high-tech assassination plot with the knowledge that the most likely killers, the Russians, had no reason to get rid of him. Adrienne had convinced him that the Russians and Dorzel were still very much in sync. He had to look elsewhere, think of someone else. Who? For what seemed the hundredth time he ran through his list of public officials with the types of implanted medical devices that could be hacked into to kill someone. What would the Russians—or anyone else—gain by murdering one of them? The vice-president: *not worth the effort*; Supreme Court Justices: *easy targets for conventional weapons*; members of the Cabinet: *Dorzel was already on his second or third round of sycophants, none of whom posed any threat to Russia*; the Speaker of the House or other Democrats in the Congressional leadership: *maybe, maybe there.* Could this be about getting one of them out of Dorzel's hair without leaving any fingerprints that could be traced to the White House? OK, that was one possibility. What else, what else could it all mean?

He had to think out of the box, come up with some new idea. What was it Adrienne had said about a surge in Russian propaganda? Bots pushing phony rumors, feeding conspiracy theories, posting realistic fake photos. Could all that activity be related to a possible assassination? Or was it just a coincidence? He had taken Hank Cotter's statements at face value that the Russians did that sort of thing to send Western democracies into disarray, to look strong by making the West look too confused to be powerful. What was he missing? Could there be more to all the disinformation than undermining people's faith in government? Why would they resort to assassinating someone if they were already winning the battle with disinformation?

Think, think, think. The germ of a thought began to grow in his mind. He bolted from his computer and ran down the hall to Belinda Winnisome's cubicle. He knocked quickly, then stepped inside as soon as he heard her say, "Yes?"

"Belinda," he said, catching his breath, "Tell me more about those data aggregators…"

"Hello to you, too, Will."

"Sorry, my bad. Hi Belinda. I hope I'm not interrupting you."

"Of course you're interrupting me," she quipped, "but it's fine. I was just giving you grief. What's up?"

"You told me about the tracking services, the data aggregators that pull together all kinds of seemingly unrelated information and market it to people who figure out how to tie it together in ways that are commercially useful. We get their stuff through Homeland Security, but who else has access to it?"

"Anyone. It's available on the open market. None of this is regulated, at least not yet. It's a free-for-all out there, the Wild West of data. Whoever pays gets what they want. The only requirements are on some of the original sources, like your bank or credit card company. They have to publish annual notices of their data policies."

"Those little booklets that go directly into recycling, right?"

"Exactly. If you don't go to the trouble of opting-out—and they don't make it easy to do so—you give consent for your data to be put into circulation. Same thing every time you log onto a website and click '*Accept*' to their terms or send an email or go jogging with your smart watch on your wrist. And forget any privacy if you've got smart appliances or light bulbs at your house. The aggregators assemble all the bits and pieces from a gazillion different sources and anyone with enough money can buy it in a nice, neat package to do with as they please. Why do you ask?"

"We're still at square one trying to figure out who might be the target for assassination by the Russians. Dorzel would seem like the top candidate because of his high level of security, but they want him to stay alive and stay in office. If you were the Russians, how would you use all that data to select a target?"

She was silent for a moment. Then she said, "Well, this doesn't speak to picking a target, but they could certainly use the information to decide when and where to strike. Remember I showed you how easy it is to know what time you usually show up for work here? It would be a piece of cake to figure out what your habits are and when someone could find you in a vulnerable location."

"So if they picked me as a target they could plot a course directly to me. Scary! What about the prior step, picking a target?"

"I'm not sure. First question that comes to mind is what would they want to achieve? What is it they want most from this country? I mean, would they want to start a civil war here? Or make a lot of money for some Russian oligarch? Like you said, Dorzel's their buddy, they're already getting their way with our government with him in office, so that's not it."

"Wait a minute—maybe that *is* it! What if they are afraid of losing the goose that lays their golden eggs?"

"Come again?"

"Dorzel. What if he gets defeated in the next election? My contact at the FBI told me chapter and verse on all the propaganda the Russians are spewing to help him get reelected, so much that they must be desperate to keep him in office. What if they find out it's not enough? Could they use all the new data sources to predict the outcome of the election?"

"Absolutely. I have three friends from grad school, real nerds, never had an interest in politics except legalizing marijuana, that sort of thing. Well, they're all making huge dollars consulting with political campaigns to read the tealeaves. They build algorithms and keep making them stronger and stronger until the margin of error is almost zero."

"How can they do that?"

"So, back in the day that my father went to college and studied political science it was all about theory—socialism, capitalism, communism, colonialism, all the *-isms*. But for at least the last forty years the political scientists have become data freaks, assembling and interpreting incredibly detailed data on who was likely to vote, who voted, where and why they voted. Polls out the wazoo before the election, exit polls afterward. When my nerdy friends tied that kind of information together with all this new stuff that's available they proved that they could predict the outcome of the last election. Nobody paid attention until afterward, then it was instant credibility when people realized what they had done. Now they've got it made in this election—everybody's buying their stuff."

"Are you saying someone already knows who's going to win the next election?"

"I'm saying *everyone* knows, if they have the money and want to know badly enough to compete for people like my old classmates."

"So if I wanted a certain person to win and your buddies convinced me that my candidate was losing, losing for sure, what would my options be? Change people's minds if possible—that's what the massive disinformation crap is all about. But you're telling me that if I used the right data I could see that it wasn't working, that I didn't have a snowball's chance in hell of changing people's minds no matter how many bots I set up. What then? What options are left?"

"I see where you're going, Will. That's a terrible thought: the only option left would be to get rid of the candidate that the data analysts say is a sure winner."

"That's it, Belinda: kill off the threat."

"And who would that be?"

"Time for us to do our own fancy analysis and figure that one out. I'll get everyone together in Ned's office."

Chapter 27: Back In The USA

Sasha's training at Farmatsevticheskaya Volga was not at all like what she had undergone at Zarya Dacha. No videos of Dorzel's sexual escapades, no Natalia Kostenka glaring at her with ghoulish eyes, no stocky attendants in dark suits. And no one like Valeria Klara to befriend her.

This time she had a series of seven instructors who were uniformly efficient and remarkably candid. Not surly, but stone-faced and doggedly on message. All she knew about them was that none were placed with the pharmaceutical company, they had each been called in from outside locations to inculcate her properly, if rapidly, into the ranks of the secret police. She saw them only for their part of her instruction, then they vanished back to wherever they had come from.

Much of the class time was dedicated to teaching her how to encrypt and decrypt messages in different media. One entire morning was taken up going over ways to recognize and evade counterintelligence operatives. Other sessions covered how to communicate with her handler; how to carry out her nominal job so as not to jeopardize her deep industrial cover; and, how to raise an alarm in a crisis. A presentation on establishing friendly relations with Americans without getting overly close made her chuckle when she recalled the lectures on getting intimate with doctors for her earlier life as a detail rep for that other drug company, *Marquis-Herrant*.

Sixteen days passed quickly. Sasha spent long hours in the classroom and even longer hours there at night reviewing materials she had to commit to memory—none of the documents could leave the building or be copied. By the seventeenth day she was exhausted as she settled into her seat for the ten hour flight from Sheremetyevo Airport to JFK. She had been surprised, and a bit disappointed, to

124

learn that there were no nonstop flights between Moscow and Washington, but when they came in over New York City she was immediately captivated by the sight of the famous skyline. Unlike most Americans taking in the same view, she saw no ghosts of the Twin Towers and indulged no fantasies that the majestic structures might somehow reappear before her eyes. She marveled at the Empire State Building, the Statue of Liberty, the endless rows of skyscrapers.

Her elation did not last long. The uniformed officers at customs and passport control seemed to know nothing about her privileged status with the US State Department. They shunted her into lines as slow and tedious as she had wrongly expected to find in Milan. To make things worse, her suitcases did not arrive on the conveyor belt at baggage claim with the others, so she spent a full two hours waiting at the lost luggage window filling out paperwork, only to have the bags show up out of nowhere. By then she had missed her connection to Washington and was informed that all the other flights were fully booked until well after 10PM. She decided on a new plan: she would enjoy a night in New York. Take a taxi into the City, have an elegant meal, book a room at one of the hotels owned by her new paramour, then take the Amtrak Acela to Washington the next day.

Her spirits improved briefly when she climbed into the taxi and heard the old Chuck Berry song about being glad to be back in the USA playing on the radio. The rest of her evening, however, had mixed results. Her room in Dorzel's hotel was small, had been decorated with neither class nor flair, and appeared rather shopworn. Then she had a nuisance of a setback when she opened her suitcases to find that her belongings were no longer neatly arranged the way she had packed them. An impersonal printed card informed her that an employee of the *SafeSkiesScreening Company, Inc.,* had examined the contents *"in the interest of keeping everyone safe."* She emptied the suitcases, then refolded and repacked everything for the trip to Washington, hoping that there would be no such sloppy inspection of her belongings for a domestic train ride. After a hot bath and a long shower she felt better and realized that she was famished.

Sasha dressed for dinner and went down to the lobby to ask for suggestions on where she should go to eat. The tall, blond man at the concierge's desk wore a dark suit and a nametag that displayed the Dorzel hotel chain's logo and, printed on a card inserted into the plastic window below the logo, read "Welcome. My Name Is Alexi" just above "St. Petersburg." He smiled and asked in native Russian, "Are you from Moscow, Ms. Parushnikova?"

"I just arrived from Moscow, yes." She had no intention of letting a fellow Russian know that she had grown up in Novolugovoye.

"And are you planning to stay long in this country?"

"Yes, but not here in New York. Why do you ask?"

"You may find this a most unusual suggestion, but if you will bear with me, I'd like to suggest that you consider the Russian Tea Room. You are not likely to have another opportunity to eat our fine Russian cuisine while you are in this country."

"That is most certainly an unusual suggestion. I had rather thought I would have an American beefsteak or perhaps some Italian food. This Russian Tea Room serves more than tea, I presume?"

"Of course, a full menu. You will have an excellent meal in exquisite surroundings. My friend Dmitri is the *Maitre D'*—would you like me to make a reservation for you?"

"So I have come all the way from Moscow for Russian food! Very well, I will do as you suggest and let you know how the American version compares."

"You will not be disappointed."

He was soon proved correct. She indulged in a bowl of traditional borsch followed by grilled lamb with turnips, and topped off her meal with a caviar and vodka tasting. She made a mental note that the next time she was in New York she would return to the Russian Tea Room in time for the Royal Afternoon Tea that was mentioned on the menu.

When she arrived back at the hotel she smiled at the concierge and flashed a thumbs-up gesture. He smiled back and returned her greeting. The man was good-looking, she thought, but quickly decided she really needed a good night's rest and headed directly to the elevator. "And so," she said to herself as she fell into a deep, contented sleep, "today I found a little bit of Russia in America. Tomorrow I will leave Russia behind."

Chapter 28: *Searching for Certainty*

Once Lauren and Ned had joined Will and Belinda in Hank Cotter's office Will said, "Thanks, everyone. I want to throw something on the table that came up in a conversation Belinda and I had this morning. Here's the situation: we think the Russians are the prime suspects, that they're testing a way of killing people by hacking into their medical devices, but we can't figure out who their ultimate target is. We'd been thinking that Dorzel is the only one who has enough security around him to require something as sophisticated as that to get to him. But that explanation doesn't compute...*so to speak.* Sorry, gang."

Everyone nodded and smiled at Will as his face flushed red.

"Anyway, we decided that scenario doesn't makes sense because Dorzel is the last person the Russians would want to get rid of. What we're thinking now is that maybe we've got it backwards, maybe the target isn't Dorzel at all, it's someone who's a threat to Dorzel getting reelected. In short, they're getting ready to kill whoever would defeat him in the election. So the question before us now is how to identify the candidate who is so sure to beat Dorzel that the only way of stopping him is to kill him—or her—with an elaborate scheme like this."

"Exactly," said Belinda. "We need predictive analytics that we can be really confident in. That means we have to know just what the chances really are of Dorzel losing, and to whom. We can't just rely on the polls. The polls say that Colonel Robin Jenkins is looking strong, but Annabaker Minion has a lot of supporters, and there are still several other Democrats that poll in the double-digits. But the polls aren't reliable enough. The numbers vary from poll to poll and they all have lots of caveats about possible bias for one reason or another. Even the biggest polls have relatively small sample sizes that lead to pretty big margins of error. We need certainty, or as close to certainty as possible if we're going to push the panic button on an impending assassination."

Will added, "The Russians certainly have the capacity to do analytics that would show whether there's someone who would definitely dislodge Dorzel. Definitely enough to go to all this trouble to assassinate whoever it is. We have to know as much as they do if we're going to pursue this idea."

"Yes, they undoubtedly have access to mega-data like the trackers and aggregators collect. And they have the personnel and supercomputers to do the analytics," added Belinda.

"Wait a second, Belinda," said Ned. "Don't you know people who do this for a living? I thought you told me you have some former classmates who are rolling in dough from doing this kind of work. Can't you just ask them?"

"We might have been good friends once, but they didn't get rich giving their stuff away. It's all proprietary, totally protected. If they've figured out who's 99.999% likely to beat Dorzel, they aren't going to tell me for free."

"That's for sure," said Will. "The zillions of data points they aggregate are more or less stolen from all of us without our knowledge, but once they have them, they own them. And their algorithms are even more closely held than their results. They'll sell you their findings for a pretty penny but they'll protect their algorithms like Coca-Cola protects its formula. We need a backdoor."

"Ironic, isn't it?" said Hank Cotter. "Somebody collects my heart rate from my smart phone or my kid's photos from social media and next thing I know they're using our information to control what medicine I'm taking or where my kid is going after school."

"Actually," interjected Lauren, "you said 'next thing you know,' but the truth is you *don't* know that they're using your information to control you and your kids. You give, they take, and they get to keep what they collect and make money off of it. And you have no idea any of that is going on. I mean, look at us—we know as much as anyone about data and data analysis and we still have no clue exactly how our personal information is being used. Remember those stories about the digital giants running experiments to see how they could influence behavior in different populations, all without anyone's permission? That's how 'artificial intelligence' is being constructed: behind our backs."

"All true," said Will. "OK, enough lamenting that other people have control of us through our own no-longer-private data. Now, let's get back to work. What are we going to do about identifying the target?"

"We're going to do exactly what we're complaining about," said Hank Cotter. "We're going to use as much of the data on how people are likely to vote as we can get our hands on, and we're not going to get anyone's permission."

"Ends justify the means?" said Ned, with a distinct note of irony.

"You might put it that way," responded Hank. "At least we can tell ourselves that our motives are good."

"I think preventing an assassination is a good enough motive," said Will. "After all, we're not in this for the money."

"Uh, we are getting paid," retorted Lauren. "*Cybersleuths, Inc.* isn't exactly a charitable organization."

"That's right," said Hank Cotter. "It's our job, and we need to get on with it. No more moralizing, no more omphaloskepsis. Who's going to do what?"

"I'm going to look up omphaloskepsis," said Ned, laughing.

Lauren said, "Stop gazing at your bellybutton to think, Ned."

"OK," said Hank Cotter, "no more words of more than three syllables when Ned's in the room. Back to divvying up the work."

"I'll see if I can have a more-or-less generic conversation with my old friends," volunteered Belinda. "They won't give any results away but maybe I'll get some leads on how they think about this stuff."

"How about suggesting that you might be interested in leaving *Cybersleuths, Inc.* and coming to work with them?" said Lauren.

Everyone turned to look at their employer, Hank Cotter. He laughed and said, "Fine with me. Not the idea of Belinda actually leaving, of course not that, but as a ploy to help our operation, sure. Besides, I think you've all read the do-not-compete clause in your contracts—you can leave *Cybersleuths, Inc.* anytime you want to, but you couldn't take a job with any company that even owns a decent computer for at least three years."

"All right, Lauren, I'll give it a try," said Belinda.

"I'll start work on designing the algorithms," said Will. "We should get going on them while Belinda is trying to squeeze some ideas out of her friends. If she comes up with something that would improve on what I manage to develop we'll take a look and adjust accordingly. Lauren and Ned can make sure I've got access to the right data and keep me on track."

"One last question," said Hank Cotter. "Supposing we're successful and we figure out that there really is a candidate who poses a sure threat to Dorzel. What exactly do we do with that information?"

"Another job for me," said Will. "I'll keep my contact at the FBI in the loop. I've been meaning to brief her anyway on our idea that the target is not Dorzel, it's someone waiting in the wings who is about to throw him out of office. I'll also tell her what we're doing and she can start planning how to handle anything we come up with."

"Done," said Hank Cotter. "Good job, everyone. Now get to work."

Chapter 29: Undercover Vodka

Sasha was grateful that the train ride from New York to Washington in Amtrak's Acela late the next morning was comfortable and uneventful. She arrived at Union Station a little after 4 in the afternoon, climbed into a taxi and told the driver she wanted to go to the Watergate. He replied, "What building you want, lady?" Confused and a bit irritated. she repeated "the Watergate" and he again asked, "Which building?" They talked past each other, their voices rising with each exchange, until she finally understood that he was trying to explain that "Watergate" referred to a hotel and an office building as well as apartments. "I apologize," she said. "Apartments, please," and settled back to enjoy another famous skyline. She loved the close-up view as they drove by the US Capitol and the Washington Monument, then she was stirred with unexpected emotion by the majesty of the Lincoln Memorial just before they passed by the Kennedy Center and turned in to the driveway of the Watergate.

The apartment did not disappoint. It was not huge or lavishly decorated, but as Valeria Klara had promised, it had a long, curved balcony that looked out over the Potomac River. Like the apartment in Moscow, the floor plan was wide open. She did not even bother trying to locate the hidden cameras and microphones. The kitchen was small but modern, the bathroom had new fixtures, and the bedroom provided another panoramic view of the Potomac. The bedroom was furnished with three large maple dressers and a matching bed. It also had a huge walk-in closet bigger than her bedroom back home in Novolugovoye. Her suitcases had remained with her for the train ride so she did not have to face the prospect of having to re-fold her clothes this time as she unpacked.

About five-thirty she began to consider what she would do for dinner. Should she walk around the neighborhood and see if there were restaurants nearby? Maybe there was some food in the kitchen and she would just fix something simple and plan on a good night's sleep before reporting for work at Pharma Volga in the morning. She found sugar, coffee and other staples in the cupboards and ice cubes in the freezer, but nothing for dinner there or in the refrigerator. Three kitchen drawers held silverware, cooking utensils, and dishtowels, while a fourth was packed with flyers and pamphlets from local restaurants. Thumbing through the papers she was drawn to an ad for *Bartolomeo's Authentic Pizzeria*. The flyer triggered a memory of a simple pleasure she had always enjoyed during her previous life in America as a detail rep for the Russian drug company: she would have a Margherita pizza delivered to her. Forty-five minutes later she heard a loud buzzing sound coming from a speaker near the front door. She pushed the red button below the speaker and said, "Yes?"

"Ms. Parushnikova?"

Again, "Yes?"

"There is a delivery person here. Are you expecting a pizza?"

A third time: "Yes."

"Very good, I will send him up."

For one moment she fantasized that a young man as handsome as Major Maxim Grigorovich Dragomirov would appear and provide her not only with food but also with a more gratifying welcome to Washington. The delivery person, however, turned out to be a short, not-so-young man with long fuzzy grey curls sticking out from his battered Washington Nationals baseball cap. Sasha counted out exact change for the amount on the bill, but the man did not say "Thank you" or walk away, he just stood in the doorway. "Ah," Sasha, "I forgot. I must give you a tip!" She handed him a five-dollar bill and at last was alone with her pizza. "Welcome to America," she said to herself as the door closed.

The next morning Sasha followed her instructions on how to travel to the offices of Pharma Volga. When she was told the offices were in a place called Crystal City, the name evoked distant images of Superman's ice cave from the old film she had watched at Zarya Dacha so many years ago. She had been advised that the best way to travel was on the Metro rather than fight the rush hour traffic that slowed Washington to a crawl every morning. She walked about a quarter-mile to the Foggy Bottom-GWU station, a name that evoked no images whatsoever, and rode five stops on the Blue Line, crossing the Potomac to Crystal City, in Virginia. Midway through the trip she was surprised that there was a station called 'Pentagon,' and wondered whether she would be subjected to a search and have her passport confiscated if she disembarked there.

Crystal City did not shimmer like the ice cave in the movie, but the endless run of steel-and-glass buildings explained its name. She walked a few short blocks north, then onto Crystal Drive, and soon found the five-story office building with a silver plaque that read, "Pharma Volga." She identified herself at the guard's desk and was told to wait for someone to escort her upstairs. Her day slipped quickly into a predictable new-employee pattern: orientation at human resources; collecting her credentials, keys, and monthly Metrocard; inspecting her assigned office; and, attending a gathering of a dozen or so of her co-workers and telling them about her past, which she did with a carefully abridged version of her life. She examined every new face and wondered which of her co-workers might be the person who knew what her real assignment was.

She didn't have long to wait. About four-thirty a plump, balding man wearing a baggy brown coat that was an obvious mismatch for his brown pants came into her office. He extended his hand and said in an easygoing voice with only a faint trace of a Russian accent, "Welcome. I am Leonid Denisovich Arkady. I thought it would be a good idea for us to get acquainted over some vodka after work, yes?"

Under other circumstances she would have been put off by such a seemingly brazen invitation from a man who aroused no interest in her whatsoever, but she had been well trained with a proper response to test his intentions. "Perhaps," she replied. "I do enjoy a glass of Ruskova Vodka once in a while. Do you know that brand?"

He replied, "Of course, an excellent vodka from the distillery in Nizhny Novgorod. Whatever you like would be fine, although I prefer Alimov from my home town of St. Petersburg."

The exchange of code words had gone perfectly on cue—there was no doubt, Leonid Denisovich Arkady was her contact in Pharma Volga. She looked at him with new eyes: his nondescript appearance and mild demeanor provided extraordinary cover for an agent of the secret police.

A little after five the funny little man knocked on her door again, then opened it a crack and said, "May I come in?"

"Of course. I was just packing up. Where shall we go?"

"I know an excellent bar with a first-class selection of vodka. It is not far from your apartment."

So, she thought, he knows everything about me. Of course he does.

"Excellent," she said. "And do they also serve food for dinner? I have not yet done any grocery shopping."

"Ah, yes. They serve a wonderful borsch and I am quite fond of their grilled lamb with turnips."

Sasha was not sure whether he was speaking by chance or emphasizing that he did, indeed, know everything about her, including her meal at the Russian Tea Room. She smiled and said, "Sounds delicious. I cannot wait to see their full menu."

He smiled back at her with a curiously inscrutable smile. That smile could have been a subtle reminder that mentioning the food she had just eaten in New York was intended to confirm that she had no secrets from him whatsoever, or it could have been no more than a polite, if enigmatic, gesture. No such thing as coincidence, she decided; the man was warning her that she could hide nothing from him.

They rode the Metro back to the Foggy Bottom-GWU stop and walked down 21st Street. When they passed a huge bronze sign with a bas-relief profile of George Washington and "The George Washington University" written in classic old English type, Sasha deciphered the 'GWU' part of her Metro stop's name. But when she tried to translate 'Foggy Bottom' into Russian, the only phrases that she could think of evoked images she was sure were not proper for a public place. She shrugged, anticipating that someday she would discover what the words referred to, just as she had finally come to understand the meaning of Crystal City. Then she laughed as the thought inexplicably reminded her of puzzling over how to translate "holy shit" in her head the first time she had heard that expletive.

Leonid Denisovich Arkady stopped in front of one of the aging townhouses in the area. He pointed with a flourish to the steps leading down a short flight of stairs to a dark storefront just below street level and announced, "Here we are, Alexandra Arkadyevna. Please, go ahead."

"Thank you, Leonid Denisovich." She took one step down, then stopped and turned toward him. "Please, call me Sasha."

"Delighted, Sasha. And my friends call me Leon."

A sign on the glass door read Бар Наташа below *Bar Natasha*. A woman bartender, imposing and yet quite attractive in her lumberjack's shirt, greeted them with a hearty, "Leon! Welcome. It has been too long." Glancing at Sasha then back at him she winked and said, "Perhaps you have been busy, my friend?"

"Not so busy, Missi," said Leon, with the same curious smile Sasha had noticed earlier.

"Tell me what you would like to drink and then, please, sit anywhere, my friend."

"Two large vodkas. My usual for me, and Ruskova for my colleague."

They walked past the bar to the single row of booths in the back and settled into the last booth. Leon said, "And so, is everything to your satisfaction so far?"

"Indeed. The apartment will do just fine, and our colleagues seem pleasant enough."

"Now for the real work. I am in touch with my counterpart. He has heard from the person in charge of these things for the man..."

Sasha interjected, "His *'procurer'*?"

"Please, my dear Sasha, there is no need to be harsh on yourself. You are performing a great service for out motherland."

Sasha laughed. "I did not speak ruefully, Leon. That was my idea of a bit of humor. Please, continue." She wondered if the man was as incapable of appreciating a joke as the ghoulish Natalia Kostenka Anatolievna.

The opaque smile crossed his face one more time. "The man wishes to see you again. There is an event that he wants you to attend. Do you have your elegant evening gowns from Milan with you?"

"I travelled with only my everyday things, but the gowns and other evening wear should arrive in the next few days. When is this event of which you speak?"

"In one week. I have some things for you." He removed an expensive-looking jeweled wristwatch and a small thumb drive from a zippered pocket inside his suit coat and handed them to her. "Here are your most important tools. On the thumb drive you will find the details of the event that you will attend. More important, it also contains the messages that you are to deliver to him. This wristwatch is a triumph of our technology. It will record sounds for up to five hours. You are to wear it when you are in his presence, or set it nearby if it is inconvenient for you to have such things on your person. It does not have the capacity to transmit, so it cannot be detected by electronic scanners. That means that you must transfer the recordings from this device to the thumb drive, which you will then return to me. I will exchange the one you give me for another that will provide further instructions."

"How am I to operate those devices?"

"In your apartment you will find a safe below the floorboards in your bedroom closet. You know that big closet?"

Sasha nodded. "Indeed. It is most spacious."

"Inside the safe is a computer that can decode the contents of this flash drive and encrypt your entries. It will also copy the recordings on the wristwatch. The computer, the flash drive and the wristwatch must remain in that safe at all times except when you are using them. The computer is never to leave the apartment. If it does, the hard drive will self-destruct and the machine will be permanently disabled."

"That is as I would expect, thank you. And this compartment in the floor—how do I open it?"

"The alarm system in the apartment is controlled by two keypads, one inside the front door and another in the bedroom closet. You can use either one to activate or shut down the alarm when you enter and leave the apartment. The keypad in the bedroom closet, however, has an additional function. When you enter a second code in that keypad a red light will blink three times and you will hear a single beep. At that point you will enter another code and the entrance to the compartment under the floor will appear."

During her training at Farmatsevticheskaya Volga in Moscow Sasha had been briefed on security systems like the one Leon was describing. "Yes," she said, "I am familiar with the operation of such a system." She smiled and added, "And I presume that someone will be alerted that I have opened the compartment in the floor?"

Leon blinked twice and said, "You have been a good student, Alexandra Arkadyevna."

The bartender arrived and set two large frosted glasses of crystal clear liquid on their table.

"To your health," Leon said in Russian, raising his tumbler of vodka.

"Yes, to *my* health," she replied, lifting hers.

This time the smile on his round face was decidedly friendly. She was pleased—apparently Leonid Denisovich Arkady could take a joke after all.

Chapter 30: Making Plans

"Will! Will! Up and at 'em, Sweetheart."

Will rubbed his eyes and sat up in bed. "Sorry, Honey, what did you say?"

"Good Morning, Sweetheart," replied Sally. "Don't you need to get up and go to work?"

"Uh huh, thanks. Sure. What about you?"

"What about me?"

"When do you start work?"

"I'm on Colorado time, remember? I don't start for another couple of hours. Why? Do you have something in mind?"

"I always have something in mind…but at the moment I'll have to settle for just talking."

"OK, talk."

Will rubbed his eyes again, ran his fingers through his long red hair, and said, "It's about this woman who asked me out."

"Woman? What woman…" Sally stopped in mid-sentence when she saw the playful smile on her husband's face. "OK, you got me. Finish that thought before I pick up a lamp and crown you with it. What woman? What's this about?"

"Adrienne, it's Adrienne. She asked me to escort her to an event at the White House. I said I'd run it by you first, of course."

"I'd hope so. But sure, if it's Adrienne, how could I object? You know how much I like Adrienne, and she did save my life, after all. Why does she need you to be her escort?"

"The event is a formal affair, black tie and all. Her colleagues are bringing their spouses and she didn't want to be the only fifth wheel."

Sally nodded. "Got it. Sure, no problem, you can always do whatever will help Adrienne. I can't help asking, though—do you really want to go to this White House? With Dorzel as president?"

"No, I have no desire to get anywhere near the place. Or near him. Actually, Adrienne's really ambivalent about going herself. She's always wanted a picture with the president, and now she's finally got the chance but she doesn't relish having Dorzel's face immortalized on her wall. Tough choice. She came so close last time, just a couple of people away from shaking the hand of a real president, and then he got called away. So who knows if she'll ever get another chance? Anyway, her bosses and colleagues are going, so she's pretty much boxed in. It would seem disrespectful if she turned down the invitation."

"Gotta do what you can when the opportunity presents itself, I guess. Of course, I have no problem with you escorting Adrienne. But good thing you're not asking me to go, I'm like you—much as I would enjoy a fancy party, I have no desire to be anywhere near Dorzel."

"That's what I told Adrienne."

"Are you sure you can still fit into your tux?"

"Hey, I still weigh the same as when we got married!"

"Sure, Honey, sure—you haven't gained an ounce."

"I will have to check and see if it needs to be dry-cleaned, though. I hope the moths haven't gotten to it. Thanks, Sweetheart, I'll let Adrienne know."

"Give her my best, and tell her to focus on the presidency, not the president."

"Pretty much what I already said. I'll pass along your greetings. Now, it really is time for work."

Will decided to walk the short commute to *Cybersleuths, Inc.,* and was rewarded with crisp fall air and bright sunshine. He arrived at his office refreshed and upbeat and was about to call Adrienne when his phone rang. The caller ID display showed the "Number Blocked" notice that generally meant the call was coming from a restricted government phone.

"Will Manningham," he said into the receiver.

"Hey Will, it's Adrienne. Got a minute?"

He laughed, "I sure do. Good timing, I was just going to call you. I've got a couple of things. First one's quick: Sally said to say hello to you, and hopes we have a good time you-know-where."

"Ah," she said, "That's exactly what I was calling you about. Just wanted to make sure we're on track. Tell Sally I said thanks and I'm sorry I'm putting her husband through this."

"She's fine, no problem. And, like I expected, she made it clear she would have no interest in going under the current circumstances."

"Understood."

"Second one's going to take a bit longer. Probably best in person. Can I come over sometime today?"

"Come on over. I'm free all morning."

"I'll leave now. See you in a bit."

Encouraged by the bright blue sky with no rain in the forecast, Will decided to take another walk to the J. Edgar Hoover Building. No bad weather, but the sunny day was already bringing out crowds of tourists and other pedestrians, so the short two-mile trip took him almost twice as long as usual. When he arrived, Adrienne said, "Took your time, huh?"

"Not by choice. The sidewalks were jammed with people. Cops were holding pedestrians on the sidewalks to keep them from blocking traffic and I had to wait for two or three lights at every crosswalk. Anyway, is this still a good time?"

"Sure. What's up?"

"I wanted to bring you up to date on our work. We're looking seriously at targets other than Dorzel."

"Who do you have in mind?"

"Someone who poses a serious threat to Dorzel—and thereby to the Russians. You told me that the Russians are going all-out to get him reelected, that there's no chance that they're at odds and are planning to kill him. What if they're convinced their current efforts to keep him in the White House can't succeed? What if there's a candidate who will knock him out of office? They'd have only one way to keep that from happening: kill off the challenger."

"You're thinking like an FBI agent again, my friend! We've been bouncing the same idea around here for the last couple of weeks. But nobody really knows who's going to win this election, or any other. The polls are wrong so often it's impossible to be sure. At least not sure enough to mount a complex assassination plan."

"Uh, that's what I thought, but my colleagues at *Cybersleuths, Inc.* know better. They've disabused me of that idea, convinced me that it's way out of date. It turns out that the artificial intelligence folks can come pretty close to 100% with their predictions."

"Interesting. Tell me more, and keep it simple. Remember, I'm just a law enforcement officer, not a geek like you."

"Ha! You guys are getting pretty good at this stuff. Anyway, here's the basic idea: if you amass enough bits and pieces of seemingly unrelated data, you can make associations that no one could have predicted ahead of time. You know all the press about how smart appliances are intruding on our privacy? Building up artificial intelligence systems to market all kinds of stuff to us?"

"Of course. I don't even keep my 'dumb' toaster plugged in when I'm not using it anymore. I just read a newspaper article about a guy who got most of the information that one of the smart devices had been recording and couldn't believe it when he saw verbatim transcripts of what he thought were private conversations in his house."

"Exactly. And I saw another one about someone who requested his own files and got somebody else's! Turns out every click on a link is money in the bank for somebody, and it's all being stored somewhere. Get used to hearing about 'clickstream data.'"

"Not another term to learn!"

"Yeah, well, it's real And it's not just about selling you things anymore. There are very smart analysts who specialize in using all that stuff for all kinds of purposes nowadays. And it turns out to be very useful when it comes to elections. Even I had no idea just what they can do, how accurate their predictions are. And if they can do it, so can the Russians."

"For sure. But you're beginning to lose me—give me an example, something concrete."

"OK, here's the one that convinced me: let's say you're searching the web for info on the election between Candidate A and Candidate B, so you click on your search engine and enter Candidate A's name first in the search box. The analysts know that you're far more likely to vote for that person than for B. And if you click on one of those cute little pop-up links that look like a game to test yourself on what you know about each candidate, game over. You're really putting in more and more information on your likely preference. They tie tidbits like those together with countless billions of others and they know how you're going to vote. They probably know even before you do!"

"So, assuming all of that works like you say, who's going to beat Dorzel?"

"We don't know yet. Looks good for Jenkins, but we don't have the kind of certainty it would take to go around killing someone. Same goes for you guys interfering in someone's campaign. We just aren't that sure yet. We're working on improving our level of confidence right now, should have something soon."

"I trust we'll be among the first to know when you do."

"Absolutely. I just wanted to bring you up to speed on what we're doing since this is all new."

"Thanks. Is that it?"

"Just to close the loop, we wanted you to know about all of this stuff we're working on so you could start thinking about the consequences if we were to find something conclusive. That is, supposing we come back to you and say that we are sure that Jenkins or Minion or someone else would be unbeatable against Dorzel. If we are absolutely confident about the outcome, then so are the Russians. So we thought you'd want to start thinking about—no, to start planning for—what to do to protect that person."

"That makes sense. But it also raises a couple of questions. If the Russians are sure that X is going to beat Dorzel, why don't they just do it the old-fashioned way with a gun and just shoot X? Why go to all this trouble to hack into someone's medical device?"

"One reason is fingerprints. No fingerprints this way, nothing for a Warren Commission to investigate. We are looking into the sudden deaths of a number of people who had implanted devices that failed. But we don't know why the devices failed. We can't prove that anyone hacked into them, and even if we could, we couldn't say who had carried out the hacking. It's a perfect way for the killers to avoid leaving any trail back to them."

"I'm with you so far."

"And what's more, if a candidate were to get shot, that would evoke a huge public outcry that might backfire. The one who got murdered would become a martyr overnight. The killing would likely generate a lot of suspicion and anger at the other candidate, especially the incumbent president. Not many people are likely to accept a 'lone gunman' explanation anymore. There might be a surge of sympathy for whoever is next in line for the opposition. But if it looks like a death from natural causes, the response might be entirely different, or at least muted. And, if the implanted device was blamed for the death, the public might well direct their outrage at the manufacturer instead of the other candidate."

"Obvious question: which candidates have implanted devices that would make them vulnerable?"

"Practically all of them. We had already run the data you sent us against lists of public officials, so it was a simple step to do the same thing for the candidates who aren't in office now. There's one fringe candidate who didn't turn up with anything, but several of the ones you're familiar with have one of the devices that matter: insulin pumps, pacemakers, defibrillators. Actually, I should say at least one device since the oldest candidate has both a pacemaker and an insulin pump!

"No surprise there. OK, Will, I think you could be on to something. Next question: what can we do to disrupt things, prevent the assassination from happening?"

"That's mainly what I wanted to get you thinking about. We should know soon if we're going to be able to predict the outcome of the election with sufficient precision to warrant you guys taking some action. For our part, all we can do is identify the likely target. It's really you guys who would need to intervene and keep the assassination from happening. We just wanted to give you a heads-up to start considering options for what actions you might take."

"We'll start thinking, sure. But all of our traditional protective measures are aimed at counteracting conventional weapons, guns and bombs, and now, of course, suicide bombers. Any thoughts on how to block someone from hacking into a medical device?"

"Not really. My little group is good with the numbers but I'll have to check with others in the firm on the technical aspects. You must have a lot of resources on that side, don't you?"

"We have a tremendous amount of technical expertise, sure. And so do others in the government. But this is a new problem, I don't know that anyone's been considering this exact situation. I'll start asking around as well."

"That's all I have for now. More to follow." He smiled and said, "So, on this fancy event we're going to, any luck finding an evening gown? If I'm going out with another woman I sure hope she's going to be stunning!"

"Don't count on stunning, buster. You'll be lucky if I make it to 'not embarrassing.' And no, I haven't had a chance to shop yet. I'm thinking of going to one of the second-hand stores for fancy evening wear so I don't invest an arm and a leg on a dress I'm going to wear only one time. And one I might burn afterward."

"Want me to ask Sally if she would go shopping with you?"

"I'm already asking a lot just borrowing her husband."

"Actually, it might be a good idea. I think she would enjoy spending some time with you when no one is looking to toss her into the trunk of a car and put a bullet into her."

"If you're sure, go ahead and check it out with her. But please let her know it's fine to say no."

"She's a big girl, she will say what she thinks. Happy to ask."

"Thanks, Will."

"I'm looking forward to our non-date. Who knows what might happen at the White House?"

Chapter 31: Two Jobs

Sasha mulled over Leonid Denisovich Arkady's words: "Now for the real work." Yes, that was her life: two jobs. One phony, one genuine. One mundane, one life-threatening. In the mornings she would dress in her business attire and take the Metro to the offices of Pharma Volga in Crystal City or head out to visit the offices of various doctors in the area. In the evenings, she would attend to the demands of her 'real work.' Best not to think too much about what she would do in the latter hours of those evenings, the part she did to gratify Dorzel. She had to focus on the other part of her real job, the work that gratified Dorzel's Russian masters. Her Russian masters.

Leon had told her to prepare for such an evening in one week's time. When she returned home from her day job she was pleased to discover that the gowns and other evening wear from Milan had been delivered to her apartment while she was at work. Six huge boxes, including three stand-up wardrobe containers, awaited her in the bedroom. She opened them carefully and hung the long evening gowns on padded hangers on the highest rod in the enormous walk-in closet. As she did so she looked down at the floorboards and wondered exactly where the concealed trapdoor might be. She would find out soon when she opened it to get to the safe and the computer she needed to decode the flash drive Leon had given her at Bar Natasha.

When she finished hanging the dresses and packing the other clothes and accessories in several of the dresser drawers, she moved the empty boxes to the hallway outside her apartment for the Watergate staff to haul away. She returned to the closet and examined the exquisite gowns, picturing how she had looked in each one in the studios of the famous designers. Her shopping trips with Valeria Klara now seemed a lifetime away. When she came across the gown she had worn that first time her scalp tingled where Dorzel had ripped out clumps of her hair. This time the dress she was going to wear would have no criss-crossed straps, and she would never again wear a tiara. She decided on a silver-and-black gown. The narrow streaks of silver contrasted brilliantly with the black background, making the dress shimmer in the light. In the salon she had thought that the design seemed perilous—the plunging neckline was held closed by only two snaps that threatened to pop open and unleash her breasts if she sneezed too hard or even took a deep breath. After her first night with Dorzel she now realized the quick access would come in quite handy, and be a lot safer than straps tied behind her neck. If only she and Valeria Klara had thought to select all the dresses based on how easily they would give way!

So much for the part of her real job that would get her into the man's inner circle, now she had to attend to the part that would store the recordings of his words and her reports for Leon. She examined the closet floor. The light oak boards fitted together perfectly, with no hint of a gap or a hinge, giving no indication that there was a hidden door somewhere. The carpenters for the Security Service were master craftsmen, she thought. She turned to the keypad and entered the first code. As Leon had said, a small red light blinked three times, and she punched in another code. Within seconds she heard a powerful whirring sound coming from one corner and watched with amazement as a section of flooring angled up on a hinge, opening a hole in the floor about one meter on each side. The trapdoor was straight on the side with the hinge and the one opposite it, but snaggle-toothed on the two ends where the boards on the lid had interdigitated with the boards that remained fixed in place.

Sasha knelt down and examined the cavity in the floor. The sides were made of concrete several inches thick and the bottom also was concrete. The lid itself was a thick, imposing structure, the underside of the floorboards lined with what looked like several inches of lead sheeting. In the middle of the space under the floor was a dark gray safe with two dials and a keypad on the lid. She twisted the dials through their number sequences, then entered yet another code into the keypad, and the top of the safe popped open with a metallic '*click.*' She lifted the lid and reached in to retrieve the laptop computer, then stood and took it to her dining room table. The computer case had no logo—she knew it would have been custom-made in the Security Service's shop. The keyboard had both English and Cyrillic characters. She powered on the computer, entered a series of passwords, and watched as the screen blinked, went dark, then lit up with a message welcoming her by name. She slipped the flash drive into a USB port and a series of file folders appeared on the screen.

When she clicked on the folder with the date of the forthcoming event Leon had referred to she saw two documents: one provided details on when and where she should arrive at the White House and what she should say to gain access through the side entrance. It also informed her that a car would be waiting to carry her home at such time as she would leave the residence. She wondered whether she would be returning to the apartment that same night or the next morning.

The other document contained the directives about her conversation with the American president. She read it several times, understanding the words perfectly well but not comprehending the meaning of the message. She was instructed to confirm his agreement with launching some sort of contingency plan that he had requested and that had been under development for some time. The discussion was to flow in two directions: she was to inform him that her side was ready to carry out the action that he had sought; and, she was to verify that he was in full agreement with taking the final steps. There were no details on just what the action was that they would be implementing, but she was to let him know that there could be no turning back once it had begun. When she saw the final words she shuddered: she was to warn the President of the United States that if he wavered or tried to disavow his involvement, he would suffer the most dire consequences.

Chapter 32: Surprise

"Not too bad," said Adrienne, preening modestly in her full-length mirror to see how she looked in an evening gown instead of the customary dark blue FBI business suit that had become part of her identity. She thought back to the handful of times she had dressed up in a formal gown, feeling awkward and uncomfortable on every occasion: a few proms, and three weddings as a bridesmaid. And those dresses! Always some shade of fuchsia or aqua and embarrassingly low-cut. This one was a tasteful midnight-black with a high scooped neckline, perfectly tailored to her athletic body without being revealing. She looked down and saw that the dress was long enough to cover her low heels and figured it would be long enough that she could have strapped on her ankle holster if she had been going to the White House on duty. But no weapons, not tonight.

Just before 6PM her cell phone beeped, signaling a text message from Will that he was in a taxi and should be downstairs in front of her building in about three minutes. She draped the pashmina shawl her mother had given her many years ago across her shoulders, picked up the tiny black purse Sally had chosen to match the dress, and headed down to meet her non-date.

As soon as she stepped out of the apartment building Will jumped out of the taxi and greeted her. "Well, Special Agent Penscal, you are quite stunning."

"Give me a break, Will. '*Stunning*,' is seriously overdoing it, but maybe I made it to '*not embarrassing*.' You look pretty good yourself, young man. Nice tux!"

Will held open the door to the taxi for her, playing the gentleman with an old-fashioned act of chivalry neither of them would have dreamed of under normal day-to-day circumstances. But this evening was special, so they both went along with the charade.

Marine guards in classic Dress Blues lined the driveway leading up to the White House. Will and Adrienne exited the taxi outside the gates and joined a long line of guests in formal wear waiting to pass through security. After watching a number of people be pulled off to one side for an additional check, Adrienne said, "Uh, Will, looks to me like security is ramped up tonight. Maybe someone special is coming."

"Or maybe you-know-who is nervous about having so many FBI agents around," he smirked.

"Could be," she laughed. "But I'd guess it's for some mucky-muck. We'll see."

When Will and Adrienne finally cleared security two Marines escorted them to the reception in the East Room. The largest room in the White House, it was packed with round tables each with seating for ten or twelve, arrayed close together in front of a long, elevated head table. The place settings were elegant: traditional White House silverware and crystal glassware, paired with flamboyantly colorful plates and bowls. A large round vase of red roses, white carnations and blue calla lilies dominated the center of each table.

They looked around for table number 16, the one that a Marine guard at the entrance had directed them to. "I think I see it, follow me," said Adrienne. She headed toward the front of the room, just off to one side of the main table. Will first spotted her boss, Chief Garry Hollingshead, then was delighted when he also recognized a number of the Special Agents on Adrienne's FBI team that he had spent many intense months with: Tom Murphy, an enormous, jovial, bald man; Denise Washington, a short African-American woman whose deceptively small size belied her physical and mental toughness; the impressively muscular Fred Renford, sporting a tuxedo so form-fitting it might have been molded directly onto his powerful frame; and Fran Trainor, a big woman whose size was magnified by the mound of black hair piled on top of her head. Will liked the group of agents. He thought of them as friends as well as dedicated public servants whom he respected—and felt heavily indebted to. They greeted him heartily and introduced him to their spouses and significant others with genuine enthusiasm.

When the introductions and greetings were finished, Will realized someone was missing: Anil Maliq, the slender, wiry agent who had rescued Sally just in time to keep her from being raped. "Where's Anil?" he asked, alarmed that something terrible might have happened.

"Anil's on a special assignment," Adrienne replied, with a serious look that softened when she saw the concern on Will's face. "He's fine, just impossible for him to come here."

Will nodded, wondering what she was telling him—or wasn't.

"OK, thanks. If you see him, give him my best."

She nodded, but said nothing.

He knew it was time to change the subject. "So, where's the FBI Director?"

Adrienne pointed to the unoccupied main table and said, "He'll be up there."

The front table remained empty for the better part of an hour while guests continued to filter in. The affable Tom Murphy proved adept at charming the waitstaff to head his way as soon as they entered the room with each new tray of hors d'oeuvres. He grabbed five pigs-in-a-blanket, his favorite, and piled them onto his overflowing small plate. Will passed up the bubbly in favor of what proved to be an excellent California Cabernet. Adrienne sipped only sparkling water and repeatedly said, "No thanks" to offers of appetizers and drinks. She was about to regret having even the sparkling water in her mouth at that precise moment. Before she could swallow, President Hugo H. Dorzel entered the room and when Adrienne looked up she gagged and spat out the water, barely catching it in a linen napkin she somehow grabbed in a split-second reaction. It was not seeing the pendulous Dorzel waddling in to the strains of Hail to the Chief that made the shell-shocked Special Agent retch, it was seeing his companion: Alexandra Parushnikova.

Alexandra Parushnikova, the Russian beauty Adrienne and Tom had spotted cavorting with a corrupt physician they had trailed to a lavish boondoggle in Cabo. Alexandra Parushnikova, identified by Will's sophisticated analytics as a key part of the Russian mob's deadly scheme to sell phony drugs and counterfeit medical devices. Alexandra Parushnikova, who belonged in jail as far as the FBI agents and Will were concerned, but instead was not only free and in the United States, but sitting at the main table in the White House in the company of the American president.

To them she was not just another female trophy brought in to feed the president's ego and bolster his image. To them she was a hardened Russian operative who had brazenly distributed defective products that had killed and maimed countless victims. Seeing her at the White House cozying up to the president could only mean one thing: she was there on a mission from her Russian masters.

Struggling to clear his throat of partially chewed pig-in-a-blanket glop, an equally flabbergasted Tom Murphy mumbled hoarsely, "What the hell…! What's that one doing here?"

Adrienne patted her face with the balled-up napkin, then looked up and mouthed the words, "Good question."

As shocked as his companions, Will felt a thin stream of red wine working its way from his throat up into his nasal passages and buried his face in the crook of his elbow just in time to catch a wine-laced sneeze. Through a chorus of "Gesundheit" and "Bless You," he whispered to Adrienne, "We'd better find out why she's here."

Adrienne nodded somberly. Getting her picture taken with the president no longer seemed of any importance. She said softly, "So she's the reason for all that extra security. Unbelievable. This is serious, very serious. Will, you've got more work cut out for you."

Chapter 33: Delivering The Goods

Alexandra Parushnikova looked out at the sea of guests and remained impassive, just as she had been taught. You are not a celebrity, she was told, but you will be a cause for curiosity. Stay above it. No eye contact, no emotion. Be distant, unapproachable, mysterious. That was exactly what the crowd saw. Nearly every guest was dazzled by the blond beauty on Dorzel's arm. To them she radiated regal elegance, an icon remaining entirely within herself. But inside, she was struggling to maintain her composure. She was performing, playing her assigned role. Her apparent serenity masked her inner turbulence, a raging storm of anxiety over the two very different tasks she was yet to carry out that night.

The evening dragged on. There was no handsome Major Maxim Grigorovich Dragomirov to stir her imagination, only the pendulous Dorzel stuffing himself with handfuls of fried chicken and French fries. She sat next to him but most of the time he was leaning forward over the table to shake some fawning admirer's hand or pat them on top of the head and address them by some colloquial nickname that she did not recognize. Sasha was not called upon to engage in anything that could be considered conversation—all she had to do when he turned toward her was sit still while he ogled her breasts and boasted endlessly about all the reasons everybody considered him the greatest American president of all time. He snorted that they were planning to build a monument to him that would be so much bigger than Mt. Rushmore it would put those four old guys to shame. That much she understood, but she had no idea what he meant when he added that it would be "bigger than that damn Indian thing that Polack was building."

She felt as though she had received a reprieve when Dorzel abruptly left the table to mingle with the crowd, but she had very little time to relax. After some ten minutes a Marine approached the head table, a handsome man so tall that the two of them were eye-to-eye even though her chair was on the elevated platform. He stood almost as straight as if he were standing at attention and said, "Ms. Parushnikova?"

"Yes," she said, smiling for the first time all evening, and letting herself entertain the titillating thought that she was indeed to have the company of an American version of Major Grigory. She was quickly disabused of her fantasy.

"Please come with me, Ma'am," he said, his voice courteous but clipped, businesslike.

Sasha stood, walked to the end of the raised platform, and descended the three steps to the main floor. The Marine offered her his arm and guided her toward a side exit. When he opened the door for her she wondered where they were going. Was this military officer actually in charge of procuring women for Dorzel? But then a man stepped from behind a statue in one of the recesses in the hallway. The Marine said, "Good evening, Mr. Jones. This is Ms. Parushnikova." Mr. Jones muttered, "Mmmhh," and did not extend his hand in greeting. The Marine lowered his arm, gently dislodging her hand. Then he turned to her, said "Ma'am," and walked back into the Blue Room.

It took Sasha only a few seconds to decide that, unlike the clean-cut Marine officer, Mr. Jones fit the part of a procurer of women perfectly. He was slight, at least two inches shorter than Sasha, so that she looked down on his shiny black hair that was so thickly gelled it appeared as sculpted as the hair on the marble statue that had concealed him. He wore a three-button dark gray suit with wide pin-stripes and a silver tie over his cobalt-blue shirt. Sasha had seen many men like this one, but he was only the second that she had not turned away from immediately; the first had been a pompous little plastic surgeon she had cozied up to under orders from her previous employer.

Mr. Jones led Sasha down an elegant hall, then turned to his right and they passed through a tiny office with papers stacked on every surface. They exited on the other side into a hallway that was so narrow they had to walk single-file. Around another corner they entered a stairwell and ascended two flights of uncarpeted wooden stairs. Sasha was beginning to think that she was being taken to the White House servants' quarters when they left the stairwell and she magically found herself in an elegant hallway with ornate doors on either side and thick red carpeting. Mr. Jones stopped in front of a door that had no name or number affixed and removed a cluster of keys from his pocket. He selected one, opened the door, and ushered Sasha in. The room was lit by two low lamps on either side of a huge, plush bed. Mr. Jones indicated an interior door on one side of the room and said, in a civil if not friendly voice, "That is the bathroom." Then he pointed to an identical door on the opposite side and said, in a distinctly less accommodating tone, "That is for him to come and go. Never open that door. Do you understand? *Never.* After I leave, you will turn the bolt to lock the door to the hallway and wait in here. Do not open the lock for any reason until it is time for you to leave. That is all. Do you have any questions?"

"Just one. When may I expect him?"

"Any time between now and sunrise. You should be ready at any moment." He walked over to an antique chifferobe standing in front of the wall near the bathroom and said, "You will find suitable clothing in here. Anything else?"

"No," said Sasha, "I'm good. Thank you for your attention."

She was relieved when he left, and engaged the deadbolt as ordered. She needed to collect her thoughts. Should she let Dorzel have his way with her before or after she delivered the messages she was tasked with? There seemed to be no good answer. If she tried to speak with him before they had sex he might be so anxious to get past the delay that he would pay little attention to what she was saying. But if they had sex right away he might disappear immediately after through his private door and she would miss the opportunity to complete her mission, a failure she could not risk. She made a strategic decision: she would proceed in two stages. She would wait to undress until he came into the room, then keep his attention by speaking as she disrobed. He needed to understand that she had an important message for him, a message that required a response. Then once they were done with sex she would tell him the details and gauge his reaction.

Sasha wondered how long she would have to wait. She looked at her wrist and examined her high-tech watch, hoping it would record their conversation as Leon had said. She sat on the edge of the bed, kicked off her shoes, and ran her plan through her head over and over: keep his attention by stripping slowly, tell him that she had an important message for him, then put up with his repulsive desires until the moment came to deliver the message and get his response.

As it turned out she did not have long to wait for him to appear, but all of her planning proved to have been wasted. Barely fifteen minutes passed before the side door was thrown open and Dorzel flew into the room, unbuckling his pants as he waddled toward her. She stood and reached up to undo the snaps at her neckline, but his stubby hands grabbed the straps and tore them apart with a fury. He pulled off the gown before she knew what was happening. She tried to speak but he was on top of her, burying his face in her breasts, pulling her thong off to one side and sliding himself into her. It was all over in less than two minutes. He lay panting on top of her, crushing the breath out of her. She struggled for air until at last he rolled off and she was able to suck in several deep breaths.

Suddenly he rolled once more and stood up. She had a moment of panic—would he leave before she could deliver her message? She gasped and was about to speak when she realized he was not gathering his clothes, not heading back through the private door, he was fumbling in the drawer of the bedside table for something. "Ah," he said, pulling a pill vial out of the drawer and dropping a large dark tablet into his hand, "here we go." He twisted the cap off a plastic bottle of water from the table, popped the pill into his mouth, took a long swig of water and swallowed. "That baby'll take about forty-five minutes, then we can go at it again," he said triumphantly, and began fumbling for his pants.

Now Sasha had a serious panic. What if some other woman attracted him at the reception and set off the Viagra? He might never return, or someone might escort her out to make way for a second dalliance. She found her voice. "I must say something," she said, suddenly realizing she had no idea how to address him. "I bring an important message. You…"

He cut her off. "Yeah, yeah, I know. We gotta go ahead, tell them to go ahead if they're ready. That guy, Jenkins. If they don't do something I won't be around here anymore."

That was it, as far as talking was concerned. He pulled on his clothes and was out the side door before she could say anything about not turning back or issue any warning about the dire consequences he would suffer if he walked away from their arrangement.

She lay back on the bed for twenty minutes or so, thinking. Then she decided to get dressed and return to the reception. She inspected her clothes and was amazed that they had not been torn to pieces in his haste. She went into the bathroom and was pleasantly surprised to find a bidet. She sat and ran cool water over her sore tissues until they calmed down, then cleaned herself with the gentle soap. Next she washed her face at the sink and fixed her hair, slipped back into her evening gown and was about to slide her feet into her heels when the side door to the bedroom flung open.

He was back for more.

Chapter 34: Quick Response

Even if Adrienne had still wanted to get the photograph with POTUS she would never have had a chance. Dorzel disappeared from the East Room from time to time, and when he reappeared he never stood in a reception line, just wandered around slapping people on the back, shaking hands, smiling for the photographer who followed him. During one appearance he did seek out the FBI Director, whispered something into his ear, then was off without bothering to meet any of the Special Agents. What she should have taken as a rebuff came as a welcome relief to Adrienne. There would be another time and another president—a president whose picture she would be proud to have on her wall. For now they needed to find out what this one was up to. In a hurry.

"OK," she said to Will, "my team is going to head directly to headquarters from here. Can you join us?"

"Sure. I'll let Sally know I'm going to be much later than I expected…and I'll explain that I'll be with the whole group."

Adrienne grinned briefly, then her game face returned. "Let's go," she said. "I called for a car. Tell your spouses they need to get home on their own."

The guards stationed at the rear entrance of the Hoover Building couldn't help laughing at the sight of five Special Agents and Will Manningham entering the building at eleven-thirty at night in formal wear. One quipped to Tom Murphy that he never knew they made tuxedoes that big, and was surprised when the perpetually jovial big man just grumbled back that he should keep his jokes to himself.

Once they were in Adrienne's office the men removed their jackets and bow ties and opened their shirts at the collar, but the women could do little more than stow their wraps, kick off their heels and let their hair down. Except for Fran Trainor, who asked

Denise Washington to loosen the clasps on the back of her gown and soon gave a loud sigh of relief, saying, "Ah, thanks, I can breathe!"

When Adrienne addressed the group she had an even more intense expression on her face than they were accustomed to seeing. "This is not going to be easy," she said. "We are going to have to tread carefully if we're to look into this situation. Any FBI action that involves President Dorzel is off-limits at our level now, as you are all well aware. And, of course, we will abide by the rules, as always."

Everyone in the room knew what she was referring to. The lackey that Dorzel had installed as FBI Director had issued a directive that any matter that could in possibly involve the White House needed to be referred to his office. The directive was accompanied by a stern warning that any violation would be treated as disloyalty and a breach of the agent's oath of office. Adrienne said nothing and displayed no body language that could be interpreted as encouraging her colleagues to defy the order. But she didn't need to. They all understood that the presence of Alexandra Parushnikova at Dorzel's side was too serious to ignore—and that it would indeed be ignored if they deferred to the Director, who knew full well that the Russian woman had been cavorting with the president.

Adrienne continued, keeping a perfectly straight face. "You are all aware that a person of interest from one of our previous cases has turned up again. Although she escaped prosecution, that person was deeply involved in a fraudulent scheme that had serious consequences for many people. We would be derelict in our responsibilities if we did not look into her current activities. But our inquiries must be carefully confined to routine matters and strictly limited to this office, since as yet we have no evidence that she is engaged in anything illegal. Is that clear?"

Everyone nodded. Tom Murphy suppressed an urge to grin in admiration at his boss's skill at being both circumspect and crystal clear at the same time.

"Will," Adrienne said, "It will be up to you to take the lead."

Will said, "Sure, got it. Loud and clear." He spoke somberly, understanding that he would provide a modicum of cover for the FBI team since he was in the private sector and technically not subject to the Director's order. He could conduct his inquiries without triggering immediate scrutiny by the FBI's internal monitors. But they both knew that if he were discovered investigating Dorzel, his links to Adrienne would be the death knell for her career. He admired her courage to risk everything to do the right thing.

She continued, as if justifying putting the responsibility on Will. "After all, Will, you know the most about Ms. Parushnikova. Any thoughts on how to proceed?"

"I think so. I should be able to recover my old files on her from my archives. I can tie them in with the mega-data Belinda and I have been using at *Cybersleuths* on the medical device deaths. We'll track her movements and look into her financials. We can generate a profile of where she's been, what's she's been doing, and where she is now. I'll also see if Belinda, Lauren or Ned have any suggestions."

"Good. I'm sure you realize we need to be quick about this."

"First thing tomorrow morning, Boss," said Will.

"You mean first thing this morning, Will," said Denise Washington, pointing at the clock on Adrienne's wall, which showed it was now well after 2AM.

Adrienne added, "And I'm not your boss. Remember that."

Will took her meaning and said, "Ah, sure. You bet."

As the group stood to leave, Will walked over to Adrienne's photo gallery and pointed to the empty spot she had reserved for her long-awaited picture with POTUS.

"Better luck next time," he said, with a wry smile.

"Let's hope we all have better luck next time, Will."

Chapter 35: Tracking Sasha

Will opened the front door of their house as quietly as he could, stepped in and removed his shoes, and tip-toed toward the bedroom when he heard Sally's voice from the living room. "I'm in here."

"Hi Honey," he replied, heading toward the voice.

Sally turned on a lamp next to the sofa. She was curled up under her favorite knitted wool comforter but sat up as Will bent over to give her a peck on the cheek.

"So, how was it? You guys stayed out to party afterward?"

"Hardly. The whole thing was unpleasant, then it got worse. The man is beyond belief."

"Tell me something I don't know. But what kept you so late?"

"I can't tell you all the details, but something happened that we need to look into. It's, uh, a very delicate situation."

"Let me guess: it has something to do with the Russians."

Will's bleary eyes opened wide. "How on earth did you come up with that?"

"You don't have to be a cybersleuth to know that he's in bed with the Russians."

Will burst out laughing. "Ha! You have no idea how right you are! His 'companion' at the reception was a Russian woman we know very well. And not his wife. I can't say a lot more than that because..."

"No explanation necessary. I take it she's sexy?"

"Quite...uh...attractive, but not as sexy as you."

"Cut the crap. Let's go to bed."

"Sure. I need to be in the office early, so I'm only good for a couple of hours of sleep."

"My hard-working husband! Want to cuddle up right here on the couch?"

"Very appealing, but not tonight, Honey."

"OK," she said, standing up and wrapping the comforter around her shoulders, "bed it is."

The next morning Will hit the snooze button when his alarm rang at 8AM, then dragged his weary body out of bed when the buzzer sounded a second time ten minutes later. He texted his team to get together at 9 but didn't make it to his office until 9:15. He entered with a sheepish grin and greeted them with, "My apologies, everyone. Late night."

"Have a cappuccino," said Lauren, handing him a cup with the Peet's logo.

"And a croissant," added Ned, opening a paper sack that filled the room with the smell of fresh baked goods.

"We figured you could use those," said Belinda. "So, what's the word?"

Will bit off half of a croissant and sipped his cappuccino, then said, "Big time problem at the White House. Very big. Dorzel showed up with a woman who was at the center of one of the biggest cases I worked on with the FBI. A Russian, part of a terrible scheme that sold counterfeit drugs and phony medical devices. Her job was to, uh, let's say, to *convince* doctors to order the stuff."

"If you busted that operation what's she doing with the president?"

"We were sure she'd go to jail, or at the very least get deported and banned from ever returning to the States. But then the new administration came in and suddenly the Russians are our BFFs. Even so, you can hardly imagine how shocked we were to see her at the White House."

"Roger that," said Ned. "What do you think is going on?"

"That's what we need to find out. I'm sure she's there for a purpose. She was an operative for the Russian mob, and now she's horsing around with the President of the United States. Whatever else, she has to be on a mission, and it can't be good. We need to figure out what she's up to."

"Why us? Why not FBI?"

Will took a moment to couch his words so that he could give his team enough of the picture without saying anything that would cast Adrienne in a bad light. "Uh, they're more or less going to rely on us. Anything involving the Russians is pretty sensitive these days. Trust me, this is something for us to do."

Belinda shook her head slowly, then said, "What about our investigation of the medical device deaths? Are we going to put that on hold while we look into this Russian agent thing?"

"No, not at all, we can't slack up on that. We don't want to miss an opportunity to prevent another person from being killed. We'll have to double up, keep going on the medical device front while we explore this new problem."

"We don't get paid overtime," Ned said with a grin.

"Nope, it's all for the joy of solving problems," said Lauren. "And saving lives. How were you thinking we'd proceed?"

"How about Belinda and I jump start this Russian thing to get it going, while you and Ned keep chugging away on the medical device deaths? Will that work?"

"Yup," said Ned, at the same time that Belinda and Lauren both said, "Sure, Will."

"Good, thanks. The woman's name is Alexandra Arkadyevna Parushnikova. She's highly educated and extremely attractive."

"In that case, I'd like to trade roles with Belinda," said Ned.

Lauren smirked, "You really think she'd go for you over Dorzel?"

Everyone chuckled, including Ned.

"As I was saying," continued Will, "Ms. Parushnikova is no dumb blonde. Whatever she's doing it's probably a high-value operation. I thought Belinda and I would develop a comprehensive profile on her and see if it gives us any clues as to what she's doing here with Dorzel."

"I thought we knew what she was doing with Dorzel," said Ned.

"Ha! Yeah, well, in addition to that sort of thing," said Will. "Now, back to the medical device stuff. Anything new?"

"Yes," said Lauren. "Following up on your idea, Will, I built a neural network to explore links between some common point and the different victims. Lo and behold, there seems to be exactly that— a single point at the center of it all. We don't have a map that leads us to Oz, not yet. But there's definitely a Wizard who was amassing information on all the people who died. Whoever it is went poking around in their lives in minute detail."

"And that's not all," interjected Belinda. "Wait till you hear what else she found. Tell him the rest, Lauren. You aren't going to like this, Will."

"Yes," she said, her deep voice dropping even deeper, "it's not just the deaths we know about that the Wizard was looking at—there are also people who are still alive."

"Shit," muttered Will. "Just what we feared: potential targets. Anything noteworthy about them?"

"Not yet. I just detected the pattern a couple of minutes ago. Some of the names sound familiar but I haven't had a chance to look into them."

"Any overlap with our list of public officials who are being kept alive by their implanted devices?"

"No. I did take a quick glance at those names to check on whether there were any matches but there weren't any."

"Very interesting. So maybe the Russians aren't gearing up to kill one of our leaders."

"One more thing," said Belinda. "I managed to make some progress with my former classmates, the ones who are using AI to predict the outcome of the election. Just like I thought, most of them wouldn't give me any specifics, but a couple of them agreed to listen to what I had come up with and tell me whether I was on track or not. So I ran my ideas by them about the kinds of analyses I was planning to run. I took my plans back to them and got a couple of winks and nods, and even a hint or two. Then, as Hank suggested, I burrowed into everything I could about all of the candidates and ran a number of my algorithms. My findings confirmed what the polls have been suggesting: Robin Jenkins would trounce Dorzel, no doubt about it. And I also found that it's equally clear that no one else would win a face-to-face with him. So I went back to those same friends and told them my results, and got another couple of winks and nods. Bottom line: if the Russians are aiming to eliminate any threat of Dorzel losing the election they'd have to be pointing at Jenkins."

"Great job, Belinda," gushed Will. "That's fantastic! I mean, that's what we pretty much expected but it's great to have it confirmed. I hope you didn't say anything about wanting to leave here and go work with them!"

"Nope, no teaser. Never had to tell my little white lie. What now?"

"Uh...what you just told us gives me a thought. Let me have a few hours to do some thinking and run some data. Then let's reassemble. OK?"

Belinda looked hurt. "I thought you and I were going to work on this together, now I give you something and you're cutting me out?"

There it was: Barry's sulk. The furrows across her forehead from the top of her eyebrows to her bright red hairline, the raised lower lip, the shrug of her shoulders, it was exactly how his dead twin used to react when he felt Will was shutting him out of something. And, Will knew, it mirrored his own look of disappointment when Barry seemed to be shutting him out.

"Just an idea," Will responded, "no big deal. Really. I just need to think about something while the idea is hot." Then he felt silly, apologizing to a colleague as if she were his late brother. "I'll let you know later if I get anywhere. How about back here at 3?"

"OK, sure," she said, and she was all Belinda again, no more Barry. For now, anyway.

Once Will was alone in his office he slid his long legs under his computer table, leaned back in his chair, and stared at his blank monitor while the fingernail of his right index finger found its way to the thinking spot on his scalp. Too many coincidences to unravel. Parushnikova at the White House. The Russians the most likely source of the medical device murders. Parushnikova having distributed counterfeit medical devices. The Russians unleashing all kinds of tricks to keep Dorzel in office. Was there a connection? Was it possible that they had only one problem to investigate, not two?

He sat like that for fifteen or twenty minutes, letting the bits and pieces fly around in his head like radioactive particles circulating in a nuclear reactor until the right ones smashed into each other and emitted a flash of light. Then it happened: *bang!* He bolted upright and within seconds his fingers were flying across the keyboard.

Chapter 36: The Bubble

"No!" shrieked Colonel Robin Washington Jenkins. "No fucking way, Andy. That's the craziest goddamn thing I've ever seen." He swept his arm furiously across the table, sending a stack of blueprints and drawings flying onto the floor.

"I told you that you were going to have to live in a bulletproof bubble, Colonel," said Andy Ackroyd, holding his heavy glasses on his nose with one finger as he bent over to collect the papers from the floor. "So, that's what it looks like. But this isn't coming just from me, it's coming from the pros. Let Captain Billy Jean explain."

"Thank you, Mr. Ackroyd. Colonel Jenkins, we regret to have to tell you but we believe you are in imminent danger of an attempt on your life during the last part of the campaign. We think there is a high probability of a potentially lethal assault unless you agree to our security arrangements or you forego all public appearances. Short of confining you to quarters we need to deploy an impenetrable defense. The containment capsule is the only way to assure your safety if you go out in public."

"Look, Captain Billy Jean, I have the highest regard for everything you and your team of Secret Service agents are doing to protect me. But this, this is just too much. I figured Ackroyd was speaking, you know, figuratively about living in a bubble. But this is for real, an actual goddamn bubble. For god's sake, how can I campaign in that thing?"

"Funny you should mention God, Colonel," said Captain Billy Jean, attempting to calm Jenkins by speaking in an unusually lighthearted tone for the plainspoken, rough-and-tumble Marine. "I was just about to mention the Pope. Not even the Pope relies on God to protect him in public. Ever since the attempted assassination of John Paul II nearly forty years ago, the popes have only gone out in their bulletproof popemobiles."

"Not Francis—he works the crowd and eats the food that people hand him."

"True enough, and his security detail has cautioned him many times that he is putting himself at risk every time he does so. He's happy to rely on God's will, he says. But even Pope Francis rides around in one kind of popemobile or another nearly all the time."

Robin Jenkins folded his arms on his chest and shook his head, a scowl of intractable defiance on his face. "Why? What's going on that makes you think things have gotten that bad? Do you have information on a specific threat to my life, or what?"

"Do we have the name of an assassin out to kill you or the date and time it an attack will take place? No, we do not have anything that precise, Colonel. But we've been picking up serious warning signs from many different sources. Electronic surveillance has detected a surge of worrisome traffic. Our human assets tell us that their contacts say there will soon be a strike at a high-value target. Putting all the indicators together, we have elevated your danger level to the top of the scale."

"It's the fucking Russians, Colonel." Andy Ackroyd spat the words out. "They're doing everything they can to keep Dorzel in office and now they're shitting their pants because your lead is insurmountable. I showed you what the data people are telling us, you're up to over 99% unbeatable against Dorzel. They must be seeing the same numbers and it's gotta be driving them nuts."

Jenkins continued to shake his head. "So I am to send out Tweets and run ads on TV and social media but no one will get to see me in person? Either that or you want to wall me off behind glass like a damn goldfish in a bowl? The people will think I'm a real coward hiding like that."

"Actually, Colonel, they wouldn't. We ran some quick focus groups and were pleasantly surprised by the reactions we got. We had people discuss how they would feel about various responses to different levels of threat to you. When we escalated up to a situation as serious as the one we're currently facing, your supporters overwhelmingly said they would understand your taking just about any defensive measures. In fact, they thought protecting you was so important they would willingly accept removing you from all public appearances if necessary. Lots of people mentioned JFK, and one said he had just read a book about how Kennedy might not have died if the Secret Service had left the plastic top in place over the convertible that day in Dallas. They also talked about Martin Luther King and Reagan getting shot, and said they never wanted something like that to happen again. And we heard a lot of comments that getting Dorzel out of office was worth going along with anything that would keep you alive."

"I still don't like this, not at all. It's not right. I didn't hide from the goddamn snipers when we were engaged in combat and I don't feel like hiding now."

"You won't be hiding, you'll be safe," countered Andy Ackroyd. "And, actually the damn bubble isn't all that different than the huge ballistic shields that other presidents have used for big public appearances. You can think of the containment chamber as, you know, an incremental improvement, not something entirely new. It's just, well, more complete than a single sheet of plexiglass. Those shields are great if somebody tries to shoot you head-on, we don't have to worry about every rooftop or open window. But someone can still lob a grenade over the top or set off a bomb under the stage. The bubble protects on the top, bottom and back as well as the front."

"Safe? You're telling me this is foolproof? There's no way to kill me if I go around in your bubble?"

"That plus all of our other security measures, yes, Sir," said Captain Billy Jean. "We refer to the containment chamber as plexiglass but it is actually made from an advanced composite material tougher than the windshield of a supersonic jet. It is impervious to ordnance of all types, and able to withstand explosions far more powerful than any suicide bomber could deliver. And of course your security detail will be in position to retaliate with lethal force to any assault."

"One more thing, Colonel," said Ackroyd. "The chamber is not exactly invisible, but almost so. The front is gently curved and the material it's made of doesn't reflect light, even camera flashes. Once you're inside and talking the audience will hardly know it's there. And it is pretty much invisible to people watching on television."

"But I'll be trapped in that thing. What if someone barges into the bubble with a bomb or poison gas, what then?"

"Retinal scan. You'll look into a retinal sensor and the door in the back will pop open, then it'll seal itself once you're inside. It's absolutely impermeable. You're the only one who can open the door and get into the bubble quickly once the sensors are activated on-site. Anyone else would have to stand there for several minutes trying to get in and we'd blow them to smithereens by then."

"And getting me into the thing? Couldn't they get to me first?"

"Very, very unlikely that any assassin could get that close to you."

"What about Indira Gandhi? Wasn't she killed by one of her bodyguards?"

"Colonel Jenkins, Sir," said Captain Bill Jean, a clear note of annoyance in her voice, "with all due respect, the very idea of a rogue Secret Service agent is unthinkable. They are the most highly vetted and loyal men and women in the world. They would all give their life to save yours. And they always work in pairs that are rotated randomly, so they're watching each other while they're guarding you."

"No offense, Captain Billy Jean. Just making a point. I know the last thing on earth I have to worry about is a Secret Service agent fragging me."

"Anyway," said Andy Ackroyd, "it's the bubble or no public appearances."

"Can it be ready for my rally back home in Happy Valley? No way we're postponing, that rally is too important to me."

"No problem, the bubble will be there and ready to go. All the arrangements are in place already."

"So that's it, huh? You thought of everything. But shit. I hate the whole idea." He went silent and buried his head in his hands. After a long minute he looked up and said, "Still…if you're absolutely sure I'm targeted for assassination, I guess I have no choice. I have my family to think of as well as the country. OK, the damn thing better work."

"Anything short of a tactical nuclear weapon and you're safe, Colonel," said Captain Billy Jean. "No worries."

Chapter 37: The Target

There it was. The answer jumped off the screen. It was so obvious, Will kicked himself for not thinking of it sooner. How could he have been so dense? Just a few simple runs through Jenkins' medical records and there it was: *"Atrioventricular node contusion resulting in cardiogenic shock and arrhythmia."* Everyone knew Colonel Robin W. Jenkins had been seriously wounded in combat. His heroism while sustaining life-threatening injuries had earned him the Medal of Honor. It was all in the public record, the makings of his legend. That was the story everyone heard a thousand times over. But the public did not know the details, how his body had been slammed chest-first against a wall when incoming shells exploded next to him, severely damaging his heart. The tissue in his heart that causes it to beat had been destroyed. Only swift and prolonged CPR by a medical corpsman had kept him alive until a surgeon back at home base inserted a pacemaker. Now his life depended on that device working correctly.

That was it: Jenkins was the target. He was vulnerable—no electronic pacemaker, no heartbeat. And Belinda had confirmed that even the tsunami of Russian disinformation couldn't keep Jenkins from trouncing Dorzel. The only way for the Russians to keep their flunky in the White House was to get rid of Jenkins. No need to go after any hostile public officials, they'd get all the friendly ones they wanted and more if Dorzel got reelected.

So it all added up, except for the big question: why did the Russians need to go to the trouble of devising such an elaborate scheme to kill off a presidential candidate? Sure, Jenkins had an enormous security detail but it was nothing like the protection for the president. One suicide bomber at a campaign stop and he would be toast. Literally. Heck, he thought, it would have been a lot cheaper and less complicated to have some operative give Jenkins a huge campaign donation and get access to a private event for the biggest fundraisers. That meant personal access in a small group, guaranteed easy pickings for an assassin. Maybe Adrienne would know why the Russians would have gone to such extreme measures to get to Jenkins. He'd go see her as soon as he briefed his teammates.

At 3 o'clock Will's group reassembled in his office. As soon as Belinda saw him she said, "You've figured something out, haven't you?" She was reading his mind—just like Barry used to! The twins had shared their own personal communication channel, a wavelength of their own that no one else could tune in to. Until now. Someday he would find out just who this Belinda Winnisome was, he had to. But not now. First they needed to protect someone who was likely to be the next President of the United States—if he lived long enough to get elected and take office.

"Guess that's obvious, huh?" he said, putting off his urge to explore Belinda's genealogy until another time.

"Written all over your face," she replied. "What did you find?"

Will explained how her findings about the likely outcome of the election had finally made him realize where he should look, and once he did, the answer was right in front of him: the target was Colonel Robin W. Jenkins. He was defenseless to an attack that shut down his pacemaker, which in his case was an implantable defibrillator that also functioned as a pacemaker.

"Actually," said Lauren, "That fits with something Ned and I just came up with. While we were waiting for you to do your runs, we went over the people that the Wizard has been tracking and discovered that Jenkins was on the list. At that point we looked into the kinds of data they were collecting on him and saw that he has a pacemaker/defibrillator they had gathered extensive information on. They're also keeping close track of his campaign schedule"

"Uh oh, I think we've got the target," said Will. "They've got Jenkins square in their cross-hairs."

"What next?" said Ned. "Alert the Jenkins campaign?"

"Well, somebody needs to, but I don't think it's up to us to tell them, at least not yet. I'll brief my contact at the FBI and let her decide what to do. For now, let's focus on the Russian woman who surfaced at the White House, Alexandra Parushnikova. I can't help thinking she's got to be involved somehow. Think it through. The

Russians are going all out to keep Dorzel in office. We discover that people are being killed by hacking into their medical devices, and we know the Russians are just about the only ones who have the capability to mount a high-tech killing spree in this country. Parushnikova used to sell medical devices. Maybe not implantable devices that got hacked exactly, but still they were phony ones that she knew would kill people when they failed. And, well, let's just say she has talents that make her a natural for getting close to a guy like Dorzel, so suddenly she's at the White House. Strikes me as too many coincidences."

"I had the same thought," said Belinda. "So I was also busy while we were out. I dug into her activities—you know, just like I showed you I could do with data on you. Well, Parushnikova is not only back in the States, she's back in the medical device industry. Her day job is with a Russian company called Farmatsevticheskaya Volga. In this country it goes by Pharma Volga. How's that for another coincidence?"

"Scary," said Will. He wondered if Belinda knew that he meant scary in more than one way since she had mirrored his very thought.

"I found out a few more things as well," she added. "She lives at the Watergate—pretty pricey digs, a seriously expensive apartment with a great view. And she frequents a little Russian dive called Bar Natasha. Want to know what her favorite drink is?"

"You're kidding, right?

"Yeah," she laughed, "I have no idea what she drinks. But I can find out if you'd like to know!"

"No interest, thanks. OK, great progress, everyone. Now that we know it's Jenkins they're coming after let's focus on him in as much detail as possible. And we need more on Parushnikova."

"Anything in particular?" asked Lauren.

"Anything at all. The more we know, the more likely we'll be able to keep him alive. I'm off to the FBI as soon as my contact can see me."

.

Chapter 38: Final Preparations

The tall, thin man extended his long legs under his workbench and fingered his dark beard as he studied the leather tool pouch that held the tiny, high-precision implements of his craft. He positioned a dust mask on his face and pinched the metal stay over the bridge of his nose, then slid his hands into a pair of skin-tight surgical gloves. He picked up his magnifying loupes, which resembled eyeglasses with small black binoculars attached to the lenses, and slipped them onto his face, pressing the nosepiece down over the top of the mask and shaking his head up and down several times to make sure the awkward contraption would not slide down his nose while he was attending to his delicate work. Then he unrolled the pouch and pulled the finely honed tools out one by one, methodically examining each one before wiping them with a clean chamois cloth and carefully returning them to their slender individual pockets.

This was it, the final stage of his operation. One last check of the miniature transmitter. Everything had to work perfectly, there was no room for failure. Failure would have consequences not just for him but also for his family. The Security Service had housed his wife and two children in a modest flat in the Barrikadnaya Area of Moscow, not far from the American Embassy. If he carried out his assignment successfully, he would be promoted and rewarded with much larger and more pleasant accommodations. A very different destination would await him if he did not succeed.

But he was confident there was no reason to worry about failure. He had spent countless hours over the past two years perfecting the equipment in the technical workshops of the Security Service, deep under the Farmatsevticheskaya Volga building. At first no one told him what the little transmitter was for, or when and how it might be used. All he knew was that it needed to send signals of a certain wavelength to a particular type of receiver. When he had convinced them that it was working properly they called him in for a meeting that was to change his life forever.

"Iosef Vladimirovich Dorofeyev," said General Petyr Leonidovich Volodin, "you have done well, and now you are to be entrusted with a mission so vital that it is not overstating things to say it is of existential significance to the Russian Federation." The words alone would have shaken him to his core, but delivered by a renowned military leader who spoke in a voice so icy it sent chills up his spine, he knew immediately that his life depended on what he was about to hear. "You must be prepared to carry out this assignment without regard to the consequences. For you, or for anyone else."

He stroked his black beard absent-mindedly to calm himself before replying. At last he said, "I am here to serve, General. I will do as I am instructed to the best of my ability."

"You will do as you are ordered, and you will succeed. You must not fail." The General turned to the ghoul-like skeleton of a woman standing next to him and said, "Natalia Kostenka Anatolievna will provide you with the details. Regard carefully what she says. You will be responsible for a particular part of this operation. Others are carrying out different pieces, which you do not need to know about. All must go as planned."

Natalia Kostenka Anatolievna stepped forward and looked at him with eyes that burned through to the back of his skull. In a strange way he found her to be even more intimidating than the General. Like many Russians he was familiar with imposing military figures like the General, men who bombarded them with directives and warned of grave consequences for failure to obey orders. But this woman had an other-worldly presence, an aura dissociated from human form. The General evoked fear of being tortured and murdered, one human being threatening to destroy another. But she emanated an eerie, alien menace, an unnerving intuition that she would drain his blood and suck his very soul out of his body.

With no more emotion than if she were ordering him to swat a fly, Natalia Kostenka revealed the grim particulars of his assignment: his equipment had performed well in the laboratory, now he was to test it on human beings. The signal from his transmitter would cause instant death by shutting down medical devices implanted in people whose lives depended on them. He would soon be sent to the United States of America, where other operatives in the intelligence service had identified twelve test subjects to be sacrificed for the good of the Russian Federation. "Their lives," Natalia Kostenka said with a sneer, "were of no consequence whatsoever." She told him in elaborate detail what he was to do, but not why. He was given no idea what purpose was being served by the murders he was to carry out to test his killing machine. Over and over she stressed that he was to be merciless, to shed any concerns for the lives he would be destroying. He must do whatever was necessary to assure the success of his mission. He listened more attentively than he had ever done, fully understanding that the same disregard for human life would be shown toward him and his family if he failed.

The sessions with Natalia Kostenka continued over the next five days. At the end of the last day, the General returned and said, "Iosef Vladimirovich Dorofeyev, once the tests on the Americans are conclusive, as we are sure they will be, one of our agents will contact you and give you one last target. When your mission is successful, you will return home in triumph."

At first this savage assignment did not sit easily with him. He was a mild-mannered, electronics engineer, not someone who had been trained to be an assassin. Would he be able to slaughter innocent people? He wasn't sure, but he knew he had no choice but to try. The stakes were too high. In order to preserve his family he would steel himself to go through the motions, stifling his loathing of the evil work. A devout Orthodox Catholic, he would risk eternal damnation and Hell to save them from harm.

As it turned out, Iosef Vladimirovich Dorofeyev took to the work quickly and carried out his wicked tasks with full resolve. He found that he was capable of snuffing the life out of other human beings without a second thought. He did not need to bloody his hands like a soldier running a bayonet through someone's belly or blasting a man's head to pieces with a bullet at close quarters. All he had to do was push a button and watch what happened, a familiar course of action for an engineer. Standing stone-faced as that woman fell to the sidewalk and died writhing in a grand mal seizure while her husband howled in mortal anguish, he realized he had been transformed into a cold-blooded killer. He felt no sympathy for the woman he left to die while hooked up to the dialysis machine, and was not in the least troubled by the thought that she would sit there dead for a full day until her body was discovered. Then he knew he had sunk to an even lower level of depravity when he actually enjoyed the chaotic scene on the subway car watching all those people in the uniforms of their sports heroes go crazy as that man who seemed to be some sort of celebrity collapsed and died.

Within a few months he had morphed from a loving family man and accomplished engineer into a cold-blooded serial killer. Twelve practice runs, twelve corpses. And now it was time for the *pièce de résistance*, his final victim. Who would it be? When would he be given his last instructions? He was growing impatient of living in this strange country. He wanted to be done with this and return to his wife and two children. They would be happy as never before in their new apartment. The children would play in the park and go to the best schools. His wife would be proud of him.

But he was a new man. What would they ask of him when he returned? Surely they would not expect him to resume what he now saw as the banal existence of a plodding, backroom engineer. Maybe he would be taken into the Security Service, be given other deadly assignments, become a Russian James Bond. It was all so thrilling, so much more exciting than he had ever imagined.

Then he received a message: a man named Leonid Denisovich Arkady would provide the final target.

Chapter 39: Assault Weapon

Will knocked on Adrienne's door and opened it enough to make eye contact.

She looked up and smiled. "Hi, Will. What's up,?"

"Quite a bit, Adrienne. We've made progress on a couple of fronts. Complicated stuff."

"Hmmm. Come in and tell me everything."

He took his usual seat facing her desk and said, "It's a bit of a jumble, I'm afraid."

"Spit it all out and we'll sort through it when you're done."

"Let's see if we can. First, we have a pretty good idea about the medical device killings. As you know, we think that the Russians are the most likely ones with the capacity to pull off something like that. We now believe that the deaths so far were target practice, just as we had feared."

"What put you over the top on that one?"

"We found a trail to what looks like a control center. Someone—we're calling him the Wizard of Oz—had been hacking into information on the people who died. Information from their medical records and the device manufactures on their implanted medical devices. Also a wide array of sources on their habits and whereabouts leading right up to when their devices failed and they died."

"Very interesting. But what leads you to think your Wizard is one of the Russians?"

"A bit of a leap of faith, supported by another set of analyses. We were thinking that the Russians would put something like this together only if it would serve their purposes. And they would resort to a plan this sophisticated only if they thought it was necessary to get to their target. Under normal circumstances, that would have led to the conclusion that they wanted to assassinate the President of the United States. POTUS alone has the level of security that would require such a novel weapon to penetrate. The USA has long been Russia's nemesis in the world, and they want to weaken us by disrupting our democratic system. But these aren't normal circumstances. Hugo H. Dorzel is not their nemesis, he's their best buddy. His presence in the Oval Office is disruptive enough to our way of life."

"I'm with you so far. So if not Dorzel, who?"

"We reasoned it would most likely be someone who threatened to interrupt the cozy relationship they have with Dorzel. So we started looking at highly-placed officials who had implanted devices that would be vulnerable to a hacking attack. We found a bunch, but none of them fit the profile that would justify mounting such a complicated operation. The officials we identified have easily penetrable protection, for one thing, so a high-tech weapon would not be necessary. And, besides, a lot of them are loyal Dorzel appointees and therefore not someone the Russians would want to eliminate."

"You're right about the security gaps in protecting officials other than the president. We've been pointing that out for many years, but we keep butting our heads against the usual two barriers to making a change in the government: money and turf. Secret Service keeps chewing up more and more of the budget by scaring the members of the Appropriations Committee that they could be responsible for a presidential assassination if they diverted funds to any other agency. Sore point with us, sorry for the sermon. Please continue."

"Understood. So then we started thinking about who would pose such a serious threat to the Russians that they would go to this extreme, and the answer seemed clear: a candidate who would defeat Dorzel in the election. We jumped into that with both feet and undertook a complicated analysis that led us to Colonel Robin Washington Jenkins."

"Are you telling me your predictions about the outcome of the election have reached that level of certainty we discussed a while ago? You're absolutely certain Jenkins would defeat Dorzel?"

"Exactly. Without boring you with the numbers—since," Will smiled as he spoke, "as you said, you're only a law enforcement officer—our result shows that Jenkins is almost 100% sure to beat

Dorzel if he gets the nomination. And, a further analysis showed that if they can stop Jenkins, they will assure Dorzel's reelection because none of the other candidates would stand a chance against him."

"Maybe that also speaks to why they would want a murder weapon that makes it look like an accidental death. Just like we talked about: no fingerprints, and no chance of making Jenkins into a martyr and generating sympathy for his successor."

"Exactly."

"OK, so you're sure Jenkins would defeat Dorzel. Why do you think he's the target?"

"Jenkins is vulnerable—he has a pacemaker, one that's also a defibrillator. He's totally dependent on it since he has none of the tissue left in heart that would make it beat on its own."

"I didn't even know that. I'm impressed—someone's got his information really bottled up, even from us."

"But that's not all. The clincher was that we found Jenkins front and center in the Wizard's hacking operation. They know everything there is to know about him and his heart device. And his comings and goings, including his campaign schedule."

"So what should we do? Can't the manufacturer update the firmware on the device to protect it from hacking?"

"No, that's a serious problem, not with his old model. The one he has does not have the most advanced encryption capability and the new software cannot be installed remotely. He's extremely vulnerable—and the Russians must know that since they have collected all the specs on his pacemaker. He absolutely has to have it surgically replaced with a new version. You need to convince Jenkins to take a day or two out from his campaign schedule to get the procedure done. In the meantime you'll have to protect him even more than you're already doing."

"Now it's my turn to tell you something. We're way ahead of you on upping his protection. We alerted the Secret Service that our sources, both electronic surveillance and undercover agents and informers, indicate that an attack on Jenkins is highly likely. So they've implemented an entirely new way of protecting him. From now on when he goes out in public he'll be sealed inside a containment capsule. It's transparent and pretty much indestructible. Bullets and bombs can't scratch it. No candidate has ever had this level of protection."

"But will it block hacking signals?"

Will saw the color fade from Adrienne's face. "No, I don't think so. Actually...it can't. One of the specs for the capsule required that wireless microphones would not be affected by the composite material it would be made from. Radio waves have to pass through the walls."

"If we're right, then, the new shield..."

"Containment capsule, not just a shield."

"Whatever it's called, it won't work. Not if someone gets close enough to send a signal to shut down his heart."

"Will, this is very troubling. Anything else? I hope that's all you wanted to tell me."

"Uh, sorry, but there's more. Since your hands are tied, we looked into Parushnikova. She's back in the medical device world, working for a company called Pharma Volga, or Farmatsevticheskaya Volga back home in Russia."

"You're shitting me!"

Will was shocked. He could not remember ever hearing Adrienne utter an expletive.

"Adrienne—what's wrong? What did I say?"

"We're very familiar with Farmatsevticheskaya Volga. They operate under the guise of being a legitimate pharmaceutical company but they're really a front for the Russian Security Service. They run training sessions for the highest-level operatives. We've had an undercover agent on-site there for years. That clinches it— Parushnikova is here on a mission. What more do you know about her?"

"She lives at the Watergate and she frequents a Russian dive bar called Bar Natasha."

"We also know that bar very well. We've planted a series of dishwashers, waitresses, janitors there from time to time. All Russian speakers, of course. We don't keep them there long enough to raise any suspicions. I'm not sure if we've got one in place right now or not, though, since our surveillance of the Russians has been severely curtailed. I'll check and see what I can find out. Ah, Will, this is a lot to digest."

"Yeah, it's a lot. We've got a Russian operative in the White House and a candidate for president who's about to be the target for assassination and we don't know if we can protect him."

"And under the current president we've got one hand tied behind our backs when it comes to the Russians. It's time for me to speak with Chief Hollingshead. He's disgusted by what we're being subjected to and I think he'll be supportive. But there's only so much he can authorize us to do. In any case, it looks like we've got to count on you, Will, even more than I had thought."

"Let's hope we come up with something before it's too late."

Chapter 40: Sending Signals

Sasha was still walking gingerly when she arrived at the offices of Pharma Volga the morning after her ordeal at the White House. But she needed to keep up appearances at her day job, and—more important—report to Leon. At ten-thirty she was standing at the elaborate coffee dispenser in the company's upscale break room when she heard a voice behind her say, in Russian, "Good morning, Alexandra Arkadyevna. How was your evening?"

She waited until her cup had filled with creamy cappuccino, then turned to the chubby little man wearing his trademark mismatched brown outfit and replied, "Just as expected, Leonid Denisovich."

"Shall we discuss after work?"

"Indeed. Some vodka would be excellent."

At five o'clock Leon came by her at her office and the two of them left Pharma Volga and walked in silence to the Metro. When they arrived at Bar Natasha the voluble bartender smiled as she greeted them with an off-color vernacular expression in Russian, then said, in English, "The usual, my friends?" Leon returned the greeting with a vulgar colloquial phrase of his own, then added, "As always, Missi, my dear."

Leon led Sasha to the last booth in the back of the dimly-lilt room. They walked past a number of burly men and women standing at the bar tossing down vodka shots, and a handful who were sitting in the single row of booths beyond the bar. She paid no attention to the thin man with a dark beard who sat in the next-to-last booth, his back turned away from their view.

"You delivered the message as instructed, Sasha?"

"Of course. And I carried out everything else that was required of me as well, but that is not for us to discuss."

The friendly smile that she had seen once before returned to his round face. "Very good. And he understood?"

"He talks incessantly, but just about himself. Even so, he did acknowledge what I said and expressed his agreement. He said that we should go ahead if we're ready."

"Do you recall his exact words?"

"Certainly. You can listen to them for yourself. I have something for you," she said, reaching into her purse. She handed Leon the thumb drive.

"Adequate."

At that moment Missi appeared with a tray. "One Alimov, one Ruskova," she said, placing two double jiggers of vodka on the table along with two glasses of water. "Anything else, my darlings?"

"Thank you, no, my dear," said Leon.

"My pleasure."

As Missi turned and walked back to the bar the thin man with the dark beard rose from the adjoining booth. Had Sasha not been sitting with her back to him she might have noticed that he made brief eye contact with Leon, who nodded ever so slightly at him. But she paid him no attention as he walked silently out of the bar, leaving with his drink still untouched.

Leon returned his eyes to Sasha and said, "And I have something for you." He slipped an identical thumb drive into her hand.

"Is this another assignment?"

"Your current instructions remain as they have been. You will note several dates over the next few weeks when your presence may be required as it was last night. Without the formalities of a gala event, I might add. There are also details on the arrangements that have been made and how you are to proceed each time."

"Anything else?"

"You will also find some guidance on actions you are to take if certain complications arise."

Sasha was alarmed. "Do you foresee complications?"

"We always prepare for the possibility. There are many layers to this matter, many opportunities for something to arise that will require a response. That is all."

Leon signaled to Missi to bring another round. Sasha had welcomed the first shots of vodka to help her recuperate from the previous night. Now she had the feeling that more vodka was needed to prepare for something yet to happen.

Chapter 41: Homecoming

"No fucking way, Andy," yelled Robin Jenkins. "I agreed to go along with that goddamn capsule thing, but there's no way we're going to postpone my rally back home. It's tomorrow, for god's sake. Lenoir tells me he's got more than fifteen thousand people coming. They've gone all out, cancelled school, chartered a shitload of buses, closed City Hall and cancelled leave for all the city workers, and hired a couple hundred rent-a-cops. And they've already paid to rent I don't know how many porta potties. Besides, those are my people, my homies. I can't let them down. I'm going to Paradise Valley, that's it."

"Look, Colonel, the Secret Service says they can't guarantee your safety. Something's going on that they don't want to tell me about, but it's a big deal. We can't risk it."

"Secret Service doesn't tell me what to do. No offense, Captain Billy Jean."

For this meeting, Captain Billy Jean broke her rule about not being in the room with Andy Ackroyd. "None taken, Colonel. But Mr. Ackroyd is correct. The information we have is that you are at grave risk. The Service wants you to go to Walter Reed immediately for a procedure that is necessary to protect you."

"Procedure? What procedure? Some sort of vaccine? Like that goddamn Anthrax vaccine they gave me that got me so sick I said I'd rather have died from the fucking disease? What now? What the hell is this all about?"

"I have not been given the details, Colonel, but I am assured it is urgent."

"So what about the damn capsule? You said it was impossible to get to me in that thing. Isn't that enough?"

"It certainly provides far greater protection than ever before. But, apparently, something else is necessary."

"Well, it's just going to have to wait. The convention starts this weekend. I can't interrupt my momentum at this point, that would be a disaster. And if I shut down the rally and go anywhere near a doctor there'll be all kinds of speculation that I'm not healthy enough to take on Dorzel. That's all Annabaker Minion would need to undermine my nomination. No, absolutely not. The day after the convention, maybe we can do it then. At the earliest. Tomorrow it's hometown boy makes good, and that's going to happen come hell or high water."

"Sounds like hell and high water both, Colonel," said Andy Ackroyd. "But it's your call, of course. No more public events until the convention, OK?"

"Nothing's on the schedule anyway, so sure, we won't add anything."

"Then we'll schedule a trip to Walter Reed for the day after the convention and say our prayers until then."

"Let's hope there's someone listening to your prayers, Mr. Ackroyd," said an obedient but frustrated Captain Bill Jean.

Chapter 42: Deadline

As soon as Will answered the phone Adrienne Penscal said, "Something's happening, Will, and sooner than we expected." Her voice was so strained he could picture the tension on her face. "I just heard from the Secret Service. They wanted Jenkins to postpone his public rally until his pacemaker is replaced but he refuses to reschedule."

"Didn't they make it clear that he's in terrible danger? That the containment capsule can't shield him?"

"He's a warrior, Will. To him this is another battle that he can't shy away from, no matter how heavily stacked the odds are against him."

"So when is this rally? How much time do we have to come up with something?"

"That's why I'm calling. Tomorrow, the rally is tomorrow."

Will shivered and said nothing in reply.

After a long pause Adrienne said, "Will? Are you still there? Did you hear what I said—tomorrow, it's tomorrow."

Will remained silent for a few more seconds. When he finally found his voice he said, "Yes, I heard. That's…that's terrible. We don't have any way to protect him, none at all. Can't they shut down the rally over his objections?"

"He's the candidate, he has the final say unless we have absolute proof that he's about to be attacked. And we don't. It's not like we've uncovered a specific plan. At this point we'd have to admit that all we've got is a high level of suspicion. That's not enough to make him cancel everything. It's too close to the convention, he can't afford to put his campaign completely on hold."

"So it's all up to him and there's nothing you can do?"

"That's right. The government cannot interfere with political activity unless there's an imminent danger to someone's life or public safety. Our hands are tied."

"Shit, Adrienne. Pardon my language, but *shit, shit, shit!* What do you want me to do?"

"Work your magic, Will. Come up with something. You know the situation better than anyone. The Secret Service is sending every agent they can spare and calling in the cavalry but no one knows what to expect. If they're planning something for tomorrow we've got no way to keep him safe."

"Worst case scenario: we...I...don't come up with anything and they hack into his pacemaker and shut his heart down. What then?"

"Medics will be ready to react immediately. But there's another complication."

"What? Tell me?"

"The capsule is designed so that only Jenkins can open it easily with the retinal sensor. Anyone else has to go through a series of complicated steps that can take a few minutes. And of course it's impossible for them to smash it open, that's the whole idea. We'll be ready if something bad happens, but the response won't be quick. The doctors say that if his heart stops for more than 4-6 minutes he'll suffer irreversible brain damage even if he gets resuscitated beyond that point. And it might not even be possible to save his life at all. We've got to keep them from hacking into the device, period. It's his only chance."

Will's fingernail was scratching feverishly at the crust on his scalp. "I don't know, I just don't know. But I'll give it a try. Maybe..."

"No room for maybe, Will."

Chapter 43: Double Double-E

Will ran through the hallway of the *Cybersleuths, Inc.* offices pounding on doors and yelling, "Big emergency, everyone. I need you all right away. Hank's office, now." He took a breath and shouted, "Please!"

A few minutes later his team once again was gathered around the table in Hank Cotter's office.

"What's the emergency?" said Hank.

Will was breathless, as much from the anxiety building in his chest as from his quick sprint from office to office.

"Tomorrow," he gasped, shaking his outstretched hands in the air. "We only have until tomorrow. If we don't do something to protect Jenkins the Russians might kill him. Tomorrow!"

"Calm down, Will," said Cotter. "What do you mean? What's going on tomorrow?"

Will lowered his hands and placed them palms-down on the table, then took a deep breath and hesitated for a moment. He shook his head slowly, a look of desperation on his face, and said, "It's my FBI contact, I just spoke with her. Jenkins is holding a big public rally tomorrow and refuses to call it off. He'll be a sitting duck for the hacker."

"He's had lots of public appearances—why do you think tomorrow is so important? Do you know for sure something is going to happen then?"

Another deep breath. "No, not absolutely sure, but the timing is right, the odds are they'll do something tomorrow. It's his last appearance before the convention, so if the Russians want to stop him from getting nominated, they have to strike tomorrow. His pacemaker is an old model, easily compromised, and they're going to replace it with a much more secure one. It'll be much harder to hack into the new one. But he absolutely refuses to go into the hospital for the procedure until after the convention. So everything points to tomorrow, that's their last window of opportunity to hack into the old pacemaker. FBI, Secret Service, they all agree that tomorrow could be D-Day."

"What about at the convention? Couldn't the Russians get someone in there?"

"Possibly, but the delegates are vetted thoroughly. Much easier to get an assassin into a public rally."

"And they can't stop him from holding the rally?"

"It's his call unless they are very sure that he's about to be attacked. This rally is a big deal, thousands of people in his hometown. Jenkins is absolutely adamant, he won't budge at all."

"This is crazy, Will. How much time do we have?"

"It's four o'clock now, we only have until noon tomorrow."

"Not much time. Just what do you hope to do between now and then?"

"We have to find a way to save Jenkins. The most important thing is figuring out a way to block the hacker's signal from getting to his pacemaker. And, if at all possible, we'd also like to detect where the signal's coming from so we can identify the killer. I mean, whoever is behind this has killed at least a dozen people so far."

"So let me get this straight—you want to block a sophisticated piece of equipment but you have no idea how it works, and find some killer who you don't know anything about in a huge crowd, and do both at the same time?" Lauren Sveiks was incredulous.

Will nodded. "I know, it sounds impossible. But we have no options."

Ned Hall chimed in. "Why do you think the killer will show up in person? Can't they send the signal from some remote site?"

"We don't think that's possible. Jenkins has a common type of pacemaker that doesn't send or receive signals over a long distance. It communicates via radio frequency signals with a home monitor. The monitor then reads the data from the pacemaker and transmits it over a Wi-Fi network or phone line to the physician. That's how the doctor keeps track of how well the device is working. That's also how the manufacturer can send software or firmware updates."

"So a hacker needs to be fairly close by to interfere with the pacemaker. How close is close enough?"

"That's a big question. Truth is, we aren't sure. Most of the lab tests on hacking have been done at short distances, but highly sophisticated intercept equipment might be able to create interference from hundreds of feet away."

"What exactly does the hacker do, anyway?"

Belinda Winnisome answered: "Jenkins' pacemaker and defibrillator is vulnerable to external attack via radiofrequency interference. Older medical devices like his were not designed to meet the newer international electro-technical standards for devices implanted in humans. The hacker creates an electromagnetic disturbance that interferes with the performance of the device."

"Ah," said Ned, "The electrical engineer in Belinda speaks. And for us non-technical folks without a double-e degree like you and Will?"

"The assassin has a transmitter that sends a signal to the pacemaker that shuts it down."

"Simple enough, thanks. So what do we need to do to protect him?"

"Two things," replied Will. "As I said, we need to block the hacker's signal from getting to his pacemaker. We also want to track the signal back to the killer. I think of this in fairly simple terms, things we're all familiar with. We need something that works like noise-cancelling headphones to jam the deadly incoming signal, and something like the find-my-iPhone app to locate the killer. I have no idea how either of those work, but that's the way I think of it. Am I making sense, Belinda?"

"Yup, perfectly clear."

As Belinda spoke her cheeks drew back slightly into a faint smile that seemed to signal that she and Will were in lock-step, communicating on their private channel—at least, that's what Will read from her look since he had seen the same expression on Barry's face countless times. He sucked in a breath through his teeth and said, "Ah...thanks, Belinda. Tell me, how are you on practical things, like actually putting together the equipment we could use? I know the theory but I was never great in the labs."

"I love to tinker!" she said, this time with a big smile for all to see. "Seriously, I'm pretty good with my hands, loved to put together basic computers with my dad when I was a little kid. All depends on getting the specs, and then I'll know if it's something I can build."

"Great. So, maybe we should start by contacting the manufacturer and double-check on whether there's a way to reprogram Jenkins' pacemaker so it can't be hacked. I'm doubtful that's possible, given that the doctors think the old model he has needs to be replaced to make it more secure. But hopefully they can provide some useful information about the signals that the device responds to and help us devise a way to recognize and jam an incoming one."

"I'll be happy to make the call with you if you'd like."

"That would be great, thanks."

"How about the rest of us?" asked Ned.

"We'll need everybody, there's a lot to be done and no time to do it in. Just to be clear—we need to design and construct two pieces of equipment, one to block signals from disabling Jenkins' pacemaker and another to track incoming signals and locate the source."

"That's a lot on such short notice," said Ned.

"Yes," said Hank Cotter, "but if that's what we have to do, we'll give it our best effort, however impossible it might seem. OK, we'll need some supplies if we're going to build working models of whatever design Will and Belinda come up with. Ned, you go down to our technical shop and see what hardware they have in stock that could be useful. Tell them I said to give you whatever you want, and to be ready to pull an all-nighter. Nobody's going home. We'll also need some pacemakers like the one that Jenkins has so we can run tests on our gizmos after we piece them together. Lauren, see if you can track down some of those devices from the local hospitals."

"Thanks, Hank," said Will, his voice quavering. "And thanks, all of you. I don't mind telling you that I'm getting very nervous—what we're up against is really starting to come home to me. Figuring out what might work and coming up with a workable design normally could take weeks, let alone putting something together and testing it. But we don't have weeks or even days, we've just got a few hours. We're pretty far up a creek and I'm not sure we're going to find a paddle."

"Hey, we can do this. You have to believe," said Belinda.

Will stared at her and nodded, but could not respond. Her words and the expression on her face precisely echoed Barry's way of supporting Will through difficult moments. Will shuddered, unable to think or move.

Mercifully, Hank Cotter broke the spell and released Will from the paralyzing vision, saying, "OK, everyone, get to work. There's a lot at stake. The odds are against us, and we may come up short, but let's give it our best shot."

At last Will found his voice. "Belinda, let's go down to my office and call the manufacturer from there. Ned, go ahead down to the shop. And Lauren, start tracking down those devices, please."

Once he and Belinda were in his office, Will pulled a chair up to the opposite side of the desk and said, "OK if you sit here and we make the call on the landline?"

"Sure."

"Would you mind taking the lead? I think you'd handle the call better than I would."

"Happy to. I'll put it on speaker."

"Good idea."

He slid the desk phone in front of Belinda. She logged onto her smart phone and after a few seconds said, "Found it, here goes." She dialed a number on the desk set and they both listened, first to the dial tone, then to the ring tone, and as soon as the call connected, to a computerized voice that said to hang up and call your doctor or dial 9-1-1 or go to an emergency room if you were calling about a problem with an implanted device. When the warnings ended the voice began a litany of all the reasons why the caller should go to the company's website instead of waiting for one of their busy agents to speak on the phone, followed by options on a telephone tree that offered no guidance on what to do if the call was about a threat to someone who might be the next President of the United States of America.

"Useless!" said Will. "Total waste of time. Time we don't have."

Belinda started typing on her smart phone again, then said, "Here's something—I got the name of the CEO of the company that manufactured Jenkins' pacemaker. I'll track him down."

The afternoon dragged on into evening. Will searched on-line fervently for the pacemaker's detailed specifications, at last abandoning the effort after deciding that the manufacturer had encrypted the information beyond the reach of even someone with his advanced cyber skills. He found himself checking the time every few minutes, growing more and more anxious with every passing second.

Then things began to improve: after one hour and twenty-four minutes of dogged persistence, Belinda was at last speaking with the CEO, whom she had tracked down at his summer home in the Hamptons. Once she managed to impress the man with the urgency of the situation—without disclosing that she was attempting to avert an assassination—he referred her to the technical director of the pacemaker division of the company. Another grueling hour of dead-end phone calls passed before Belinda connected with her. Will listened as the technical director confirmed that no, it was not possible to reprogram Jenkins' pacemaker, it would have to be replaced. Belinda then asked her a series of technical questions, wrote down two pages of notes, and was promised a number of links to unencrypted industrial manuals with wiring maps and detailed specifications.

"Amazing, Belinda, great work," said Will when she hung up the phone.

As they awaited the email with the links he continued watching the time slip away, now growing frustrated as well as nervous—hours had passed, he had contributed practically nothing, and they still had no idea when they would finally build and test the critical equipment they needed. Inside his shirt he felt cold sweat running down his sides from his armpits.

When the email arrived Belinda said, "How about I forward you one set of links and you can connect to them on your computer, and I'll go to my own office and run through the others?"

Will didn't like the idea of being separated from Belinda—her presence took the edge off his mounting anxiety. But he knew that dividing things up was the most efficient way to work. "OK," he agreed reluctantly, "but let me know as soon as you find anything."

For the next ninety minutes Will sweated more and more as he followed up blind link after blind link—tons of technical information on various pacemakers from that manufacturer but nothing that was exactly what they needed. The situation seemed hopeless—too complicated, too little time.

Will was just about to scream in frustration when Belinda burst into his office carrying her laptop computer. "Got it," she said, triumphantly, clearing a space for her laptop on Will's desk. "Look at this: it's the manual for Jenkins' pacemaker, with the specs we've been looking for and the wiring diagrams."

Will looked over Belinda's shoulder and let his scream of frustration come out as a cry of joy: "*Ahhhhh*, fantastic!"

"Let's split the stuff up so both of us can wade through it."

"Fine. You focus on the wiring diagrams and I'll take the specs."

Will went back to his monitor and began scrolling through sheet after sheet of specifications. After about twenty minutes he called out, "It's good—everything we need should be here. When you're finished with the wiring diagrams we can decide whether we've got enough to build something. You keep working on the wiring while I go check on Lauren and Ned. Give me a holler if you need anything."

Will ran down the hall to Lauren's office. She sat her desk and was hanging up the telephone just as he barged in and said, breathlessly, "How's it going?"

"Started pretty slow, but I finally got something. I called seventeen hospitals and found four that have samples of the pacemaker in stock. They're happy to let us send a courier to collect them since the devices are out of date and were about to be returned to the manufacturer anyway."

"Great. Have you sent someone to get them yet?"

"Yup, that the was the call I was finishing just now when you came in."

"OK, let me know as soon as they get here."

Will flew down a flight of stairs to the workshop where he found Ned rummaging through heavy file boxes stacked on industrial-strength metal shelves. "Find anything?"

"Just finished rummaging through our inventory. I managed to pull out some things I think might work." He stepped back and gestured to two mail carts laden with a variety of electronic equipment and boxes of spare parts. "I was just about to come up and show you. You wheel one cart and I'll take the other."

"Let's go."

As the two men waited for the freight elevator, Will looked at his watch: 2:30 in the morning. Nine-and-a-half hours until the rally. He felt his heart racing and couldn't catch his breath. They were running out of time, they weren't going to make it, Jenkins was going to die. Then his panic suddenly got even more acute:. "Omigod," he cried out, "we don't have nine-and-a-half hours. Paradise Valley is in suburban Maryland, it's over an hour away without any traffic. It could take twice that long with the rally. We're screwed, Ned, totally screwed." He pounded on the elevator door as if that would make it move faster. When the door finally opened he said, "Hurry up, get in. I've got to get hold of Hank."

As soon as they pushed the carts into his office, Will buzzed Hank Cotter's office. "Hank, we need help," he blurted into the phone.

"What is it Will? What help?"

"Hank, this is taking way longer than I had hoped. We're running out of time, we don't even have a prototype yet of either the signal tracker or the jamming device. We're going to need every minute and we can't risk getting caught in traffic. Can you get a helicopter to fly us up to the rally?"

"I have no idea, Will, but I'll see what I can do."

"Thanks, Hank," he said, and abruptly disconnected the phone. He turned to Belinda and said, "Are you ready to get going with building something?"

"Almost. I need to finish my designs."

Another endless half hour crept by before she said, "OK, let's do this." As Ned and Lauren watched, she told Will what equipment she had in mind. "Will, you take that cart, I'll go through this one."

They began pulling electronic equipment helter-skelter out of the baskets of the mail carts and tossing them onto Will's desk or the floor. When Belinda saw a thick tablet computer she said, "Bingo! That's one." At almost the same moment Will spotted a large black metal box in the lower basket of the other cart. When he reached to grab the instrument he saw that his hands were shaking.

"OK, that's the other one," he said, struggling to keep his voice from breaking. "Now let's see if we can make them both do something they were never intended to do!"

Will took another glance at the clock: 3 AM. Now his forehead was as wet as his armpits. He looked at Belinda and steeled himself to ask the question he wasn't sure he wanted the answer to. "So, what do you think?" His voice was quavering. "Are these going to do the trick?"

"I'd give it 50-50," she said.

Chapter 44: Attack

The fifteen thousand people packed elbow-to-elbow in the hot June sun were growing restless waiting for the guest of honor to arrive. They were drenched in sweat and weary after standing for endless hours, tired of hearing the Jefferson High School band pound out its repertoire of John Philip Sousa marches over and over, and had long since tuned out to the endless parade of minor local officials boasting about their pet projects. And on top of their growing impatience a palpable edginess began to spread through the crowd as people realized that, in addition to a heightened police presence, a small army of men and women in dark suits with curly black wires running from their ears were looking directly at each of them one-by-one, constantly scanning their faces with suspicious eyes.

Some four hours before Colonel Robin Jenkins was scheduled to address the gathering, a tall, thin man with a dark beard had arrived at the entrance to the Paradise Valley Memorial Bandshell. Iosef Vladimirovich Dorofeyev stood patiently waiting in line as the crowd passed slowly through security. The spectators were admitted one at a time into the controlled space between two newly-erected rows of chain-line fencing that now encircled the park. Each person in turn emptied their bags and pockets into bins that were fed on conveyor belts through the X-ray machines, then walked through metal detectors, collected their belongings, and waited to be cleared to enter the Bandshell grounds. Neither human eyes nor the screening equipment detected any difference between Iosef's small black device and the countless mobile phones that had preceded it. But no pictures would be taken with his device, and no phone calls made. It had only one function: to end Colonel Jenkins' presidential campaign prematurely.

Iosef scanned the grounds and noted that in addition to the usual uniformed security guards who looked like TSA agents in airports there were several additional layers. Men and women in dark suits, curly wires running from their ears, chests bulging with weapons and Kevlar vests under their jackets. SWAT Police wearing flak jackets over their uniforms and carrying assault weapons that reminded him of Russian AK-47s. He glanced up and saw people walking back and forth across the roofs of the surrounding buildings; probably snipers, he concluded. And as he was looking up he spotted a reflection of sunlight off of a stationary object far above them—a drone, he thought. An observation drone, or was it also weaponized?

He scoffed at the heavy security. What good was an army if they did not know he was there? He would just be one man among many thousands holding a mobile phone, snapping photos, sending texts and Tweets. Once he entered the fatal code into his transmitter, Colonel Jenkins would collapse suddenly and no one would have any idea what had happened to him. There would be no noise, no gunman for the crowd or the Cossacks to capture, no indication that Jenkins had been assassinated. The crowd would go wild with confusion, the security guards would be stunned and have no idea what action to take, his attendants would rush to start emergency procedures trying to save his life. No one would notice Iosef Vladimirovich Dorofeyev quietly leaving the grounds, soon to be on his way back to a hero's welcome in Moscow.

Neither Iosef nor anyone else in the crowd had paid attention to the tall, lanky redhead who held what looked like a thick iPad as he maneuvered swiftly through the growing throng of Jenkins supporters. Will Manningham glanced back and forth repeatedly between the screen of his device and the faces in the crowd. The screen displayed ever-widening concentric circles radiating out from his position and bright green dots like blips on a radar screen. He did not know anything about the person he was looking for—short or tall, man or woman, old or young—not a clue. All he knew was that his device was scanning the airwaves for an aberrant pattern, a signal that would interfere with Jenkins' pacemaker and kill him immediately.

Adrienne Penscal was close on Will's heels, her hand on her 9 millimeter Glock17, her trained eyes searching the crowd for any signs of suspicious behavior. Suddenly her grip tightened on the handle of her weapon—she saw a dark-haired man feverishly poking at his cell phone, clearly agitated that it was not responding the way he wanted it to. "Will," she called out, "over there." She ran over to the man and shouted, "FBI. Hands up, drop the phone!" The man's head jerked back in terror and the phone fell from his hand, shattering as it hit the ground.

"Daddy!" howled a little girl, pointing at the ground. "You broke my phone, you broke my phone!"

"Please, please," cried the man, his arms raised high above his head, "it's my daughter's phone, it wasn't working. She's been bugging me about it all morning and I can't get it to work—no signal."

Will picked up the phone, looked it over quickly, and said, "It's just a phone, Adrienne. No problem."

"Thank you sir," said Adrienne. "You can give your daughter back her phone. Just being careful. Have a nice day."

Will and Adrienne resumed their search, moving systematically along the lines of spectators, starting from the people jammed against the barriers at the front and working their way deeper into the throng row-by-row. Will double-checked that the supplemental power pack was still attached to his instrument and that it showed a full charge. The screen continued to show the concentric circles and pinpoint green blips, but nothing unusual appeared. Will was growing increasingly tense—what if he did not detect the deadly signal in time?

At last it was showtime. Maryland Governor Francis X. Lenoir walked to the center of the stage in front of heavy curtains and said, "MY FELLOW DEMOCRATS, join me in welcoming THE NEXT PRESIDENT OF THE UNITED STATES OF AMERICA, OUR OWN FAVORITE SON, A TRUE AMERICAN HERO, COLONEL ROBIN W. JENKINS!"

The curtains opened to reveal a thick plexiglass cylinder twelve feet high with a curved front and a domed roof. The crowd screamed in delight when Robin Washington Jenkins appeared inside the containment capsule. He skipped gracefully up the three steps of the podium to the lectern, grinning from ear to ear and waving his upraised right hand briskly. When he reached the bank of microphones he leaned forward and asked, "What do you think? Are we going to win?"

The crowd roared its approval, chanting "Jenkins! Jenkins!" until he quieted them again.

"I can understand your excitement. I share it, you know I do. We've all had a deeply unsettling four years. All of us, the people of the United States who really care about this country, are desperate for relief. We've had enough of that guy—you know who I mean."

The crowd went wild with catcalls and booing as Colonel Robin W. Jenkins, their hero, castigated the incumbent president. "I am ready to answer your call," he said. "That avaricious, foulmouthed, ill-tempered man cares only about himself, not about you and not about this wonderful country. We will restore the rule of law in an even and fair-handed way. We will hold him and his corrupt gang accountable for their crimes. We will right their grievous wrongs."

Robin Jenkins was ready to take the reins. The populace was desperate to be rid of President Dorzel. All that remained was for him to lock up the nomination and live through election day.

Iosef Vladimirovich Dorofeyev laughed when he saw the containment capsule. Such a foolish waste, he thought with smug satisfaction, knowing that it could not filter out his radio frequency waves. The deadly weapon that he held in his hands would be unaffected by the plexiglass barrier. A dozen bodies testified that his system was perfect, infallible. Iosef savored the moment. In less than a minute the threat to President Dorzel would be over. Colonel Jenkins would collapse, writhe in a grand mal seizure, then go limp as the life drained out of his body. No one could save him now.

Looking for all the world like a man innocently placing a call on his mobile phone, Iosef typed on the keyboard and pressed the "send" button. He watched and waited. Waited and watched. Nothing happened. He sucked in his breath—what could be wrong? There had never been a delay before, not once in twelve times. Had he entered the wrong code? He typed the numbers carefully, hit "send" again, and stared in disbelief as Colonel Jenkins continued speaking and opened his arms to thank the crowd for its support. He tried a third time, keeping his finger down on the "send" button. Still nothing. Then he panicked. Failure could mean the end of his own life. Or worse. His skin tingled, his bowels churned in pain, his hands trembled.

Iosef did not have long to agonize over his fate. A very tall man with bright red hair burst through the crowd and ran up to him pointing and yelling, "Here he is, here! The guy with the beard." Almost as soon as the words came out of Will Manningham's mouth,

Special Agent Adrienne Penscal tackled Iosef, wrested what looked like a cell phone out of his hands, and threw the bearded man to the ground. Instantly a phalanx of a half-dozen heavily armed men and women swarmed over him. Will picked up the device and entered a series of keystrokes, then watched it go dark. He turned to Adrienne and said, "It's off, it's off." She hugged him reflexively, then let loose quickly and held open a plastic bag. She said, "Here, Will. Evidence bag. Drop it in here."

By now the bearded man was face-down on the ground, his wrists handcuffed behind his back, agents patting him down to check for weapons more rudimentary than the one he had thought could not fail. With a heavy Russian accent he screamed, "No! No! This is impossible, this cannot be."

"Ah, but it is possible," said Adrienne, "and it is happening." She bent down to the agents holding the man and said, "Pick him up and get him out of here. Take him to the van and then to the basement of Hoover." As the tight circle of agents with their prisoner in the center burrowed through the throng of Jenkins supporters, Adrienne smiled at Will, resisted the urge to hug him a second time, and said, "Good job, Will. Mission accomplished."

Back at FBI headquarters Denise Washington, Fred Renford, Tom Murphy and Fran Trainor joined Will and Adrienne in her office. Tom Murphy popped open a bottle of champagne, prompting a smiling Fran Trainor to say, "That's strictly forbidden on federal property, Special Agent Murphy. You have just committed a federal crime."

"So arrest me, Special Agent Trainor," he replied, handing her his handcuffs. He filled six plastic water glasses with the bubbly.

"You'd better pour another," said Adrienne. "Chief Hollingshead will be here any second."

Murphy blanched momentarily, then went pink and said, "For real?"

"Yes, but don't worry. He won't arrest you."

"Or fire you," came the unmistakable voice of Chief Garry Hollingshead. Adrienne had not noticed that their boss was already standing in the doorway. "Unless you don't pour me one, that is."

After a round of toasts Denise Washington said, "OK, Will, now you have to tell us how you did it. You only found out last night that the event was going ahead today. How did you manage to stop whatever was supposed to happen?"

"I knew you were good at computers," added Tom Murphy, "but I didn't know you were also an electrical engineer."

"Well, yeah, I am, but this was a real team effort. Turns out one of my colleagues at *Cybersleuths, Inc.*, Belinda Winnisome, is also a double-e and she's really skilled at building things. She managed to track down the technical specs on Jenkins' device from the manufacturer. Once she had that information she came up with the idea of reconfiguring one of our powerful tablet computers as a tracking device and figured out how to reprogram it to identify suspicious signals and pinpoint the source. The last piece was to design and piece together a jamming device to block any incoming signals. Fortunately another colleague had located just the right pieces of spare equipment for Belinda to repurpose. Another colleague managed to locate samples of the same pacemaker as Jenkins has and collected them from a couple of local hospitals. We used them to test our prototypes. We only finished testing this morning and took a helicopter up to the rally."

"So the tests were positive? You knew Jenkins would be safe?"

Will smile sheepishly. "Frankly, no. We weren't sure it would all work even down to the last second, but we had no choice other than to give it a try. Fortunately, it did. When we got to the rally we put the transmitter sitting right next to the podium and counted on it to create interference that would block the hacker's signal. Then I went running around looking for the source of a signal on the pacemaker's wave length. We hoped the signal blocker would protect Jenkins even if we couldn't spot the hacker."

"If I'd known you were so unsure," said Chief Hollingshead, "I would have cancelled the rally at the last minute."

"Really?" said Will. "Jenkins would have been seriously pissed...whoops, sorry Chief, pardon my language."

Hollingshead took a long sip of champagne and laughed. "Yes, he certainly would have been pissed. But we would have had no choice. All I say is, I'm glad it was the one and only Will Manningham that we were relying on."

"Thank you for that note of confidence, Chief, but as I said, I had a lot of help."

"You're too modest, Will. Now, I believe Special Agent Penscal has something to tell you that you should find of interest."

All eyes turned toward Adrienne. "The would-be assassin is Iosef Vladimirovich Dorofeyev, an electrical engineer from Moscow, turned serial killer. He arrived in the States a few months ago on a tourist visa—just before the string of unexplained deaths started. It's a great relief to have caught him, but he's not the only one we've taken into custody. We also collared Alexandra Parushnikova and her handler, one Leonid Denisovich Arkady. Turns out we do have an operative at Bar Natasha and she saw Parushnikova and Arkady together there not long ago. She also spotted Dorofeyev in the booth next to them. He left before they did, but she was able to identify him. We put a tail on Arkady and nabbed him before he could find out that their plot had failed and Dorofeyev had been arrested. Then we went and got Parushnikova."

"So, what happens next?"

"We're already hearing rumblings that Dorzel wants to pardon all three of them."

"Maybe Dorzel would keep Parushnikova in prison if he could make conjugal visits," quipped Tom Murphy, to a chorus of laughter.

"In all seriousness," said Chief Hollingshead, "the abuse of presidential pardons is most troublesome. But there may be a way around the pardons. The local District Attorney is charging the three of them with multiple counts of murder and one count of attempted murder under state law, which should preclude a federal pardon. But we'll have to see—the president has other tools at his disposal, and the three Russians are currently under his control in federal custody."

"They should ship them all to Guantanamo," said Fred Renford.

"The Jenkins people have requested that we not say anything publicly about the attempted assassination," said Chief Hollingshead. "They don't want Dorzel to start complaining that Jenkins is getting some kind of advantage from a sympathy vote. Oh, there's one more thing that has to remain completely confidential: the cardiologists at Walter Reed are going to do something with Jenkins' pacemaker that will make it less vulnerable to hacking. OK, everyone, you deserve a break. Go home and enjoy yourselves."

Will took a deep breath and exhaled. He felt gratified that Robin Jenkins was safe, yet he had a distinct feeling that things would not end on a happy note.

Chapter 45: Endgames

Election night turned out to have both good news and bad news as far as Will and Sally were concerned. The good news was that Hugo H. Dorzel was soundly trounced by Colonel Robin W. Jenkins, who swept into office with a margin of almost ten million in the popular vote and 289 of the 538 votes in the Electoral College for a comfortable, if not overwhelming, majority. And Jenkins' coattails were strong enough to eek out a 50-50 tie in the Senate, where Jenkins' Vice President, who was not Annabaker Minion, could cast tiebreaking votes. The Democrats were also on track to garner a 232-203 margin in the House of Representatives.

"That's it, Honey, we're back to normal," crowed Will as they saw the final results come in about 1 AM and clicked champagne flutes. "Maybe now we'll be able fight the crooks instead of taking orders from them."

"Don't be so glib," said Sally. "It'll take some time to get things back on track. And no matter how you look at it, we're not exactly a united country. There will be a lot of Dorzel supporters who aren't going to take this lightly."

"Aw, rain on my parade, why don't you? But, unfortunately, you're right, there's more than to healing the country than one election. That's what troubles me the most, that so many people in this country could idolize a man who's blatantly incompetent and, seriously, has no redeeming social value whatsoever. I mean, he's, let's see, misogynistic, xenophobic, avaricious, capricious, volatile, mendacious—what the hell, I could go on and on describing how awful Dorzel is."

"Wow, what a run of ten-dollar words! Not that Dorzel would actually understand any of them, but they're all spot on. Actually, I think it's even worse: to me, it's not that they idolize him *despite* his incredible shortcomings, it's that they idolize him *precisely because* he is all of those things, and unabashedly so."

"All too true, unfortunately. Makes me wonder if Dorzel dragged this country down to his level or just exposed who we really are."

"Dismal thought, Honey. Don't let it keep you from enjoying the result. We've still got a tough road ahead but it sure feels a lot better tonight than it did four years ago."

"No argument there. My god, what an awful night that was."

They clinked champagne glasses one more time. Then the bad news came.

Will was surfing the news channels just before heading to bed when he heard a broadcaster say, "And in other news, we've just learned that the soon-to-be outgoing Dorzel Administration has issued 130 pardons and another 247 orders of clemency. We haven't had time to review them all but some of the names are ones we are quite familiar with, people Mr. Dorzel has had business and personal relationships with for many years. The White House acknowledged that Mr. Dorzel did not follow the long-established procedures for reviewing pardons and clemency petitions, but explained that he was determined to, as they put it, 'see justice carried out before it was too late.' On a different matter, we have also learned that a Russian woman widely reported to be involved romantically with the president has disappeared, along with two of her associates. All three were facing state criminal charges including multiple counts of first-degree murder, but they had remained in federal custody for the past five months while the Russian government claimed that they were entitled to diplomatic immunity. Sources close to the situation, who spoke with us anonymously because they are not authorized to discuss the matter, told us that the three Russians had been in the process of being transferred to state custody when they disappeared. There is speculation that they are on their way to Russia but we have not yet been able to confirm their whereabouts."

"Holy shit," yelled Will. "No way! That son of a bitch. Those three are flat-out nothing but murderers. Dorzel's letting them go back to Russia! Goddamn it all."

"Calm down, Honey. I know it must hurt for yet another gang of Russian crooks to escape scot free after all your work. But at least you stopped them from killing Colonel Jenkins. And," she said, lifting one eyebrow and smirking coyly, "maybe life won't be so rosy for those three when they get back home, huh?"

Will nodded. "You could be right. The Russians don't take kindly to failure. I only hope I never have to deal with any of them again."

Will was not to get his wish. As he and Sally headed toward their bedroom he heard his phone buzzing in his jacket pocket. "Dang," he said, "I forgot to turn that thing off. You go ahead, I'll silence it." Will shook his head when he saw that the caller ID read "Number Blocked." He hesitated, then touched the green button to accept the call.

"Yes?"

"Will. It's Adrienne. I need you to meet me right away."

"Adrienne, it's almost 2 in the morning and, well, we've been celebrating. This was a really uplifting night—at least until I heard about our three friends disappearing."

"That's why I need to see you. Now."

"OK, if you say so. Let me tell Sally and I'll catch a cab."

"Tell her you're leaving but don't say anything else. Nothing. And don't bother with a cab, there's a car on the way to pick you up."

"*What?* What's this about?"

"Three minutes, max."

"OK."

Will was about to explain to Sally when she took one look at him and shook her head. "Don't tell me. Something's up and you're going out, right?"

"You are just as smart as you are sexy."

"Cut the crap. Don't forget, Metro's shut down by now."

"I know. Someone's picking me up."

"Some mysterious Russian blonde?"

"Ha! Nothing that exciting. I'll text you when I'm on my way home."

One quick kiss and Will ran out the front door to wait for his ride. But the oversized black Suburban was already double-parked in the street, engine running. As soon as Will came down the walkway the rear door opened and Adrienne said, "Get in, quick."

Will ducked his head to climb into the back seat and froze: Sally had been right after all. The mysterious Russian blonde was scrunched down in the third row.

Chapter 46: Sasha

Will shook his head in disbelief and didn't move. Fred Renford's powerful arms grabbed Will's jacket and pulled him into the big car, then Renford reached over and pulled the door shut as Tom Murphy slammed the accelerator to the floor.

"What...what on earth, Adrienne? What the hell is going on?"

"We'll tell you when we get to your office."

"My office! Why *my* office?"

"We need a secure location."

"The Hoover Building isn't secure?"

"The Hoover Building is federal property. You have your keys with you?"

"Yes, but all I need is my fingerprint. Adrienne..."

"Just wait. We have a lot to do tonight, and I only want to go through this once."

The streets on Capitol Hill were jammed with revelers, thousands of people setting off fireworks and brazenly violating the District's open container liquor law. The Suburban inched through the crowd and pulled to a stop in front of the *Cybersleuths, Inc.* brownstone. Will jumped out and walked up to the front door, touched the doorbell sensor with his finger, and pulled the door open. Fred Renford was right behind Will. Fran Trainor and Denise Washington emerged from the rear of the Suburban, their arms tight around a woman with a shawl over her head. Adrienne followed close behind. Tom Murphy, walking backward, trailed the group, scanning the surrounding area, his hand at waist-level inside his unbuttoned coat.

When they had settled in Will's office Adrienne said, "OK, Will, thanks. I knew we could count on you."

"Count on me for what, Adrienne? Tell me what the hell we're doing here."

"I believe you know Ms. Alexandra Parushnikova."

"Of course. Well, I know who she is, but we haven't actually met." He looked at Sasha and nodded.

Sasha pulled off the shawl, combed her hair with her fingers, and said, "Yes. I also know you Mr. Manningham. Thank you, thank you so very…" Her voice trailed off.

Denise Washington put a hand gently on the Russian's shoulder and said, "It's OK, you're safe here."

"Please, continue, Ms. Parushnikova. We need to hear what you want from us."

"I am a dead woman if I go back to Russia. Please, I cannot go back. My mother…they have already…"

"What about your mother. Please, do your best."

Will took a bottle of water from a cabinet and handed it to her. "Maybe this will help," he said.

"Thank you," she said, twisting off the cap and taking a long drink. She set down the water bottle and took a deep breath that she let out with an audible sigh. "My mother is dead. She was taken from her home by the Security Service. They told me that she would be held until I was back in the country, then she would be released. But I have heard from…from a friend, someone who knows that she is dead. Her heart gave out soon after she was taken."

"Our condolences for your loss. I must ask, who was your source?"

"Just a friend. Please, that is all I can say. She is the only friend I have in that country. Please." Sasha was terrified that if she mentioned Valeria Klara her name might somehow get back to the Security Service.

"We understand. Please, continue, what matters is that you are confident that you know the truth about what happened to your mother."

"My friend would never deceive me. You will let me stay here? You will not send me back?"

"If you provide information that is useful we will see what we can do. But you must tell us what you know before we can make any promises."

Tom Murphy chimed in. "After tonight's election we are hopeful that we will no longer have to be so, eh, so friendly with the Russians."

"Exactly," said Adrienne. "OK, tell us what you know that you think will be useful."

"That man, Dorzel. He is no longer powerful?"

"He's still president for about another two months, but then he will be a private citizen."

"He is disgusting, a horrible man. I never want to see him again."

"That much we can assure you of."

"I was required to...to let him have his way with me. I cannot tell you how much I suffered. I..."

"He is no threat to you now. We are on private property in the District of Columbia. He has no power over you here."

Will was beginning to get the picture. Sasha would be in danger as long as Dorzel was still in office. He could use her as a pawn to gain some advantage for himself from the Russians. Anything was possible with that man.

"Thank you, thank you so much."

"Tell us what you know about him, and anything else you think we would be interested in. The guards at the federal penitentiary who brought you to us said that you told them you had important information for us."

"I will tell you everything. I was sent to this country on an assignment from the Russian Security Service. I..."

Adrienne interrupted Sasha. "We know quite a bit about you from our own sources. Tell us about Dorzel."

"Your new president, the man Jenkins who was elected tonight?"

"Yes?"

"The Russian Security Service, they had some secret weapon. Dorzel asked them to help him with Mr. Jenkins and I was sent to make sure he would understand that they would take action against Jenkins."

"That is an extremely serious accusation, especially against the president. No offense, Ms. Parushnikova, but we cannot just take your word for it, we need some hard evidence. Can you prove that he was behind the attempt on Colonel Jenkins?"

She pointed to her wristwatch. "This little watch is a recording device given to me by the Security Service. I was ordered to record our conversations. I have his very words right here." She reached into her bra and removed a small thumb drive. "Here, I made a copy of the recording."

Adrienne's eyes opened wider than Will had ever seen them as Sasha handed her the thumb drive. She said, "Will, do you have something we can play this on?"

"Of course, my computer. Hand it to me."

He inserted the thumb drive into a USB port on his computer. The screen of his monitor lit up with a black box with a triangle in the center. "Ready? Here goes." He clicked on the triangle and the group listened in utter astonishment as the words of the President of the United States came through the speakers:

"Yeah, yeah, I know. We gotta go ahead, tell them to go ahead if they're ready. That guy, Jenkins. If they don't do something I won't be around here anymore."

They played the recording four times, then Adrienne said to Sasha, "And you would testify to this in a court of law?"

"Would that be required?"

"If we are to protect you, yes."

"Then I will do it. I will do whatever I need to."

Adrienne turned to her team. "We need to bring in the District Attorney. This is a bit ambiguous but if they can show that Dorzel knew what the Russians were up to, it might be enough to tie him to the attempt on Jenkins. And maybe to the twelve other deaths. Those would all be crimes under state law. Even if Dorzel were to resign at the last minute and cut a pardon deal with the interim president he couldn't escape state charges. The prosecutor might want to hold off filing charges until Jenkins is sworn in, but that's not our decision."

She turned back to Sasha. "If what you tell us can be proved we will be able to protect you, for sure."

"I will not go to jail?"

"No, you will be granted immunity. Is that everything?"

She shook her head, then said, "No, not everything. There is more, much more. But...I will have a new, as you say, a new identify?"

"Yes, that is the only way we can be sure you will be safe."

"I know many other things I can tell you. Russian agents. Spies. In your government. I know many names. I will tell you everything."

Adrienne smiled broadly. "That is very important. If you provide us with information about the Russian Security Service and give us the names of their operatives, then we will have a reason to keep you under federal protection. For the rest of your life."

Will was overcome with the urge to see whether this woman could be helpful in a very different way. "Adrienne, if you don't mind," he said, then turned to Sasha. "Ms. Parushnikova, I would like to know if you can provide me with information on certain other matters that involve the Russians."

Adrienne knew what Will was getting at. The Russians who had escaped after killing his brother. The ones behind the black market in counterfeit drugs and medical supplies that Parushnikova herself had been involved in. "All in good time, Will," Adrienne said softly, but firmly. "All in good time." Then she looked at her team and said, "OK, guys, we need to get her to a safe house. Denise, you make the calls, please."

"Sure, Boss. I'm on it. Will—may I use your phone?"

"Good thinking, Denise," said Adrienne. "Best not to use yours just now."

Will said, "Of course, go ahead." He looked at his watch. Four-thirty in the morning. He was already in his office, he might as well doze off on the couch for a few hours and get an early start. He had a lot of questions he wanted to prepare for Alexandra Parushnikova. As he thought about what he needed to do, a familiar dialogue with Barry popped into his head:

"It's not over 'till it's over," Will would say.

Barry would reply, "It's never over."

"Yeah," Will said to the lingering specter of his brother. "It's never over."

Epilogue

Belinda Winnisome peered at Will over her coffee cup. "So, Will, how's it been so far? Interesting first few months for you here, huh?"

"You can say that again." Will wasn't thinking about Alexandra Parushnikova, who was off somewhere beginning her new life. He figured she was probably living in someplace like Omaha or Amarillo, her hair cut short and dyed dark brown, driving a Chevy to her new job. He had finally stopped obsessing about her two accomplices who had disappeared after Dorzel turned them over to the Russians. And he wasn't thinking about how the FBI moved in on Pharma Volga the day after the inauguration of President Robin W. Jenkins and arrested four Russian operatives in D.C. and others in New York, Chicago, and Los Angeles.

What filled Will's mind were thoughts about his family. His brother and parents, all dead at the hands of the Russians. Barry, gunned down right in front of his eyes. His mother poisoned with unnecessary chemotherapy. His distraught father pining away over his losses until he gave up the will to live less than a year later. And now this woman, Belinda Winnisome. She was so much like Barry— and so much like him as well. They connected with each other, read each other's thoughts, mimicked each other's expressions. Who the hell was she?

Will had done everything he could think of to track down any possible connection between him and Belinda. He had amassed every scrap of information he could find on her and her family, had run all the analyses she had taught him. He knew who her parents were, where she had been born. He had hacked into the hospital records of her birth and seen her birth certificate. She had been born in a different city than he and his brother, but more important, she was exactly four months younger than the two of them. So she could not be a long-lost triplet that his parents had never revealed. Her transcripts showed that he and Belinda had been at Princeton in the same doctoral program but for some reason she had been several years behind him so they never crossed paths. He had constructed an extensive family tree for her family and his, going back many generations on both sides. Nothing.

Well, nothing he could make sense of, just one faint connection. Will's parents had lived in New Brunswick, New Jersey, when they were undergraduates at Rutgers, and Belinda's parents had been twenty miles away in Princeton. But that was it. Their years in New Jersey did not overlap. No shared classes between the two universities, no sports or other activities in common, no mixers. And his parents had moved far away long before either Belinda or Will and Barry had been born.

And yet, there had to be something he was missing, he was sure there had to be. He had one more idea.

"Yeah," he continued, "I guess you could call it interesting. How about you? Do you often have this much excitement at *Cybersleuths, Inc.*?"

She laughed. Barry's laugh, Will couldn't help thinking.

"Not really. I mean, we take on a bunch of complicated cases that probably have some gruesome aspects, but we usually don't have any idea how our work gets used. No hands-on involvement like this time. Anyway, was there anything in particular you wanted to chat about?"

"Just that I knew Hank Cotter from before, that's how I got here, but things got so hectic so quickly I haven't had a chance to get to know you, Lauren and Ned very well. Sally and I have been thinking of having everyone over to the house for drinks and dinner, something like that, and I wanted to see if you thought people would think that was a good idea."

"As far as I'm concerned, I think that would be great. Hard to predict for the others, we don't socialize a lot together. But there's only one way to find out—just ask."

"OK, I'll get a few dates from Sally and then see if we can round everyone up. Thanks."

"Time to get back to the grind."

"Yeah, you go ahead, I'll clean up here."

"See you later. Thanks for the coffee."

"My pleasure."

As soon as Belinda left the break room Will pushed the lid down tight on her thick paper coffee cup, and slipped it into a plastic bag he pulled out of his pocket. "This is it," he thought, "one last try." He put the bag and cup back into his pocket.

Will did not return to his office. He walked out of the brownstone and headed directly for the J. Edgar Hoover Building.

Forty-five minutes later Adrienne Penscal was shaking her head, a look of frustrated tolerance on her face. "You know, Will, this is really going way too far. I shouldn't do this, not even for you."

"But you will, won't you?"

"I said I would, so, yes. Give me the materials and open your mouth."

Will handed his friend the plastic bag with Belinda Winnisome's coffee cup and opened his mouth as directed. Adrienne swabbed the inside of his cheeks and put the swab into a plastic tube that she sealed.

"Thank you, Adrienne. You know how much this means to me."

Adrienne nodded. She knew, knew all too well. Will had been living undercover and working closely with her from the moment Barry was murdered until they had broken up the Russian gang that killed his brother and mother and destroyed his father. She had even withheld critical information from her boss to keep Will working on the case.

"I risked my career once for you, I might as well do it again. But this is it."

She did not say that she had also been struck by Will's resemblance to Belinda Winnisome and that she was feeding her own curiosity as well as his obsession.

"How long?"

"I'm doing this, but I don't dare make it a priority. Maybe a week, possibly longer depending on how busy the lab is. DNA tests are quick these days but we're doing thousands and thousands of them. You'll have to be patient."

Will sighed. "I wish you could give me the results immediately, but I understand."

Every time his phone rang over the next ten days Will looked at it expectantly, hoping the caller ID would say "Number Blocked."

When at last it happened, he grabbed the phone and said, "Adrienne?"

"Yes, it's me."

"What is it? Do you have it?"

"Come over to my office."

"I'm running out the door right now."

"No, sorry, not just yet. Wait a bit. I have to do something that will take a couple of hours. Let's say around 2 o'clock, OK?"

"Aw, geez, do you have to drag this out? Just tell me now."

"Be patient for a few more hours."

At twenty minutes to 2 Will was speed-walking down Pennsylvania Avenue, his arms shaking from his fingertips to his shoulders. Adrienne must have something important to tell him. If it had been negative she would have just said so over the phone. But what, what could it be?

Will shuffled his feet impatiently while the guard talked on the telephone for several minutes before asking for his ID. Soon he was inside the Hoover Building, racing toward Adrienne's office. When he arrived, he was surprised to find the door shut and a post-it note telling him to go to a nearby conference room. He knocked briskly and the door flew open. Adrienne greeted him with a big smile and stepped to one side. When he saw the other people in the room Will went wobbly in the knees: Belinda Winnisome and Sally stood waiting for him, smiling as broadly as Adrienne. The rest of Adrienne's squad was spread out around the room along with the group from *Cybersleuths Inc.*

"What...what..." was all he could utter.

"Will," said Adrienne, "say hello to your half-sister."

"My...my *what?*"

Before he could say anything he was surrounded by three women, hugging him tight, tears in everyone's eyes, while the onlookers began clapping and cheering.

At last he found his voice. "Half-sister? My father—my father had another child?"

"Yes, Will, the DNA results are absolutely definite, she's your half-sister by your father. But don't jump to conclusions about him, it's not what you might think. Belinda can explain things."

Sally held tight to Will's hands as Belinda spoke.

"I always knew that my parents had had difficulty getting pregnant. They referred to me as their miracle baby. When I turned twenty-one they sat me down and told me that my dad was the one with the problem, a very low sperm count. So they went to a sperm bank and my mother got impregnated with sperm that had been frozen for a number of years. They never knew who the donor was, that information was completely confidential in those days." She began sobbing, then found her voice. "I didn't care—as far as I was concerned, my dad was my father, and always would be. I never searched for my biological father, but now I'm glad that I know who he was—because now I have the brother I never knew I had."

"Oh my god!" exclaimed Will. "That explains something my father said when Barry and I were about to go to college. He said that when he was in college he had been so desperate for money he had donated blood and plasma as often as they would let him. Then one time—he swore it was only once—he said he had to do something else for money, something that he regretted and never did again. But he wouldn't explain what it was no matter how much we pushed him to tell us. He just said it was not illegal, he hadn't broken any laws, he just was too troubled by what he called, 'the possible consequences.'"

"I guess I'm one of those consequences," said Belinda, triggering loud laughter that broke the tension in the room.

"Yeah, what a consequence," said Will. "He was a good man, always. The important thing he wanted to tell us was that we should always come to him if we needed money, we should never do anything else, he'd always take care of it, he'd find a way."

Adrienne added, "His sperm was frozen long before Belinda's mother was artificially inseminated. That's not uncommon—babies have been born after as many as twenty years, or even more."

"I wonder..." began Will, but Adrienne cut him off.

"I know what you're wondering, but we know the answer. We tracked down the records of the sperm bank and confirmed that your father's specimen was used just that once. No other 'consequences' running around."

"Thanks, Adrienne. One step ahead of me as always." Will turned to his wife, tears streaming down his face. "Sally, remember I said I'd like to get the gang from *Cybersleuths, Inc.,* over to the house? Looks like we're going to have to add in the FBI and have a big celebration! I've got a sister!"

Acknowledgments

Many thanks to my wife, Ta Budetti, and my long-time friend, Tim Gunn, who patiently continue to serve as my editors and thought consultants.

Any deficits in this work are entirely my responsibility.

About the author

Peter Budetti trained as a physician (Columbia) and lawyer (Berkeley) but most of his professional life he has worked on health care policy in Washington and held senior academic positions.

Having spent years as a university professor, he decided to write novels for the general public because he felt that he has stories worth telling but no desire to add to his numerous academic publications that languish in obscurity. His novels are inspired by real events, personal experiences, and his imagination.

To date, he has written four novels. *Resuscitated* draws on his earlier life as a pediatrician, as well as his legal background and experiences in Washington and academe. *Hemorrhage, Deadly Bargain,* and *Hacked to Death* form a trilogy of thrillers that grew out of his years combating fraud in healthcare.

He is now *Of Counsel* to Phillips and Cohen, LLP, the nation's most successful law firm representing whistleblowers. As a political appointee in President Obama's administration he was responsible for overseeing modernization of Medicare's outdated systems for detecting and preventing healthcare fraud; he thereby acquired the amusing moniker of *Healthcare Antifraud Czar*. Previously he served for six years as Counsel, Subcommittee on Health and the Environment, U.S. House of Representatives, under the Chairmanship of Congressman Henry A. Waxman; as a member of the health staff, Senate Finance Committee, under the Chairmanship of Senator Daniel Patrick Moynihan; and as a core legislative drafter for President Bill Clinton's Health Security Act.

In his academic life, he founded and directed health policy research centers and held tenured professorships at Northwestern University and The George Washington University, was a faculty member of the Institute for Health Policy Studies, University of California, San Francisco, and held an endowed chair as Professor in the College of Public Health, University of Oklahoma. He has published more than fifty scholarly articles and another forty-plus reports, book chapters, reviews, and editorials.

His undergraduate degree is from the University of Notre Dame. He is a board-certified pediatrician and member of the California Bar and District of Columbia Bar. He is married and has two grown children, seven grandchildren, and one Pekingese-mix rescue doggy. He and his wife live in Kansas City, Missouri, where they moved when they decided it was time to get away from Washington, D.C. They spend their free time at their lake house in Arkansas.

CPSIA information can be obtained
at www.ICGtesting.com
Printed in the USA
LVHW010851300920
667476LV00004B/232